# CRESCENT HEART

# N. B. AUSTIN

# CRESCENT HEART

## THE CIVILANDS SERIES: BOOK 3

MOORE BELL

~

*For the two matriarchs, the Irish and the Greek,*
*With pride and love as fierce as you'd see.*
*For the two patriarchs, the Cop and the Pilot.*
*With family first and as brave as could be.*

~

# CHAPTER 1

## WE BECOME WHO WE'VE ALWAYS BEEN

"Are you ready?" Daniel Keagan asked, casting a glance at Frankie Covington.

"Collin never did scare me."

*Young pup no more*, Daniel thought. Given Frankie was the one who had tracked down and apprehended the now-prisoner, Daniel didn't feel his comrade was blustering. Though Collin McCormack had spoiled the surrender of the V'ahani with his crazed vendetta, the scene would have been much worse without Frankie's actions. The young man had been treated as a hero thereafter, and Daniel was happy to raise him in the Keagan ranks, even going so far as to take him under his wing.

"Well, all right, let's go then."

It was a dark, cloudy night when they left the hotel to meet the sheriff. It'd be Daniel's first real talk with Collin since Collin's crime. A few weeks had passed since the failed V'ahani negotiation, and he felt like he'd made Collin sweat enough to finally talk.

Crickets filled the air of the otherwise silent town as they walked toward the jail.

"Things seem to be moving along here pretty nicely by the way, sir," Frankie said.

1

Daniel swelled with pride thinking about how far he'd come in earning the trust of the people of Harran. His assumption that Donald Schneider was a leading voice among the townspeople ended up being spot on, and he'd put a good amount of his time into flattering the old hotel owner. It had all been working so well, in fact, that he had even started to reconnect with his fling-turned attempted-assassin, Johanna Fontaine. When the townspeople had surrounded him at the jail, he had no choice but to agree to their demand for Johanna's release. Despite a tender moment they shared at the time, he spent the days to follow avoiding her. It continued this way until one morning she had cornered him in the hotel lobby and apologized. Though this first encounter had been awkward, there was something very different about their talks after. They felt deeper, like the two of them were being more honest and on the same page. There was a weight to their conversations now, which wasn't there before. It felt like a rekindling, even though he'd made it clear it'd take time before he'd go anywhere near a bedroom with her again.

"There's still ground to be gained, but I don't disagree."

While Daniel still felt the need to slick back his hair and fix his Lion's Paw pin to his vest, he'd been doing so less and less over the last few weeks. On the rare occasions he now wore the pin, he felt a growing disgust, as if it burnt through his shirt and charred his skin beneath it.

"It's been some time since I sent my messenger off with Cassius. I'm just hoping Billy's gotten the word by now and will be up here soon. If we want any of this progress we've made to last, convincing him is gonna be the most important step we could take. The direction of our operation needs to change. Even after we get to the bottom of this situation with Collin and find out what really happened when the Morrell house burned to the ground, if we don't find a way to contain Clovis, it'll all be for nothing."

"Seems like you're doing everything you can at the moment, though, you know? And that counts for a lot more than nothing."

"Well, thanks, Frankie." The jail came into view, along with the sheriff waiting on its porch. "We're about to find out what it counts for I suppose."

The sheriff approached Daniel with a skip in his step. It was understandable he was looking forward to this. The fellow must be bored, seeing as he only had a single prisoner now. Without a word, they gave each other a nod and marched into the jail.

"All right, Collin, wake your ass up. It's high time you talk," Daniel said as soon as he spotted the man in the cell to his left, lying on his side with his eyes closed.

It was a bit of a challenge to see inside of the jail at night, with it being lit only by a single, dim candle. This candle rested next to a half-full bottle of rum on a table at the back of the building, directly to the right of the small sheriff's office. The cell to Daniel's right, where the dimwit prisoner Charles Langston once sat, was now empty. The thought of what punishment William might have deemed fit for that fool held his mind for a fleeting moment until Collin jolted to sit up straight. The deformity of the now-scarred wounds on his face was enough to make the stomach tighten.

"Been waiting in here for weeks. What took so long?" Collin asked with a drowsy yawn.

Daniel squinted down at him in the dark. "Where's your Lion's Paw pin?"

"You stripped it off me as soon as we left the negotiation. You forget already?"

"Of course not. Point is I don't owe you any explanations. I'll let you humor me on this one though … why do you think I took it from you?" The answer seemed obvious, but he wanted to hear the admission from the bastard's mouth.

The silence stretched, as Collin did nothing more than stare at him.

"He did it because Keagan business ain't none of your concern no more, Collin," Frankie said with his chest puffed. "So why Mr. Daniel kept you waiting ain't none of your—"

"Let adults talk, you little ant." Collin waved a dismissive hand in the young man's direction.

"You can keep calling me names all you want, but I ain't the one in the cell."

"No, but you're in another type of cell altogether, and you always will be. By the way, what color do your eyes interpret my finger to be now?" Collin raised his middle finger at Frankie, who with a curse went to grab for his gun, but Daniel and the sheriff restrained him.

"Frankie, go wait outside till I'm done here!" Daniel said, forcing him back. Though Frankie pulled away, he accepted the order with a nod. The direction of his head didn't leave Collin as his body turned for the door. In response, an even bigger smile graced Collin's face, and the finger shamefully remained in the air the whole time.

"Goddamn it, y'all are children, I swear. Now look here, Collin, it's been as long a day as any, and I'm too tired for your nonsense. So, tell me what happened to Adonis Morrell and his family."

"I'll tell you happily, but first, you know I need some kind of assurances. At this point, the whole world will be after me, and you saw what Frankie did, grabbing at his gun like that. He's so blinded by his *unwarranted* hatred for me, he'd move to draw on a defenseless man. And to think, all I did was pull his tail a little bit."

Daniel rolled his eyes, but the negotiation had already begun in his mind. "He hasn't done a thing wrong up to this point, and he's too set on making his way in the world to make a mistake like that. I'll accept the danger you feel from elsewhere, but no member of the Keagan gang is gonna be any kind of threat to your life. For the rest, first thing tomorrow I'll assign two men to assist the sheriff in guarding your cell."

"Armed?"

"Now, what kind of guards would they be if they weren't? Yes, *armed.*" Regardless of the information Collin had, Daniel believed there was no real way this man could repay the debt of what he'd done. Shooting a V'ahani warrior dead from a Keagan camp in the middle of open negotiations was far too costly—and his intention to hit Dominic Turner too irrelevant to the problems it caused. "They'll ensure your safety and should be all you need here. I ain't ceding any more ground either. Two's as many resources as I can afford to provide."

Collin furrowed his brow for a moment as if to ponder, then nodded. "Fair enough. That'll work."

After about ten seconds of continued silence, Daniel couldn't wait any longer. "Well? Out with it."

"Right," Collin said as he sat up straight. "See, I wasn't really one of Clovis's men."

In bewilderment, Daniel shook his head. "You weren't one of—? Oh man, you just cannot possibly ... Frankie, get in here with that pistol of yours!"

"No—no, you misunderstand me."

Frankie burst through the door, his gun already loaded and pointed at Collin's head as the man raised his hands in defense.

"Good God, do you see this? Tell him to lower that thing!"

"Not unless you give him a reason to lower it, you snake. What the hell do you mean you weren't one of his men? Were you not there that morning?"

"I was, okay? I was."

Even with Collin's desperate gasp, Daniel remained suspicious, but gestured for Frankie to lower his weapon.

"What I meant was I wasn't one of his regulars. He's got his own faction within your ranks—and they're growing, let me tell you— who are *his* men. I believe it goes as far as Walter being one of them at this point. They're brainwashed, and they're twisted—maybe not as much as he is—but they are, all the same."

"The ones in control of the Hold with him now, I take it," Daniel said under his breath to himself. A state of terror sunk in, but he was determined not to let it show. The situation was more serious than he could have imagined. "Keep going."

"Well, having started out at the mansion in Fayette ... I just wasn't getting as much out of this Territory as I'd hoped. It was all so tame and not too different from rural New Berkeley. So when William ordered Clovis and his group on to Harran, I saw it as my chance to get some excitement for a change. As we went on, though, I started to feel uneasy being around a cult like the one Clovis runs. By the time we got to the Morrells, the doubts about my decision became overwhelming. And after? Once our business was done there, I'd truly regretted having been a part of it in any way. The whole thing changed me. Made me into something I didn't want to be. Initially, I thought escaping to Harran and playing guard here would reverse it all, but it didn't."

"The rumors are true then?" Daniel raised his palm to his sweaty forehead, part of him dreading this truth. "The Morrells didn't shoot first?"

"Not only did they not shoot first, Daniel, but they didn't so much as make a threat. Adonis surrendered outright. The only wrong he did was to take too long to gather his family for Clovis's liking. And to be honest about it, a person with above-average impatience could've waited longer, given the circumstances."

Pacing the room, Daniel reflected on all the time, effort, and love he and William had tried so hard to give Clovis. Was Clovis simply ungrateful? Or did he hate them altogether? Or was it not about him and William at all but simply Clovis's unquenchable thirst for inflicting violence? And if it was the violence, could he and William still hide behind the excuse of Clovis's troubled childhood? It obviously wasn't the first time by any means their brother had caused such devastation, but it was the first time Clovis had done so at his brothers' expense. However horrible and selfish it was to admit, that's what made Daniel's concern rise to new levels in regard to his brother. In committing an act against their direct orders and against everything they had sought in coming to the Murrieta, it suggested there was no controlling Clovis any longer. It suggested he was a rabid dog—a cunning one, who had formed his own sadistic pack. And what did that mean for him or William? For their dream for the Murrieta? And beyond them, what did it mean for the people of Harran or for anyone who stood in Clovis's way on his path to chaos?

Frankie nudged him with a gentle hand. "Daniel?"

The interruption allowed him to snap back to the situation in the jail. "Thank you, Collin. You'll have your guards in the morning."

As Frankie and Daniel left the jail, the sheriff walked out with them.

"Gonna have a quick smoke," he said, already standing across the road and lighting a pipe.

"All right. Have a good night, sheriff. I'll send two boys over in the morning," Daniel replied. But the sheriff was already somewhere else, craning his neck to look up to the stars.

Daniel couldn't help but do the same while walking back to the hotel. The sky here was massive. So much bigger than anything he could imagine—so much bigger than the Murrieta, or the Keagan gang, or him.

Right before the hotel, the saloon came into view, and as they came alongside it, Daniel stopped. "I need a drink, or three."

"All right, sir, I'm a little tired, so I might—"

"You need a drink, too," he said partly as a joke, partly as a command. He didn't want to be alone with his thoughts at the moment.

"Yes, Mr. Daniel, sir."

Daniel didn't enter right away, his sight still fixed on the stars. "How do you suppose you're meant to make a choice like the one I'm presented with? Against my own blood?"

"Well, by the sound of it, I don't suppose the choice you're making is really *against* Clovis at all. The way he's carrying on is only gonna keep leading to more danger and hurt. If you could stop it somehow, I'm thinking you'd be doing what's best for him as much as anyone else."

The sentiment comforted Daniel as his eyes hopped around constellations.

"Um … sir?" Frankie asked.

"Yeah, what is it?" Daniel asked with a grin.

At Frankie's silence, Daniel brought his gaze back to his immediate surroundings. Frankie stood frozen, pointing back toward the direction of the jail. Daniel whipped around.

Smoke billowed into the sky from behind the buildings between them and where they had come from. Without a thought, Daniel took off sprinting. He heard Frankie behind him but didn't slow down until the jail came into sight. As he arrived, he stopped dead in his tracks. A raging fire flowed out the barred windows, as the already charred wood began to crumble.

*

Jeannie Morrell didn't move a muscle. Her back was to the wall, and her pistol was drawn in the dark office. Beads of sweat slid down her neck, and she repressed the urge to shudder. Despite her nerves, she was excited with what she was hearing.

"So the rumors are true then? The Morrells didn't shoot first?" she heard Daniel Keagan ask from the other side of the wall. An ear-to-ear smile overtook Jeannie's face as she glanced to Harrison and Dominic. Her eyes, now adjusted to the dark they had been lurking in, could make out their shared excitement. The revelation was such a relief after the frustrating start, when Collin said he wasn't one of Clovis's men. At the time, she'd thought Dominic might burst right in and shoot him on the spot. Now, with the truth coming to light, she thought about her parents and brother, Donovan.

*Finally, justice might be served.*

After a bit more chatter from the other side of the wall, Dominic, who leaned across the wall opposite to her and Harrison, motioned that Daniel and his men had departed the jail. Taking a step towards the exit, Jeannie froze when Dominic suddenly eased open the office door.

*What is he doing?*

They were supposed to confront Daniel with Collin's revelation now. Daniel had left the jail. Why was Dominic opening the door to head in? Confused, she reached up a hand to Harrison's shoulder just as Harrison did the same to Dominic's.

"What are you doing?" Harrison asked in the faintest whisper. "This isn't what we planned."

"No. But we need to be sure he won't go and change his story again."

Jeannie's stomach dropped and she exchanged a worried look with Harrison. She'd let her brother take the lead here.

After a moment, Harrison sighed and nodded, but he looked as concerned as she felt. She was nervous about the risk of confronting a madman as much as she was about Dominic's intentions with his enemy. But if Harrison thought they could handle it, they would.

All three of their guns were drawn, though Dominic only aimed straight in front of him once he slipped through the doorframe. Harrison emerged next in the same fashion. Jeannie finally did the same. On her exit, she spotted Collin standing on his bench and peeking in the direction of the town through the barred window in his cell, humming a merry tune to himself. She and Harrison lowered their guns, but Dominic kept his aimed at Collin.

"Get down from there. Do it now," Dominic said in a hushed tone.

Collin spun around with such a jolt that Jeannie couldn't help but jump as well. Squinting at them at first, a timid twinge painting what part of his face Jeannie could see in the candlelight, his expression turned to one of excited recognition the moment he made them out.

"Bravo, magic man, bravo." Simulating a handclap without making a sound, Collin mocked them.

"Put your hands down." Dominic cocked back his pistol as he moved toward the front door, beside a coat hanger and a spoke on the wall with the jail keys hanging from it. Jeannie narrowed her eyes at the sound.

*What is Dominic after?*

She shifted her eyes towards Harrison, but he was focused on the exchange. She returned her attention to Collin.

Collin smiled wide. "Oh but I just want to show you how impressed I am. I mean, the way you've managed to appear before my eyes here? Maybe you're half a decent illusionist after all."

"Keep your voice down. I'm not here to bicker."

"I know why you're here. You're here because this is about you and me." Collin jumped down off his cell bench. "It always has been, and it'll continue to be till the bitter fucking end. And if you think I'm gonna yelp like some toddler calling for his mammy, you're mistaken, magic man."

Dread slithered through Jeannie. She opened her mouth to demand they leave now, but Dominic beat her to it.

"You lied, didn't you?" Dominic asked, his gaze fixed on Collin.

"Not for a second. I'm here because of you, and you're here because of me."

Dominic shook his head, visibly irritated. "No. I'm talking about what you said to Daniel. You told him you regretted it."

Collin laughed long and hard. Jeannie felt sickened by his disturbing behavior, but mainly wanted to know Dominic's intent. "What are we doing here, Dominic?" she asked.

Collin fell into hysterics. "Pray you never understand it, girly."

Dominic moved closer to the cell. "Admit it was a lie," he said to Collin.

Collin stopped cackling. "No, I told him the truth ... at least at first. I actually wasn't one of Clovis's men. I wasn't before, and I wasn't later either. In fact, I wasn't even there at the raid on you children's house at all. Saying I had been was just my ticket to getting protection, since I somehow missed you and shot that native instead. Protection would buy me time to find you again and finish the job. And if I get another chance, I'm not going to miss, magic man."

Whether Collin had been a witness or not didn't matter to Jeannie—all that mattered was that Daniel believed it. "Stop calling him that," she said, having had enough of Collin's antics and Dominic's stalling. "You're in no position to talk down to him. You call him by his name and apologize."

"Okay, okay, little lady. So, where do we go from here?"

Jeannie looked to Harrison. He nodded.

"You swear you won't go back on your story to Daniel and in exchange we don't turn you over to the V'ahani," Harrison said.

Collin grinned. "I ain't gotta swear to shit. Daniel wouldn't allow you to turn me over. We had a deal. And *that* deal is the one that's gonna get me magic man's head. So that's the only deal I'm interested in."

Jeannie's thoughts were in a jumble. Would Collin benefit from changing the story? Why would he? What did it mean if he did? Would Daniel still know the truth?

"What is wrong with you?" Dominic asked, rubbing his eyes with his hand.

"I'm persistent."

"But why are you doing this? Why persist?"

"I'm too competitive. I can't let you win."

"For God's sake, why do people like you always get so deluded in this territory?"

"People like *us*. And you know it's because—"

"Stop! Just stop! If you stop, everyone can win. Can't you see that?" Dominic grabbed at one of the cell bars violently.

Collin met him. "I can't stop. I won't stop. Not until one of us is destroyed. It's the way this was always meant to go. Don't *you* see?

It's our destiny. It's the only thing that matters. These bars will not always hold me and you know it."

Jeannie felt her heart speed up. This wasn't going anywhere good.

"Dominic, forget him," Harrison said, as he came to her side. He began ushering her towards the office and the back exit. "We have what we need and we need to go talk to Daniel now while he knows the truth."

Dominic holstered his gun and Jeannie nearly sighed aloud in relief. Good. They could leave now. She and Harrison paused in the doorway of the office, waiting.

*Come on, Dominic. Leave it.*

Dominic shook his head and pulled a flask out of his pocket. He took a sip before slipping the flask through the bars of the cell and placing it on a stool on the other side. He paused a moment, his back to them, and then he stepped back. "Take a swig."

*What is he doing?*

"Dominic," Jeannie said.

He didn't look her way, continuing to stare down Collin. Collin sighed and lifted it up. "Sure," he said as he shot Dominic a look. "I suppose we can toast to your win."

Dominic turned towards her and Harrison as he unbuckled his holster and placed his gun on a table. He began rolling up his sleeves. Jeannie wanted to grab him and force him out of the jail. "You see, don't you, Morrells? If he doesn't understand by now, if he hasn't seen another path by now, he never will. This isn't about winning. It isn't even about justice or revenge. Well, it is, if I'm honest, but it's more than that too. It's about survival. It's about protecting the things I care for. I never wanted this. I've fought it and avoided it and talked myself out of it, but he's left me no choice. I will not hesitate again."

"Dominic. What are you saying?" Jeannie asked, as her heart dropped into her stomach. "Hesitate with what?"

"He'll never stop coming for me. He'll never stop trying to get me any way he can, regardless of the collateral damage. And because of that, he'll never stop coming for the things I care about—you, this town, my life." The cell door swung open to Jeannie's terror. Dominic didn't seem surprised. Jeannie looked up at the spoke by the door of the jail and confirmed what she already knew. The key was missing. Dominic had slipped it to Collin along with the flask. Collin bounced a moment on his heels, as if preparing.

Dominic turned to face him, getting into a fighting stance. "So now I have to do what's necessary. I'm not hesitating anymore."

"Finally." With a howl, Collin dove for Dominic but the illusionist was ready and threw him into the bars of the adjacent cell.

Collin shot back up and lunged again, but Dominic punched him square in the jaw, causing him to land on his backside, stunned.

"What do we do?" Jeannie asked Harrison, who had lifted his gun but lowered it back down as Dominic came running toward them, grabbing at a bottle by the office door before turning back to his enemy.

The bottle hurled towards Collin, who was back up and charging forward. It bounced off his shoulder and the contents burst over the floor near the door behind him. Despite the blows Collin had already taken, the two were soon grappling and trading punches.

"Enough!" Jeannie said, but her cry was to no avail. Harrison held her back and watched the men carefully.

An elbow to Collin's jaw was met with a hook to Dominic's belly. Arms and legs flailed about and collided. Blood began to run as knuckles broke skin. As the struggle continued, it became clear Dominic's early strikes had taken a toll on Collin. Collin started stumbling each time he rose and soon enough, one slip led to a head-locked submission by Dominic.

With a tight grip around Collin's throat, Dominic struggled to hold his enemy in place. "It's over, Collin."

"It ain't," Collin said, coughing out what words he could.

"Give up. Give up and admit the feud is done. Admit you'll stop."

She saw Dominic's grip loosen just enough to allow Collin to respond. Hope spawned in Jeannie. Maybe, maybe this was the end of it.

"If you want it done, then finish it. If you don't, I'll be back. I'll come back and I'll do my worst. Killing you ain't enough no more. That ain't enough of a win. I'll destroy you. I'll tear your worthless town to the ground. I'll hang those kids in front of you. And I'll make you watch all of it before I kill you," Collin looked up at Jeannie and grinned, "*Dominic Turner.*"

Jeannie shared a look with Dominic, finally understanding even if she didn't agree with it. His expression was one of resignation before the planes of his face hardened with determination. "I appreciate you using my name, but I think I kind of like the ring of 'magic man.'"

Dominic threw Collin headfirst against the bars, stunning him again. Without pause, he walked into the cell and grabbed his flask off the stool. In a seamless turn, he was outside the cell and in front of Collin, who was on the ground, clutching his head. Dominic took a swig from his flask. After the sip, he raised a hand to his mouth and blew out a stream of fire. It was much like the first time Dominic and Collin had met, only this stream was aimed toward the alcohol on the floor where the bottle had smashed. When it struck its target, the floor burst into flames.

"Abra-fucking-kadabra," Dominic said, before spinning towards them.

Harrison shoved Jeannie through the office door and towards the back exit. As soon as Jeannie saw Dominic run through the office door, slamming it shut behind him, she sprinted out of the jail. As Harrison and Dominic followed her, so did the agonizing screams of Collin McCormack. Jeannie winced.

Dominic pulled them to a halt just before they ran around the edge of the building.

"I'm sorry. I'm sorry I didn't follow the plan." Dominic paused. "It had to be done."

Jeannie didn't know what to say. Part of her understood, part of her wasn't sure that there really was no other way.

"Whether that's true or not, it was your decision and it's over now," Harrison said into the silence. "We won't speak of it again."

Dominic nodded. "Understood."

There was a beat and then Jeannie stepped forward, past Dominic, signaling the end of the conversation. They had something more important to focus on now—their original plan. She turned the corner of the building. Daniel Keagan and two of his men stood in the middle of the road, watching the flames.

*This is our chance to save everyone.*

"Now you know the truth, Daniel Keagan," she said, stepping forward.

Daniel slowly moved his eyes to look at her. Behind her, Harrison let out a thundering whistle.

"I'm afraid Jeannie's right, boyo," Donald Schneider said as he emerged from the shadows with some townsfolk. An array of silhouettes followed from several other locations to surround Daniel and his two men. The fire might have shocked the people of Harran, but not one of them showed a hint of it.

"There's no excuse now," Debra Kennedale said.

"And there's no hiding from it," Cassie Kennedale finished.

As Collin's shrieks subsided into silence and the others assembled, illuminated by the crackling flames of the burning building, Harrison approached Jeannie's side. Jeannie felt a strength she had never felt before. It'd been a long time since she stood in the open, utterly unafraid. Finally, after all this time, she was back among her people. They were together now, her whole town and her whole family, and they were making their stand for their home. For Harran.

"When we first met, you were looking for the head of the Morrell household," Jeannie said. "You were looking for the man who crafted the fabric holding the Riverlands together, the man who built the only place immune to the madness of the Murrieta. You found him, and then you and your brother William unleashed the devil upon his doorstep." She paused. "And now you want to call this place your home? Tell us, Daniel Keagan! Speak!"

"I do," Daniel said, his hair dripping with sweat and falling loose over his face. "I do. But y'all didn't need to ..." He glanced back at the flames.

"You must tell us, Daniel, why we should show you mercy, why you deserve the chance your brother will never have, why you want the way of life that monster nearly destroyed. Tell us why you deserve Harran," Johanna Fontaine said, in a careful approach.

At the sight of her, Daniel fell to his knees. The two men standing behind him were trembling in shock and raised their hands in surrender despite the lack of pointed weapons.

There was a moment where a look passed between them and Daniel heaved a sigh. They had Daniel where they wanted him, but Jeannie knew the goal was to secure a promise of some kind. The plan had been to make sure Collin told the truth and ambush Daniel right after—to guarantee his turning, to guarantee the truth was enough to get him on their side. Her loved ones in Harran knew the possibility existed or they wouldn't even have given Daniel this option. Yet none of them had gone through what her brother and she had. Even if they did love Adonis Morrell, they hadn't suffered the loss of a father, a mother, a brother. So Jeannie needed to hear the words—now.

"You know what your brother did, you know what he is capable of, and you know what it's cost us because *you know* what this place is. So what are you gonna do about it, Daniel Keagan?" Jeannie asked.

"I'll … I'll stop him."

"I didn't catch that, boyo," Donald said. It was likely a genuine statement due to his age, but Jeannie wouldn't mind an affirmation herself.

"I said I will stop him! Okay? I'll do whatever it takes to prove to y'all I'm changed. It was a mistake—no, it was more than that. It was wrong. We were wrong! And I'm sorry, you hear? I'm so goddamn sorry. I just thought I knew better. I didn't!" Daniel's voice broke. He was unraveling before them. He looked up at Jeannie. "Now ... *now* I know. And I want nothing but to help y'all the way y'all have helped me. I'll correct this one way or another. I'll show you, I swear it. If in a week's time William doesn't show ... if he doesn't show, I'll go south myself and will do everything I can to fix this."

For a moment, Jeannie said nothing. She was overjoyed about the change that seemed to have taken place inside him, but they needed the completion of his promise. She felt Harrison stand taller next to her, keeping his silence, waiting. Jeannie was the prosecutor and he was the judge. "Stand on your feet, wipe the hair out of your eyes, and tell all of us you will prove it," Jeannie said, firmly.

Daniel stared at her with a fierce gaze that intimidated her at first, but the closer she looked, the more Jeannie recognized an honest acceptance within him. He truly had turned. Placing a hand on his knee, he lifted himself to his feet before slicking his hair out of his face—though some of it fell right back down onto his forehead. Still staring at her, he placed his right hand on his chest, where his Lion's Paw pin was fastened. Ripping the pin right off, he balled his hand around it before unfolding it once again and letting the pin fall to the ground. Standing there with a ripped vest, he said, "I will prove it."

Jeannie exhaled in elation. With his influence, she knew they could change things.

"Welcome to Harran, Daniel Keagan," Harrison said beside her, an infectious smile breaking out on his face.

# CHAPTER 2

## WHAT ROADS REMAIN?

The red-tailed hawk had circled and monitored Harran for days, observing minimal movement. This was to be expected, though. The time would soon come to continue further south.

From what Hanzah could glean from the peaceful atmosphere in Harran, Daniel Keagan seemed to be making an honest effort to please the townsfolk. After reporting as much to Orrin and Varek, Hanzah was ordered to continue his reconnaissance further south. It was a tedious task—hence his assignment of it, he guessed. When he'd come to for breaks and rest, he often found that the limbs his weight favored were asleep. He hated the pins-and-needles feeling. Despite the minor frustration, he soldiered on and soon got back to work.

Where the lushness of the Riverlands ended, the winding plains of the central Murrieta began. The hawk flew over the occasional, smaller settlement, its broad, rich brown wings extended as it glided through the air. Along the way, it slowed only to rest and feed.

Three days came and passed with nothing of interest to report, and fatigue started to set into Hanzah's dormant body. Each time he got back to his recon, he felt like his soul was being chipped away at from sheer boredom.

As the elevation of the plains steadily rose into a terrain of cresting hills, the hawk came upon William Keagan's town of Fayette. After several hours of inspecting the Keagan mansion, of sweeping through homes and storefronts and inspecting the occasional passersby, there was not much of note. So, the hawk took up its southern path again.

From Fayette it would take all of two days of sweeping the southern lands before reaching the Hold. Still winding and weaving through the skies, there remained minimal activity for a half-hour or so south of Fayette. The occasional campsite appeared, with fire pits long past charred. On the grounds of one in particular, a vole could be seen exploring. It had been a while since its last snack, so when the hawk had an opening, it swooped down. As it went, though, it became distracted by voices in the distance, and the vole darted off.

The hawk glided back up high into the air, now looking down on a group of men on horseback who were heading north in the direction it had come from. It lowered back down to get a better glimpse of the group. As it began to circle them, its sharp vision identified Clovis Keagan at the head of the riders, along with his confidante, Devin, one of his known associates. The bird heard the men speak, and Hanzah translated the sounds. They were talking about the Riverlands.

A distant crack sounded below. With a hit to the wing, the hawk began diving. Another crack, and there was a sudden pressure in the hawk's chest, before everything faded to black.

Hanzah's eyes, which he'd been told rolled back into his head when utilizing the birds, snapped back into place. With a heavy sigh, he tried to shake the horror and the intensity of being shot. Though not in any physical pain himself, it was a traumatic new experience to be in the eyes of one of the Mother's creatures as it was killed. As he shook his head to clear it, he realized the importance of what he'd seen—Clovis Keagan was marching north, away from the Hold. Knowing Varek would be ready to go south to meet him, Hanzah felt a mixture of confidence in his people and nerves about the impending nature of his first war. He worried too about the impact such a battle would have on his friends in Harran.

Knowing there would be no time to waste, Hanzah jumped awkwardly to his feet and sprinted toward the improvised camp his people had set up just off the main Mountainlands trail. The entirety of the V'ahani fighters from Chieftain Orrin's and Grand Chieftain Varek's factions were present and had been preparing themselves for war for weeks. This news could be what they were waiting for—especially the more battle-hungry among them.

"Uncle Orrin!" Warriors sitting on either side of the path he was running down turned their heads his way. Hanzah knew he was creating a scene, but he didn't care. This was too important. "Chieftain Varek! He is on the move!"

As the main tents came into view, Varek, Orrin, Varek's masters, and Orrin's councilmen stood still around a fire. They turned their heads his way.

"Speak with precision, Hanzah. Who is coming?" Varek asked, the light from the fire accentuating the scar extending down his face.

Hanzah stopped in front of them, bringing his hands to his knees to finish catching his breath. "Clovis Keagan ... Clovis Keagan and a large group of his men are riding north."

The leaders' heads all turned from Hanzah back to each other.

"I do not know why we would have believed any different." Shaking his head, Varek leaned over, grabbed his coat off a nearby log, and threw it over his shoulders. "We told Daniel it would be war if his brother was not contained. Now the devil marches toward our home? Well, so be it. Mobilize the men. The time has come to end this."

The Mountainlands camp came alive, and Hanzah felt relieved to be active and moving again. The V'ahani fighters seemed thrilled by the prospect of a battle. Though most of them did nothing but train, living this far north meant most of the younger generation of Mountainlands V'ahani had never seen any kind of large-scale action.

*And now they would be relied upon to determine the fate of our people.*

In no time at all the camp was forming ranks, and once they had started to do so, Hanzah realized he'd lost track of the spear he'd fashioned with Orrin's help earlier in the week. It didn't matter much in actuality, as he would be utilizing the grizzlies in a fight anyway—a thing Hanzah had significant experience in despite his age—but for the purposes of presentation and impressing his superiors, he needed to find it.

When Varek wasn't looking, Hanzah approached Orrin and tugged on his sleeve. "Uncle, have you seen my spear?"

Orrin was making preparations of his own, racing around the camp to do so. Although his movements were frantic, he still wore a smile and spoke in a merry tone. "Yes, of course."

"Great! Where is it?"

"I do not have the slightest clue."

"But you said—"

With brows furrowed, he paused from his activities and stroked his thick beard. "I *did* help you craft it, did I not? So, of course, I have seen it."

Hanzah sighed, and then it hit him: he'd left it back at his recon spot. "Oh yeah, you did. I am sorry. I had forgotten my shovel it seems."

Orrin jostled him lightly, and with a laugh and a wink, he was off again. Hanzah ran as fast as he could, but when he returned, spear in hand, he was the very last to join ranks. Trying not to call attention to himself, he stood firmly in place next to his uncle, who sat atop his horse. The men around them did look fierce, despite their lack of experience. Spears and blades by their sides were made all the more intimidating by the V'ahani-white war paint, which decorated most of their faces in varying patterns. The specific pattern worn told a story, both of rank and of family. As a matter of fact, it also served as the only designation of V'ahani lineage, since they used no surnames—a tradition they'd only seen on the Easterners arrival to the Riverlands. For now, Hanzah wore no paint of his own.

As everyone waited for Varek to come with orders, Hanzah noticed his uncle's face too was bare.

"Uncle, did you not want to put on your face before we fight?" he asked in a half-whisper.

"Did you not want to put on yours?"

"No."

"Well, why not?"

"Because I … my father always used to put it on for me." Receiving no response, Hanzah looked up to see Orrin's gentle nod, his lip turned down in a frown. "I am proud enough, but I am just not ready yet. I am sorry—"

"No. Do not dare apologize." Orrin's interruption was stern and out of his usual character, prompting Hanzah to turn his head toward the ground. "Hey. Look at me. You are my family."

"Yes, I know."

"Well our pattern should be the same then, should it not? When you are ready, I would be happy to assist you in putting yours on. But for now, if you wear no paint, I wear no paint."

Hanzah looked up with a smile.

A 20-something warrior standing beside him nudged him. "Arkouda was a great man and Chieftain, Hanzah. I am so sorry for your—"

Riding past them, Varek scoffed as he scanned the ranks. "Will the enemy accept our apologies?"

"NO, GRAND CHIEFTAIN!" the entire battalion replied.

Seeing his sympathetic, now-at-attention new friend's face flush in embarrassment, Hanzah leaned over once Varek was out of sight and placed a hand on his shoulder. "Thank you. Your words are my armor, brother."

The fellow remained stiff, but he grinned.

"So we shall not give any," Varek continued. "March!"

With a massive, unified shout, they followed the order. As they departed the campsite, the torches wielded by men at different points of the line joined the moonlight to brighten the density of the dark night. One such torch was held right over Hanzah's head by the person behind him. Its heat blanketed the back of his neck.

"We had one demand after they *murdered* one of your brothers during our negotiations." As they progressed through the mountainous path, one which Hanzah was now very familiar with, Varek did not cease his dialogue with the warriors. "I thought I was being reasonable when I told them Clovis Keagan must be contained. Was I being unreasonable?"

"NO, GRAND CHIEFTAIN."

"Then the onus is on us to rid this territory of him. But not just of him. Of them all! It is clear they do not respect us and cannot live among us on fair terms. For this, they have no place in our home. Will we shed their blood?"

"YES, GRAND CHIEFTAIN."

This time, Hanzah did not join, as he thought of all his Eastern friends in Harran and worried about the meaning of the Grand Chieftain's words. It would be difficult for him to support the idea all the Easterners should leave the Territory, and he wouldn't allow any of his friends' blood to be shed simply because they were Easterners.

"And will we save our people whom they have imprisoned and tortured?"

"YES, GRAND CHIEFTAIN." Hanzah joined back in louder this time, his captive sister, Latera, the first thing in his mind.

"And will you make the Mother proud?"

"YES, GRAND CHIEF—"

"Halt!"

They had reached the opening of the mountain pass and the bridge to the Riverlands in no time at all. All stopped as Varek made his way toward the front of the line, where someone had made the call at the top of their lungs. Alongside Hanzah, Orrin lifted a curious brow before following Varek. Fidgeting with a nervous anticipation, Hanzah tried with futility to see over or around the taller men in front of him. There was silence in the group, with some frustrated chatter at the front.

The clattering of hooves marked Varek's return.

"Go back to camp, the bridge has been destroyed."

Ever loyal to their Grand Chieftain, the warriors all turned and marched back as requested, while Hanzah stood still in terror and confusion. Needing to know what Varek meant, he jumped to the side of the trail in wait. The sulk of Orrin's shoulders contrasted the stiffness of Varek's.

"Perhaps you are not suited for reconnaissance after all," Varek said, his horse charging up to Hanzah. He closed in fast enough to make Hanzah flinch.

"I do not … what do you mean?"

"You would like us to believe you saw Clovis Keagan out there, while you possess eyes so blind they failed to see the very bridge we need to cross has vanished?"

"Is it not possible he passed what he thought would be a familiar sight, Grand Chieftain?" Orrin asked with a hand raised, coming to Hanzah's defense. The gesture was one he was becoming more and more grateful for as his uncle continued to stick up for him.

"Nothing is impossible, but now we cannot trust in the validity of what he has seen. Even after the bridge is rebuilt—an activity that itself will be impossible without the quantity of axes and other tools necessary—we are talking about putting our warriors in jeopardy for a cause we cannot yet be certain will be fruitful. I will not risk it. No, Hanzah, for your mistake you will make the journey to the Mountainlands camp and fetch the supplies we need to rebuild the bridge. In the meantime, we will see if any others can verify what you claim to have seen."

Hanzah had only meant to do his part to help his people—and perhaps impress the Grand Chieftain in the hopes of cementing his place within the V'ahani. Yet impressing Varek never seemed to work out for him, and he was beginning to wonder if it was worth trying anymore. The destruction of the bridge was dumbfounding to him. Just how capable were these Keagans? It only made him worry more for his people at the Hold.

"I will go with him." Orrin hopped off his horse and placed a hand on Hanzah's shoulder.

Gratitude swamped Hanzah again for his uncle's display of loyalty.

"So be it," Varek said, before turning away.

Hanzah looked up at Orrin and smiled. At least now he'd have his uncle's humor on the journey north.

\*

The dining room at Fayette had been trashed, and it would stay trashed, per William's orders. While not much made sense to Henry Abigale anymore, he was on the exact same page regarding this particular sentiment. Unlike William though, who was still too broken by it all to come anywhere near the room, Henry returned there every day since he'd seen his own daughter's head on that very table. Though he couldn't stomach the thought, some part of him needed to maintain it and never let it go. From the now-emptied platter, to the guns on the floor, to the mess on the table, it all mattered and could never be forgotten. He stared at the dried blood day in and day out. It was blood from the veins of his precious, beautiful Judith; it was his own blood, his own life.

For hours he would sit in William's seat and stare, thinking too many thoughts and, in turn, experiencing too many emotions. It wasn't healthy, he knew it wasn't, but the resulting fury was too strong to resist, and from it his new mission materialized.

*Jackson "Forrest" Hayes.*

The fiend who shattered his entire world. There could be no path forward until he paid—something Henry had decided on within hours of the tragedy in this dining room.

So, every day, he'd stare, tapping his fingers on the table in a frantic pace and whispering to himself out loud, "Forrest Hayes— Jackson 'Forrest' Hayes … no less than all of it—the entire operation … how? Who cares? Find a way—any way—whatever it takes … tear it down—burn it, shred it, poison it—poison him—no … not death—too easy—no … torture—yes, pain, hurt, suffering … that fucking—" Losing his barely leashed control, he slammed his fist down onto the table and caught a crooked knife-fork combo, instant pain slicing through his skin. "Ah, shit!" He brought the cut up to his mouth. After replacing the silverware in the exact place it had been, he took a deep breath, closed his eyes, and let his thoughts shift back to Judith. Nothing else mattered, anyway.

"Henry—"

"Shhh!" Over his shoulder, he raised a finger, his mind hovering on a vivid memory of Judith running around their front yard as a little girl. He didn't yet want to let go of it. "Just a moment …"

"Yes, of course."

He recognized his wife Maria's whisper. Whether or not it had been intentional, Henry appreciated how the lowered volume of her voice allowed him to hear the reply while keeping his own memory alive.

After another moment, he turned around. "All right, my dear, come in."

"What happened to your hand?" Maria asked once she appeared in front of him.

Beside her was Gregory Calloway. "I'm sorry, Mr. Abigale. We should have knocked or come at another time."

"Oh, hello." Henry glanced at the man and back at his wife. "And it's nothing, dear. Simple accident. But please," Henry said, gesturing for them both to take a seat as he wrapped his hand with a handkerchief from his pocket. His focus was still too singular to linger on the concerned look his wife sent him. "There's no issue with your timing either, Gregory. I should be equally sensitive to the loss of your own child. I mean, hell, saying it now out loud, I feel like I should've been inviting you to sit with me in these times of reflection."

As Gregory sat at the table, he let out a deep sigh, one with which Henry was all too familiar. "As much as I appreciate the sentiment … reflection is the last thing I need. I wish more than anything that things hadn't turned out the way they did for each of us."

"You know, our paths have kind of been the opposite—gangster to attempted family man for me and vice-versa for you. Because of it, I think we each understand what it's like to walk in the other's shoes. So, I understand, Gregory, I do—even if that's not my trajectory right now." He paused. "Anyway, what'd you come here to tell me?"

"Gregory wanted us all to talk because he needs our help," Maria said, putting a hand on Gregory's shoulder for a brief moment.

"As you know, Billy's been in a pretty dark place since ... what happened," Gregory said. "And—"

"The few times he does come out of his room, he could be mistaken for a goddamn ghost haunting these halls." Even with his appreciation for how much William clearly loved his daughter and his own understanding of the weight of grief, Henry couldn't help but cut Gregory short. He felt more than a bit disgusted by William at the moment—the man didn't seem to understand the need for action.

For a moment, pain flickered in Gregory's eyes. "Yeah, it's been real tough to see him that way." He paused, sitting up a little straighter. "But while he recovers, I feel the responsibility's still mine to try and make sure everything runs smoothly around here. With that in mind, I could use your advice with regards to how you think I should handle Clovis in all this."

"Oh. Well, that I actually am equipped to help you with," Henry replied, a memory from their first days in Doreshire arising at the mention. "I'm not sure how in depth William went when he told you about our trip to New Berkeley, but it seemed he had a revelation or two in regards to Clovis. Some events caused him to realize his brother goes much farther in his cruelty than previously assumed, and he had hopes of altering that. So, I'd say ensuring the youngest brother is leashed and made to remain a well-behaved little demon would be ideal for now."

"Yeah, well, that's the thing … Clovis has left the Hold with a contingent of his men and is heading north to assist Daniel in Harran. It was a request we'd transmitted multiple times previously, and he's only now granted it."

"Well, shit, how close are they to reaching Harran?"

"Actually, he's not very close at all." Gregory's voice trembled as he scratched at his head. "It's worse—he's here at the mansion. I guess he decided to stop along the way north. I tried to satisfy whatever request he had and send him off, but it seems he caught on to my being curt and now he's insisting on speaking with Billy."

It was clear now why Gregory was troubled. Though the Keagans weren't close to Henry's first concern at this point, he did feel for his son-in-law and knew William's mental state would be far too fragile to deal with Clovis right now. He was also impressed with Gregory's cunning instincts to involve his wife in this request, since if it weren't for Maria's pleading eyes, he would have been far less eager to make any effort to help.

"Does he know yet?" Henry asked, dreading the possibility of an affirmative. "Does Clovis know what happened, I mean."

"No, which is kind of why I came to you. I kept them waiting out front, and I'm sure he'll be getting impatient at this point, but I needed to get some kind of input on what I should do first. Clovis is the last person Billy should be talking to right now, right? I know if we told Clovis though, there'd be no keeping them apart. You know how he is with his brothers."

Henry took a deep breath and rubbed his fingers across his greasy forehead, his thoughts now racing. "Okay, look, I'll go out there and talk to him. I'll do what I can to try and get him to continue on toward Harran, but I can't make any promises. Whether I succeed or fail, you're William's best friend. We should have sent word to Daniel sooner. But until Daniel arrives, you're all William has. He's a broken man right now, and it's on you to keep the cracks from growing. And you need to do so, not only for him, but for all of us, Gregory. We can't have a mad king."

Gregory pressed his lumbering hands on his temples and groaned. "But he's back now. Things were supposed to go back to normal once Billy got back. I can't take the lead forever—the past few weeks were difficult enough."

"On the contrary, you've proven you can," Maria said.

"You also don't have a choice if you want what's best for us all, unfortunately. You do want that, right?" Guilting Gregory was intentional, and Henry nodded, indicating its necessity, as Maria shot him a look. The resulting tension in her face was to be expected. She expected him to take control, even as she was propping up Gregory until he or William was ready. But he wasn't going to take control. Though he had been trying to avoid this conversation for some time, he knew he needed to come out and say it now—or rather he'd prefer to say it now with Gregory present. Maybe this way his wife would be more conscious to remain even-tempered. "You need to understand that you're responsible for everything until William's head is back in the game, because soon you won't have me to help you either."

"What do you mean?" Gregory asked.

The narrowing of Maria's eyes was an even more painful dagger than Henry could have imagined. He didn't want to do this to his wife, but there was no path forward otherwise.

"Yes, what *do* you mean, Henry?" she asked.

"I'm going back to New Berkeley."

"Where *the fuck* is my brother?" Clovis's livid voice rang out through the mansion. He was inside. Gregory stood in agitation and headed for the door.

"Again, Henry?" Maria asked in a sharp half-whisper, unwilling to be distracted or discovered.

Henry stood up, his eyes on his wife. "I shouldn't have to explain why to you. It's the only way I can ensure our safety. You didn't see her ... her head, Maria."

"Only because you wouldn't let me!"

"You wouldn't have been able to handle it, okay?" He couldn't help but roll his eyes at her. *He* struggled with the image of Judith's severed head, and he'd seen much more violence than his wife ever had. "Why can't you understand I'm just trying to protect you?"

"Because you didn't pro—" Though Maria cut herself off, the rest of her words lingered in the air between them.

*Because you didn't protect Judith.*

It was evident Maria regretted starting, but it didn't matter. Henry struggled to fight back the emotion rising in him. To hear her say what the voice in his head had been saying since the incident was crushing. "I *know*, I know, Maria ... which is why I need to do this. When it's done and safe, I'll come back for you and the kids, and we'll all go back home to live in New Berkeley again where we belong. There's nothing for us in this nightmare of a place. You have to understand—I can't let you all down again. He won't stop unless he's made to."

His wife approached him and took his hands in hers. "You know I didn't mean it, Henry. I didn't mean it. You haven't let us down. I'm just angry that you want to leave. We need you here. *I* need you here."

He wasn't buying it. She just regretted saying the truth. So he chose to ignore her. He'd redeem himself when Forrest Hayes was ruined.

He turned to Gregory, who was standing by the doorway, contemplating how to deal with Clovis without causing an implosion, no doubt. The latter could be heard stomping through the halls, shouting for William. "Gregory, please remember I'm relying on you to keep my family safe while I'm gone. You're the only one I can trust to protect them until I've done what I need to do. Will you handle that for me?"

Gregory blinked once, then twice, before sighing. "I mean, yeah … I'll try my best."

Out in the hall, Clovis's feet pounded the floor. "That's it! Guess I'm gonna have to go find him myself!"

"I know you will," Henry said to Gregory. After exchanging one last look of mutual disappointment with his wife, he grabbed for the door. Gregory didn't inspire his complete confidence, but he knew he had no other choice.

When he exited, he walked through a short hall, and there was Clovis—as much a mess in his appearance as ever. For some reason, there were bags around his eyes, as well. Those were new.

With as much pep as Henry could muster, he walked over to him at a brisk pace, halting his thunderous advance. "Clovis, what can I do for you, my friend?"

Bloodshot eyes turned toward him. "What can *you* do for me? Well, no one has been able to do a single thing for me besides my brothers, so you could start out pointing in the direction of the one who's living here."

"Look, I understand your frustration, but William told us he doesn't want to be interrupted under any circumstances." Henry decided to divulge a small bit of information to keep Clovis at bay. "Our journey to New Berkeley … let's just say it didn't go according to plan, and William requested time to recover from what went down. It should be him who tells you all the news, too, which I'm sure he'll do when he decides he's ready."

"You're telling me things didn't go according to plan on the trip? The trip that meant everything to Billy?" Clovis asked in a near whisper, creeping closer to Henry with his head tilted.

Remaining still, Henry's stomach twisted as Clovis approached. There was almost a physical chill that emanated from him.

"And now he's hurting, and you expect me to wait to be there for him?" Clovis continued, edging even closer. "His own *brother*? One of the only people he truly has in this world? What kind of a monster do you think I am?"

Careful to keep his voice monotone, Henry said, "Look, son, I'm not trying to divide you two in any way. If alone time wasn't what William asked for, I wouldn't have even suggested you allow him to come out on his own."

"Divide us? Now who said anything about dividing us?"

"I didn't m—"

"And what do you mean *come out*? How long has my brother been alone?"

As Clovis spoke, the futility of trying to convince him of anything crystalized. The man would never hear him. He was too far gone for it. The best course would be for Henry to end the conversation on his good side. "No, he—"

"Are you not aware of the things I've done to people? People I didn't even know? People who did absolutely nothing to me personally?"

"I wouldn't—"

"What do you think I would do to a person who did wrong me?"

Henry held his breath, going very still. He couldn't afford violence with Clovis—he needed to get to New Berkley at full strength.

"Oh, you *do* know," Clovis continued. "You definitely do. I can see it in the way you shake. I can hear your heart beating out of your chest from here. *Dah-dum, dah-dum, dah-dum.* So you *can* see them, those poor, faceless people … and you can think of what I might do to a person standing between me and one of the only people in the world to ever love me. Despite all I am, he loves me, and he's never given up on me."

Henry said nothing as Clovis grew more and more agitated.

"The last person I killed I tackled from a balcony before beating to a pulp. I guess, technically, I wasn't the one to take his last breath, but damn it, I was the one to kill his spirit. And a man without a spirit is as good as dead. I don't even remember his name. But that was months ago. It's really been far too long since I've had blood on my hands."

*Maniac.* But there wasn't any true fear left in Henry. He was past that.

With a sigh, he raised his hands and turned aside to let Clovis pass. The man could have his way; he had more important things to handle.

"Okay, okay, there's no need for all this, now. We're on the same team, and we've all been through a lot, so please know I'm only trying to protect the people we love the same way you are—people I myself have failed to protect, but no more. Maybe when he tells you all that's happened, you'll understand."

Clovis gave him a long, complacent look before heading toward the stairs. As he went, Maria and Gregory burst into the hall, shock and worry on their faces. Whether they thought so or not, he felt he'd done everything he could have under the circumstances of whom he was dealing with—which probably was little to nothing. Clovis wasn't rational. In his opinion, his odds of slowing Clovis down were also reflective of the hope left here in the Murrieta. Maybe in this way, Leonard Keagan had been right in his initial review of this place. Whatever William would or wouldn't achieve, though, was no longer Henry's concern. What lay ahead in New Berkeley was. As Clovis headed up to William's room, Henry turned away to prepare for whatever—and whomever—he'd face there.

*

The bed felt like a rock beneath William. It was uncomfortable and cold, but perhaps those qualities were what drew him to it since he felt the same. He was both exhausted and unable to sleep, a confused state he had remained in since he lost Judith. While rest and peace continued to elude him, he had found one thing in this time alone: a reaffirmed epiphany that echoed in his head.

"A time will come when you'll have to make a choice, William, between the relentless pursuit of your burning passions and your dedication to those who you love the most. Only then will you understand how difficult it is, no matter which path you might choose. Only then will you understand my choice." It was his father's voice repeating the lines over and over again, and most of the time he would reply, arguing and begging for it to stop.

As he looked around the bedroom now, which was in a state of mess he could conjure no justification or energy for cleaning up, his stomach started to rumble. *How long had it been since he'd eaten? How long had he been in this room? No matter.*

Reaching for his butler-summoning bell, a single knock banged on the door. Before he could open his mouth to prevent whoever it was from entering, the handle twisted, and Clovis barged in.

"Whose mansion is this anyway?" Clovis asked by way of greeting, as he crossed the room to pour himself a glass from a near-empty bottle of scotch on one of William's dressers. He downed the glass almost as soon as he'd lifted it to his mouth, at which point he poured another, finishing off the bottle.

"Clovis … I uh … I don't—"

For the first time since he'd walked in, Clovis looked William's way. "Man, you do look like hell." Clovis dragged over a chest to his bedside and sat atop it. "So what's the deal, Billy? What went down back in the dump Father calls a city? Why are those vermin downstairs trying to keep you from me?"

"I would ask you what brings you to Fayette, but to be honest, I don't even know why I'm here anymore."

"Brother—"

"No, Clovis." William felt a vague ramble coming on, and since he'd been rambling to himself for so long, he couldn't stop just because he was now in the company of his brother. The stream of words gave him something innocuous to do. "I mean, why are any of us here? Nothing in this world makes a lick of sense. I don't understand it. The natives control giant grizzlies, the Highlanders run around the Passage with no allegiances to anything, and New Berkeley's been transformed into a massive cinderblock. Hell, do you realize I met a guy while I was away—from the East like us— who reproduced with one of the natives?" Clovis's face twisted. "Oh whatever, that's not even the weird part. Thing is their child has the same abilities as the other natives, too. Can you even comprehend such a thing? Shit like that makes me kinda think this whole life is just more complicated than I'm willing to try and understand. I mean, what's it all for, anyway?"

As Clovis squinted at him for almost a full minute, William realized this was one of the first times he'd ever seen his brother at a loss for words. With a sigh, Clovis finally leaned back to cross one leg over the other.

"As much as the thing about the natives is, well … interesting … it seems Henry was right—this *is* serious. And here I was thinking I was the miserable, pessimistic, world-hating brother in this family. What'd Dad do to you, Billy? Whatever it was, you know I'll find him and do him worse."

"You couldn't."

"Well, now I know you're—"

"There is nothing worse, Clovis!" William stood up, unable to sit still when he was filled with so much emotion. "He never had known—nor could he ever have come to know—love like I had for my Judith. Without it, there's nothing you or I could have ever taken away from him that would be the equivalent. Ain't nothing could give him a fraction of this torment he's given me. To his own son, he did this!"

Clovis raised himself up from the chest and approached him. "He killed Judith?"

Having been long past breaking down, William looked his brother straight in the eye and nodded. It became evident to William this was the first time he felt the full brand of mental anguish Clovis had lived with his entire life. Perhaps Clovis, of all people, could now understand him more than anyone else in the world. This scared him as much as it comforted him, and though he thought himself long past it, within a moment he was overcome, sniffling and crying with his head hung.

Never the one for affectionate contact, Clovis wrapped a crooked arm around him. "It'll be okay, Billy. I'm here, brother."

"It won't be okay. Nothing will be, dammit! I went back there, and he was the same as ever, Clovis. After all those years and everything I've been able to do, it all meant nothing to him. I just became the next thing for him to conquer. I wouldn't let him take this from us."

"Damn right, you wouldn't. He couldn't handle the Murrieta anyway. And I swear to you, Billy, I'll find a way to hurt him how he hurt you. I promise."

"Clovis, you can't. You can't cause he's dead too."

"He's dead?"

"Yes," William paused, "I killed him myself."

Clovis stood frozen, his face blank.

"He left me no other choice but to kill him. It was him or me. Him or all we'd done here. I was alone there and I had to make a choice. Kill him or lose everything."

Clovis blinked once, then twice, barely reacting. Then a sudden rage contorted his face, turning it red. "How were you handling it alone? You weren't supposed to be alone! That's why Daniel and I didn't go! I know Henry was always a groveler and Forrest is attached at Leonard's fucking hip, but where was Jimmy? We've got his son—hell, we have both his sons and his daughter here with us. Walter's been my second in command. He was there for us more than our scum father ever was. Our bond with him was supposed to further support our cause. Isn't that what you said? So where the hell was Jimmy?"

He'd completely forgotten about his uncle in his shit storm of a visit to New Berkeley. William thought back to how his father had avoided his one inquiry about Jimmy. He wondered if his uncle was dead, betrayed by Leonard and Forrest like the rest of them.

"I don't know. Dead, maybe. But he wasn't there and I don't know that it would've changed much anyway. I think I would've had to kill Leonard regardless. And let me tell you something, it hurt at first to see what I'd done. But after? When we came back to Fayette? I'd never felt so much clarity in my life. It was like all those years of his mistreatment and doubt were washed away. My plan had failed, but it didn't matter because I wasn't living in his shadow anymore." William heaved a heavy breath. "But there was no escaping it. There was never any escaping that goddamn shadow!

Because Forrest, the sick narcissistic parasite, had to send Cassius and some dimwit sidekick Charles after me for retribution. And I didn't care, Clovis. When they came for me, I didn't fear death. But they didn't come for just me—they came for the one thing I valued more than my own life. And they got her. They took Judith, and they took my unborn child from me. My child! My wife! And I'm left alone and don't know why I bother breathing each day."

Rage changed to fervor in Clovis's expression as he jerked William by the shoulders. "You're breathing for the same reason I am. For the only thing we've ever truly had in this world—our brothers. You've always treated this empire like some project to earn his respect. But now its foundation has been set, and you've proven you were always better than him anyway. Once we finish our work here, Forrest will get his. You best believe that. I'll make that cocksucker eat the meat off his own bones while we watch, I swear to you. I'll make anyone else who betrayed you suffer, too. But we gotta see this thing through in the Murrieta first. You know we do."

While he wouldn't usually feed off such talk from Clovis, the thought of his brother feeding Forrest to himself was a welcomed distraction. The pause must have taken too long for Clovis, who released his shoulders and paced the room as if to think aloud.

"They tried to tell me downstairs we needed to slow things down, but what we really need is to tighten our grip now more than ever before. Hell, I know Judith was his daughter and all, but Henry used to work for Forrest too. How can we take his word for anything with Cassius turning out the way he did? No, I'm too worried for Daniel's safety to let us decrease our pace in the slightest. I know it might be hard to see now, but what we're building here is everything we've ever wanted, and we can't allow nobody to put it at risk. With what ruthless crimes I'd heard went down in the Riverlands, it pains me. A wolf skin draped over the corpse of one of our men. You remember. Shit like that isn't gonna fly on my watch. And, as you well know, Billy, with Daniel up there, we can't afford to lose another member of our family."

William plopped down on the chest, exhaling his stress and anguish with a groan. "It *will* have all been for nothing if we lose Daniel too, won't it?"

A smirk crossed Clovis's face, and he charged up to William. "That's precisely the case."

What Clovis was saying to him was right. Or it felt right. *What did right even mean anymore anyway?*

He waved a dismissive hand. "Go north, and if the culprits aren't already apprehended, apprehend them."

"Of course!"

"Keep our interests in mind, but don't let anyone responsible stand in our way. It's about time they all accepted the Keagans are here to stay. When it's finished in the Riverlands, send Daniel back with a request for however many men you'll need to reign in the natives of the mountains."

"So, still no word on any dealings with the tribesmen, I guess?"

"Seems Daniel's hands must have been tied up for quite a bit with the mess in Harran. So yeah, nothing new."

"Well, that won't be the case for much longer. My men and I will head there now," Clovis said, turning toward the door. But the door was already swinging open.

"Billy, I'm sorry to interrupt." Gregory was standing in the doorway, the knob still in his hand. He exchanged a sour look with Clovis before he turned back to William.

William only rolled his eyes at the tension. It was always the case with these two. Or with Clovis and anyone close to his brothers, really. "We were finishing up, what is it?"

"There's been whispers in town, and I've been investigating about the possibility of some folks spotting Charles Langston."

The name of his father's and Forrest's bumbling man, of the man who played a role in Judith's death, caused a phoenix to rise inside him from the decaying remains of the man he once was. The fire in its wake was furious and amplified by Gregory's silence. "He's here?"

"It's a possibility—I mean, I don't know for certain yet, but—"

"Gregory, this is a man who was involved—"

"Involved in the murder?" Clovis finished, scowling at Gregory. "And you didn't think to tell Billy right away?"

"I just wanted to wait till I had a source I was confident in. Now I do," Gregory said, more defensive now that Clovis had given his two cents. "Priest Kubler—you remember, of course, from the wedding—one of his parishioners informed me they caught a fellow sleeping in the pews some days back. Said he ran off before they could make any inquiries, but Charles fits the description. The priest basically lives there himself, so he might have heard something, too, I'm thinking."

Though he wasn't angry with Gregory in particular, not being in the know was frustrating—especially on this matter. "Keep nothing more from me. We *will* find him at all costs so I can put him down like the rabid, gimp mutt he is."

"*Ooooh*—sounds like of fun. Might you need me to stick around and assist a bit longer?"

"No, Clovis, you need to continue on as we discussed. If we do this … if we can take this territory once and for all, I know my Judith will speak with me again from the heavens and tell me how proud she is. Or maybe she'll—" William paused with heavy breath as he saw the part-somber, part-confused looks he was getting. *They could never understand. No one could ever understand what she was to me.* "Whatever the case, from here on out, we tear down any who stand in our way. This all cannot have happened in vain. I cannot let it."

Nods came from both men, Clovis's in high spirits and Gregory's indiscernible. Gregory turned and exited the room.

As Clovis went to follow through the doorway, he stopped. "Oh and Billy, this side of you … I know it might seem a little scary right now. But I like it—a lot. It's what we'll need in order to do what's right."

"I've got nothing left to be afraid of," William said, as Clovis nodded with a smile and left him to be alone once more.

# CHAPTER 3

## THE GILDED AGE

"What about the lore of the Maiden's Canvas? The legend of the Walking Widow? Oh—or our peoples' great battle of the Half-Hollowed Hills? You must have heard of that, no?"

Latera listened as Mika questioned Elan, Gannon, Shelton, Warrick, and Hammond. Walking just ahead of them, she and Winona led the others along a hilly, open basin in the southern Murrieta. Together they were utilizing the guidance of the birds to find their way to an abandoned Tokali camp. Their indirect route took them for almost two weeks of travel, northwest of the Hold. There, they would take time to plan the next move to get their people freed. Mika had been testing the boys on their knowledge of the Mother, the Murrieta, and on all things within the clans' common histories, and Latera was astonished at how little the Tokali knew. While they seemed to have a working knowledge of clan skirmishes in recent decades—stories they claimed were popular to spread in the Hold—the most fascinating, ancient wars and beliefs were lost on them. Their ignorance served as a good distraction for her, while she battled through the unfamiliar discomfort of climbing southern hills in the growing, late-spring heat.

"Walking Widow? Sounds like a ghost story," Hammond said.

*I guess he is not wrong.*

Latera glanced at Winona, who curled her lip and shrugged her shoulders, which made her chuckle. She wondered if Winona was displeased with their lack of knowledge alone or if their accent bothered her, too. Though the tribes shared the same language, certain pronunciations differed between the two. Hammond's accent was more dramatic than the other boys, and the more time she spent with them, the more curious she grew about why.

Scribbling in his notepad and whispering aloud his writing as always was Warrick. "Legend of the Walking Widow ... ghosts."

"You and your people do not really believe in ghosts, do you?" Elan asked.

While the whole conversation had been playful, there was an underlying defensive tone. Despite their apparent alliance, the prideful, competitive nature of the clans shone through.

"No, no, no—not ghosts!" Mika said, as if Warrick had blasphemed. Latera and Winona erupted into laughter, and Mika soon joined them.

"Well, it certainly has a more interesting name than the rest of your history lessons," Shelton said.

Latera found the way Shelton looked around his group of friends for approval rather amusing. It took them a moment before they realized he'd been expecting a laugh.

"Interesting it is, though it's really more so hopeful than anything—and unauthenticated," Mika explained.

Far off at the bottom of the hill they'd been scaling, the camp they had been searching for revealed itself as Mika paused his lesson. Located at the head of a large lake to its south, which had a line of trees along its western perimeter, the camp looked much like other abandoned sites they'd passed, with scattered tents and supplies here and there.

"Finally," Hammond said before he and Latera exchanged a look of exhausted relief.

"Oh, come on. You getting out of shape or what?" Elan asked, patting his friend from behind and charging ahead. The jest led Hammond to follow at a quicker pace, but he did not separate from the others, who took their time as they descended.

"Do not leave us in suspense, please," Gannon said to Mika as if he had never noticed the sight of the camp. "Be out with it."

Mika nodded. "Well, it is a complicated one, but the overall belief passed on with the legend says the Mother actually walks among us."

"No kidding?" Gannon asked. All the Tokali besides Elan, who was now far ahead, seemed intrigued—Hammond even slowed his pace to hear more.

"No kidding to speak of. It is said Her spirit inhabits one native and allows them to control all the creatures of the Territory beyond the limits of either clan distinctly and of both clans collectively."

An observed silence followed as the others absorbed the heavy intrigue of the legend.

"So which Tokali is she? Maybe Adila?"

This time, the others all were much quicker to catch on to Shelton's humor.

A brief giggle escaped Latera, but she convinced herself it was only due to his timing. She was far too infuriated to find comical even the possibility she'd been worshiping Elan's wretched mother all her life.

"There is no part of the legend that specifies the clan she is a part of," Winona said. Turning her hands in the air, her fingers started dancing. "But … she could always be a member of a ghost clan."

Hammond beamed. "I knew it!"

"Yes, I have heard the same. It is not known which clan she would belong to." Playing along, Latera went stern, killing Winona's lighthearted turn. "There is one certainty though, according to what my father used to tell me."

"What certainty?" Shelton asked.

"I know, despite the fact it is all legend, without any shred of a doubt, the Mother is most definitely, and with complete certainty … not Tokali."

They all looked around at each other, and Hammond curled his lower lip and shrugged his shoulders. "I cannot lie, my friends. I think she got us there. You win this round, royal V'ahani jester."

"Excuse me? What did you call me?" Latera asked in the most serious tone she could while trying to keep from showing her amusement.

Hammond froze until he noticed she was barely restraining her laughter. Raising a fist and letting her smile show, Latera charged at him and chased him all the way to the camp. The others in the group laughed altogether for the first time as they approached the camp from behind her. She caught Hammond just as Elan disappeared inside a tent.

A large figure flew out of the same tent a moment later, landing on his knees with a thud.

*An Easterner.*

"Stop him!" Elan cried in the common tongue as he ran out of the tent, a Keagan pin raised high in the air. "He is one of them."

*A lone Keagan ... here?*

The man made a quick attempt to get to his feet, but in no time at all Gannon's rifle was drawn. Elan readied a dagger in his other hand, a dagger he must have found in the tent. Each of the others followed, surrounding the man in battle-ready stances.

The first characteristics Latera noticed about the man were that his vest barely closed over his large frame, the bandana around his neck was filthy, and the top of his head was balding.

The man raised his hands toward them. "I don't want to hurt none of you native folks, I swear it. I've had a rough go of it, and I've been camping out here is all. If you let me, I'll just be on my way."

"Let you be on your way?" Latera asked, wondering how foolish he must think they were. "So you can run off and tell your Keagan friends our whereabouts?"

"Keagan friends?"

Lifting his hand higher, Elan took a step forward. "Could I be holding this pin any closer to the sun?"

"Oh that? No, no, no. I only have it for protection—so I can pass off as one of them should they find me." The hairs on the sides of the man's balding head fluttered in the wind, and he kept making a fruitless effort to pat them down as he stammered on. "In fact, I took it off the body of one of them on the way down here."

This man seemed too desperate to Latera. "So you killed one of theirs?"

"No, ma'am. Look, I'm not even from these parts. I'm from Harran in the Riverlands, but those bastards ruined everything and sent me on the run. I was in a position of great responsibility back north before they came along. There were people who came to me for advice and looked up to me. Even after the Keagans came and took it all away, I knew I owed it to my constituents to always keep my cool. Mayor was my official title."

"It seems difficult to trust an Easterner—even one from the Riverlands—without Adonis Morrell around to vouch for them." Pacing the circle around him, her hands clasped at her back, Latera considered how to handle this.

"What is our move, Latera?" Gannon asked, echoing her thoughts, his rifle still aimed at the man.

The man began to tremble with fear, his lip quivering. By now she was all too familiar with the position of control she held, but she was still learning how to navigate to her best advantage.

"What is your name?"

"I know they've done you natives wrong, too. I can help—"

"Are you hard of hearing?" Elan reared back his blade in intimidation. "Answer her question."

"Charles—sorry, my name is Charles."

"Very well … Charles." Coming to a stop in front of him, she delivered her initial thoughts. "The Riverlands are home to some of us, as well, so this alone will earn you mercy for now."

"Oh, thank you, so much. I—"

"However, we have too much at stake, and I do not know the

South well enough to let you go. I am sure you can understand."

"Yes, of course," Charles said, hunched over on his knees with his head bowed. "It's a dangerous place, this territory. All kinds of monsters out there."

"Thank you for your understanding. You will have to be tied up or supervised at all times, but we will make sure you have what you need to survive. We will discuss more of how you can assist us later. For now, boys, take him. Elan, please see to determining how to keep an eye on him and keep him fed."

Elan led Charles and the other Tokali into the camp, while Winona pulled Latera aside. Mika huddled in, as well.

"Do you trust him?" Winona asked.

"Maybe what he said is true, and maybe it is not. I never heard anything about the people of Harran having a mayor, though I admit, I did not know much about them or their customs. Did you?"

"Not beyond the role Adonis played," Mika said. Winona shook her head and shrugged as well.

"Well, if anyone would know it would be Jeannie and Harrison Morrell." With an expectant grin, Latera waited to see if her friends would connect the dots.

The first eyes to widen were Winona's. "Hanzah! Praise your cunning, Chieftess."

With a nod, Latera marched off through the camp, toward the trees outlining the lake. The sun was glistening on the ripples of water, which were calm and steady. As muggy as it felt here, she couldn't help but acknowledge the beauty of it—especially in her reclaimed freedom. The glassy water, the scent of wood and earth, the crunching of tree-fallen debris beneath her every step. She knew these things were all there before her time at the Hold, but it was as if her senses had been dulled during her imprisonment. Now, she absorbed and was one with her surroundings. At all costs, she was determined to ensure the rest of the V'ahani of the Riverlands would feel the beauty of freedom again. A sliver of guilt lingered inside her for being separated from them, though she was also more confident than ever in her choice. With Walter Keagan now dead and Clovis away, it was the only chance she had to regroup and plan for a rebellion. Once these Tokali warriors were better trained to utilize the gifts of the Mother, she would have the assets she needed to make her move on the Hold and inspire resistance— especially with the lack of Keagan leadership at present.

Rubbing her right thumb and pointer fingers together, she looked up to the trees. The repetitive motion was a new habit she'd picked up, a method for leaving the traumatic experiences she had undergone at the Hold behind. It calmed her. She would need it, too, as her responsibility for those around her continued to increase. Her brother returned to her thoughts as a sparrow high above came into sight.

"Hear me child of the Mother," she called to it. The sparrow craned its head in her direction and sang back in acknowledgment. "Deliver this message exactly as I speak it to Hanzah of the V'ahani, who can be found in the Mountainlands, from his sister Latera. 'Brother, Winnie, Mika, and I escaped the Hold with a group of Tokali. I believe I can trust them despite what has happened. Only time will tell, but fear not, for my eyes are open now and seeing with crystal clarity the likes of which I did not know existed.

Please send the leaders news of my escape and say whatever you must to eliminate the thought of surrender from their minds. The Hold may be taken back soon enough. Tell them Clovis Keagan is coming to the Riverlands, and a life under Keagan rule is not a life worth living. We must fight him. Also, ask the Morrells of a Mayor in Harran named Charles and return word to me as soon as possible. I can be found at a Tokali camp northwest of the Hold for now. Stay strong, and know you move forward with my love.' This is my message. Fly swiftly."

The sparrow let out a shrill chatter before darting off like lightning. Latera watched it fly away with a smile, if a quick one, as there was no time to waste. Her fingers continued to rub together as she marched back, her thoughts dancing with dreams of her people's liberation.

*

"You can't stop me now, Harrison," Daniel Keagan said with a dark grin. "You've been running and running this whole time, but you're cornered now. There's nowhere left for you to go. And don't get me wrong, y'all's daddy taught you well. I can see he did. But you never stood a chance once Daniel Keagan came to town. This is just what I do."

"How do you keep doing this?"

"Have you not figured it out yet?"

Harrison's shoulders sunk as he sighed. "I have."

"Well, good … means you're learning." Daniel moved his queen across the board. "Checkmate."

Lounging in a cushioned chair in the lobby of Donald's hotel,

Jeannie watched as Harrison and Daniel played chess for the fifth time this week. They'd started the day after the incident at the jail as a way to get to know each other. Each game, she would initially sit down to watch, intent on trying to pick up more of the strategy, but then she would pass out at some point, only to wake when the talking began toward the end. She took comfort in knowing Donald slept as much or more than she did—his silly hat drooping down the side of his head—and she couldn't help but laugh now as her brother lost for the fifth time in the five long games. Although chess had always been his favorite hobby for him and their father, Harrison's over-confidence at the start and pouting at the end of each loss provided an undeniable amusement. For Jeannie, it wasn't about her brother's misery, though. What made her appreciate the moment most was the sense of calm. Simple days like this of playing games and giving her brother a hard time were so long overdue.

Leaning back in his chair, Harrison folded his arms tight. "You think it's funny, do you? At least I can stay awake long enough to finish a game."

"I wasn't asleep the whole time; my eyes were just closed for a bit."

"Yeah right—"

"They needed to be, too, because they were pained and exhausted from all the rolling they were doing at your piss-poor moves."

Next to them, Daniel let out a chuckle while he reorganized the set. "Well, damn. You got some bite to you, now, don't you?"

"Took you long enough to think of that one," Harrison replied.

Too elated by Daniel's acclaim to care about Harrison's remark,

Jeannie sat tall. As if she was accepting an award, she started mock-waving and bowing with a toothy grin on her face. "Thank you. Thank you. You're far too kind."

While Harrison reset his own pieces on Donald's board, Daniel stood up, lifting his coat from the back of his seat and throwing it over his shoulder. Recognizing it was time for him to leave Harran, Jeannie accepted she couldn't keep stalling on her unanswered questions. To this day, there remained a natural intimidation she felt around Daniel, but she wouldn't allow herself to miss this chance for closure.

"Wait. Today's the day you promised you'd leave and talk to William, is it not?"

"Of course. Did you think I wasn't—"

"No, no, I trust you on your word for now," Jeannie said before taking a deep breath. "There's something I need to know though."

Angling the chair he was sitting on before in her direction, Daniel sat down and squared up to her. "Please."

"Thank you. It's just … if you and William weren't on the same page with Clovis doing what he did, what was your original intent for my father?"

"Well, to be frank, we wanted what he had. Only thing is, at the time, we thought to get it we could swoop in and overtake his operation as our own. What we didn't realize—and what I'm only now starting to see—is what we thought of as his 'operation' wasn't an operation at all. It was a way of life for him, and those connections he made with both natives and Easterners weren't something anyone else could walk in and pick up without an equal amount of dedication to each party. There just ain't no shortcuts in life."

"As we've learned the hard way," Harrison said as Jeannie shared a look with him. The V'ahani were their prime example, for sure, who they'd struggled to connect with during their time in the Mountainlands, despite their late father's ties. As tough as it had been to stomach, they'd need to start over in a way. It was good to hear they'd come to the realization well before someone older and more seasoned like Daniel though.

"I'm sure you have. I'm also sure Adonis must have had the intent to develop y'all's relationships into the same degree of trust with his partners as he had. Would've taken a lot of time though, for sure. Time my lot ended up taking away from y'all, and I can't tell y'all how much it eats at me inside now to accept it."

"Which leads me to my real question," Jeannie said. "I understand you can see the consequences now, and you feel sorry for them. But before, when this all began for you, why—or how—did you not consider what Clovis was doing?"

With a slow look down, a shake of his head, and a curl of his lips, Daniel seemed to admit he had no good answer. "I guess the only way I can explain it … Harrison, say you saw Jeannie getting bullied in some kind of way by some older kids. What might you do to stop it?"

"Before or after she mocks my chess game?"

"Now, come on," Daniel said with a hearty laugh.

While Jeannie was less amused, she couldn't help but grin—it was only fair he'd get her back.

"Kidding. I'd defend my sister." This time Harrison's tone was stoic.

"Just like y'all's father taught you, yeah?"

"That's right."

"I believe it. Now tell me … how would you handle the situation if it was your own daddy doing the bullying?"

Harrison's mouth opened, but no words came. Jeannie furrowed her brow as she tried to imagine her father treating them poorly. She couldn't. It made her realize how few times she'd ever tried to consider an alternative to the kind of life she'd had with her family.

"Believe me, I struggled with the answer, too. It's plagued me from the time he was young to this day. And it'll continue to until William and I find a solution."

"Well, still, you can't think it was okay to push your problem onto others," Jeannie said as the thought of the flames engulfing her home overtook any creeping empathy.

"Yeah, Jeannie's right. Whatever it is he's been through, it doesn't excuse all he's done, Daniel."

"The truth is, I never did think the entirety of it was okay, but at the time I also didn't care, if I'm maintaining my honesty. Despite how his madness exhausted me, I couldn't give up on helping him find his place. I can see now there's no excuse though, so let me be off to figure this out. Let me do what I can to correct the wrongs I allowed to go unchecked. Y'all stay strong for these folks while I'm away, you hear?"

"Much as I appreciate all these two children do for us, we're plenty strong, I tell ya," Donald said, making Jeannie and the rest jump as no one realized he'd awoken.

"My goodness, Mr. Schneider."

"Right and proper." His chirp back at Jeannie was more joyous than usual.

The door to the hotel burst open. Frankie ran in, his curly hair and the shirt under his vest both drenched in sweat.

"Frankie, perfect. I'm ready to leave now, though perhaps in a bit less of a rush than you just came in," Daniel said.

From his place at the door, Frankie swooped to the Morrells' side and grabbed them. "Jeannie, Harrison, we need to get you out of here—now. Where's Dominic?"

"We haven't seen him this morning. What's this about?" Harrison asked.

Beside Jeannie, Daniel's skin went pale before he sped to the door. "It can't ..."

Now at the back of the hotel lobby, Jeannie and Harrison were trying to fight off Frankie, who was urgently dragging them away from the door. Jeannie kept her eyes on Daniel. She saw his fearful gaze as he opened the door, closing it and pulling away an instant later. With a sigh, he slicked back his hair and locked eyes with Jeannie. In them, she saw pain, stress, exhaustion, and that's when she knew. She felt the past week of peace and high hopes slip away from her.

She turned to Harrison. On seeing the look on her face, he stopped resisting Frankie, too.

"What—" Harrison began, but Frankie cut him off.

"Donald, is there a back way?" Frankie asked.

"Straight ahead and to yer right. You best be sure to be keepin' them safe, boyo, or I'll find ya."

"Wouldn't want that." Neither Jeannie nor Harrison laughed at Frankie's under-the-breath joke as they all darted for the door.

Upon departing the hotel, Frankie led them to the same tree

line and brush Jeannie had once hid in with Hanzah. Through thorn-laden shrubs and a ground littered with pine cones, they soon found a vantage point with significant enough cover.

"All right, I have to go back. Stay here for now. We'll make sure you aren't found and have what you need."

"Wait. You have to tell us now, Frankie—what the hell's going on?" Harrison said.

Pointing at a mass of riders, a dust cloud at their backs, Jeannie replied for him. "Clovis ..."

\*

The thunderous rattle of men and their horses increased, clouds of dust rising in their wake. Clovis's out-of-control train barreled straight toward Daniel, as he stood there helpless and terrified, dreading its approach. Clovis in Harran was the worst possible scenario coming to fruition. It was further worsened by the sheer number of men flanking him. There seemed close to a hundred, far more than Daniel had in his own contingent, which was not as organized or brutal as his brother's would be.

As Daniel marched toward the beginning of the town to meet them, the gusty day caused dirt to blow up into his face. Squinting his eyes against it, he felt lost.

*This isn't the right time.*

William and he needed to confront Clovis together. How would he be able to control Clovis alone? There was enough uncertainty in his heart about having the mental strength to stand against him at all, let alone when he was so outnumbered. As much as he'd come to love Harran and its people, doubt crept into his conviction. How would he even get Clovis to hear him? Despite an unsettling kind of uncertainty about how to move forward, one thing was clear to him: He needed to get Clovis out of Harran as soon as possible.

"Daniel!" Daniel turned to see Johanna running up to him. "Daniel, is it him?"

He wanted to assure her he would handle it; he wanted to assure her it'd all be okay. But when he opened his mouth to do so, he couldn't.

As he struggled, her eyebrows turned up. "But you said … you promised us. You told us you were going to deal with him."

"I am, okay? I'm going to try like I told y'all. I need y'all to believe in me—especially you."

Johanna's expression twisted as her crisp, amber eyes glanced behind him. There was a fearful tenderness in them as the windy day blew her blue dress and wavy gold hair to the side. At times it shocked him this was the same woman he'd once viewed as a ditsy roadblock, the same woman who almost stabbed him to death in his sleep. Now he knew her for who she was and felt a strength in her that called out to him. It was like the spaces inside him were shaped in ways she fit into, clicking together like a puzzle piece. And while there were those corresponding differences to fill his voids, there were also so many similarities. It was a sensation he never thought he'd have time or desire for.

*Maybe this is what Billy feels for Judith.*

"You were about to leave, weren't you?" she asked, her whisper nearly lost into the wind. "Were you not going to say goodbye?"

"No, I wasn't going to, actually." Strands of his hair were coming undone, caught in the gust, and he pushed them back. Searching her face, he remembered everything he'd felt over the past few months and everything he still felt now, standing on the precipice of his brother's thunderous arrival. He felt his resolve stabilize just a little more. "There wasn't a need. Because no matter where I'm off to and no matter what comes of this business now, I'll always come back. I'll never truly leave this place, Jo. This is home now."

For an instant, the hopeful elation in her expression overwhelmed him. He was lost in it. She nodded, breaking the spell, and gave him a quick embrace before running back toward town. As he watched her run, Daniel could see some of the other locals, as well as his own men, lining the main street, watching for what was to come. Dropping his head back down to the ground, he reached in the chest pocket of his shirt, hidden beneath his brown vest. Inside it rested his Lion's Paw pin. After having taken it off the night of the fire, he knew he'd still need it in a practical sense. He'd need it to travel to Billy, let alone to confront Clovis. But his head hung low now as he hooked it back into the fabric of his outer visage with reluctance.

Within a moment of doing so, Clovis's horse was before him. Jumping off mid-stride, Clovis outstretched his arms as his men halted behind him. It'd been some time since Daniel had seen his brother, and he was glad to see Clovis's appearance had improved a bit. The usually absurd haircut and beard occupying his head were molded into a well-shaped beard and flowing ear-length hairstyle. His outfit was also a little cleaner and more put together than usual. What Daniel could imply from this change was that Clovis had been to the mansion—he'd never do this kind of thing on his own accord.

"AT LONG LAST, THERE HE IS!" Clovis said as he came to embrace Daniel. Daniel thudded his back in response.

"Clovis. Devin." With a nod, Daniel also acknowledged Clovis's right-hand man, who was still up on his own steed. "I have to say, I'm surprised to see y'all."

"Yeah, sorry we're a little late. We were having a bit of fun down in the south. Weren't we, boys?"

Cheers spewed from the lot behind him.

"Well, I just mean I'm surprised to see y'all at all, seeing as I sent Billy word the issues I'd been dealing with here were cleaned up," Daniel said, trying to sprinkle politeness into his tone.

"What's the matter, brother? You ain't happy to see me?"

In his time here, Daniel had nearly forgotten what their relationship had always been like. He'd forgotten what it was to interact in such a carefully constructed role. Seeing the look on Clovis's face, it came right back to him. He let out a cackle to compensate. "Oh, what? You gonna cry about it? Don't be giving me no pansy shit now. I've had enough to deal with here."

"There's the son of a bitch I know." The grin spreading across his brother's face flipped straight into a frown of utter disgust as he looked out on the town.

Daniel thought now was a good opportunity to convince him to turn around, as it was clear he didn't like the look of the place. "Now, as I said, I sent a man down to Fayette with Cassius to—"

"Cassius was here?"

"Yeah … I mean he was for a couple of hours once Billy and he got back from New Berkeley. Told me some kinda mess went down with Billy's plan and that he'd come up here for a prisoner of mine, who I'd been asking to move to Fayette for some time."

"What prisoner?"

"Charles Langston was his name. Full-on idiot that one—but a murdering idiot."

"Daniel … Daniel, Daniel, Daniel." Rubbing his eyes and contorting the skin on his face in all manner of strange, stressed-out ways, Clovis sighed. "You say you sent word about not needing me here, but you don't seem to understand."

Daniel's heart skipped a beat. In an instant, all hope he might be able to get Clovis to up and turn back came crashing down. Clovis clung to being "needed" for his specialties.

"This place, it's in even worse condition than we could've imagined," Clovis said, stepping up to him, turning Daniel's shoulders toward the town, and massaging them. It was anything but soothing. His brother only touched someone like this when he was about to deal some kind of mental blow. "There are rats here—*everywhere*. They're hiding beneath the floorboards and in the little spaces in the kitchens … under our beds and within the drawers. Can you sense their presence like I can? It's *infessssted* with all kinds of diseased rodents, each one trying to nibble away at us. At what we are. I look out at this town you *think* you hold, and I see a building burned to the ground."

"That was an accident by one of our own. Found out the hard way rum, drunkenness, and candle fire don't mix well together. I straightened him out though. It isn't nothing to—"

"Tell me this isn't nothing." Clovis let out a blistering whistle. From inside the mass of horses came one with a body slung over the backside behind its rider. The rider threw the pale pile off, which flopped like a ragdoll to the ground. There was a bullet hole right on the forehead of the dead man, though he couldn't determine the identity without getting closer.

"Who's he?" Daniel asked, not wanting to go see for himself.

"Based on what you told me, you should know your answer already."

Having little choice, he walked over to the body and saw it was the man he had sent with Cassius to deliver his message to William.

"But how? What happened?"

The story Clovis told was worse than any nightmare Daniel could have imagined. William's dream to unite the Murrieta Territory with the East—smashed. Their father Leonard—killed in self-defense by William, who only ever wanted the man's approval. And most horrific of all: William's love Judith—decapitated by the same person who was supposed to protect her family, a person William trusted.

By the time Clovis finished, Daniel had to walk off for a breath and came to a knee to further contain his emotions. After what he'd felt with Johanna moments ago, the thought of what William must be going through was gut wrenching.

*Oh, Billy.*

He needed to be there for his brother, but leaving Clovis alone in Harran was not an option. Daniel now knew what happened when they let Clovis run free. And he couldn't allow it to happen here—not again. He had people to protect.

"I've never seen him anywhere near the condition he's in now, Daniel," Clovis said, coming to Daniel's side as he was still gathering his thoughts. Clovis's voice had lowered, and it was clear he didn't want his followers to hear. "And it scared me, the way he was acting. Y'all being the minds you are—so collected and smart all the time—it was disturbing. I mean, you know me. You know what I am and how I don't have no feelings. It's just a part of who I am. No two ways about it."

"That's some bullshit and you know it, little brother."

"No it ... Well whatever. But y'all acting like y'all's selves is one of the few things I have to live for. It's the only stability I've ever had and without it ... who the hell can say? I—I love y'all, you know? I need my brother back, and only you can get him there."

"What was the last part? I think I missed it." He couldn't help but grin. This time, his fall into this teasing was a natural one. Clovis's words made everything more difficult, because Daniel knew they were true.

"Don't overdo it, asshole."

"Well hey, joking aside, I appreciate your honesty. It sounds like what he needs though, is both of us." It was the best solution, if only he could convince Clovis.

Peering to his side to gauge his brother's reaction, he noticed Clovis squinting ahead, distracted, before jumping into a forward march. "Now, what the hell is—? Hey! Don't you dare move. Stay right there."

Back at the beginning of town, Daniel saw one of the psychic sisters, Debra Kennedale, standing frozen over a sign. With a closer look he realized it was the mysterious, "Welcome to Harran!" sign, which had been placed around the wolf-carcass murder.

*Why now? Goddamn it! Why did they have to do this now?*

"Clovis, what's the problem?" Daniel followed after him, wanting to make certain he would see any foolish writing on the backside this time before his brother could. Debra, who had stuck the wooden board into place, began to back away with an angry glare on her face. Out came Clovis's revolver, which he loaded and locked to Daniel's horror. The act prompted Debra to freeze and raise her hands.

"Take another step, you mangy hag! Go ahead, I dare you to move one more inch."

"Hey, come on, man. What are you getting so worked up about?" Daniel leaped the final few steps to catch up to Clovis, and he tried to be as gentle as he was urgent when he wrestled Clovis's arm to the ground. The two were now within fifty yards or so of Debra. The scuffle between them was picking up when a dim pop noise sounded from Debra's direction. Fearing an overreaction, Daniel jumped in front of Clovis. Craning his head back, he saw smoke rising to engulf Debra. The reaction he feared came as Clovis raised the gun again, pushing Daniel out of the way. Clovis unloaded the pistol at the smoke and sign.

"What the hell?" Daniel asked when the last of the bullets fired, horrified at the thought of Debra being hit. "I told you I have this place under control. You gotta listen to me when I give you an order."

"I've always listened to you and done everything y'all's way."

While Daniel was upset with himself to have let the last part slip—portraying himself as a superior wasn't the easiest way to get Clovis in the mood to listen to reason—he was more frustrated with this lie from Clovis, considering what he now knew about the incident at the Morrell home.

"But y'all's way allowed Cassius to sneak back into Fayette with someone from *your* town and break our brother. Yeah, that's right, the halfwit Charles you mentioned was in on it with Cassius the whole time. He was one of Leonard's pawns, too."

With a gulp, Daniel undid the top button at his neck on his shirt. "This deep in the Territory? That can't be possible."

Everything he thought he knew was falling apart around him.

"We've got indigenous folk controlling bears and birds and all sorts of madness around us, and you're telling me our father being a bastard is impossible? This place needs cleansing yet, brother. And I'm the person best suited to cleanse it."

Still in shock, Daniel watched as the smoke cleared and was relieved to see no evidence of a harmed Debra Kennedale—at least it was one small relief. He'd have to figure this out though, because there would be no getting rid of his brother until Clovis felt he'd completed the task he'd assigned himself. Following Clovis's group as they meandered into town, he passed the sign, which was now littered with four bullet holes. Even though it was once a great symbol of stress for him, he was now upset to see it in such a condition. Devin dismounted from his horse nearby the sign and, with two other men, proceeded to light it on fire. Wanting to tell them off, Daniel stepped forward to do so, but at a questioning look from Clovis, he froze. His brother turned away, as did the others, and shame swamped Daniel. He'd sworn to protect this town from his brother, but he felt paralyzed by the enormity of the task. From the time the sign was lit afire until the moment it fell to the ground in a pile of ash, he remained there, standing slouched, fearing his own welcome to Harran might have burned away with it.

# CHAPTER 4

## GHOST

The trek back to Orrin's camp in the Mountainlands wasn't a short or easy one—though Hanzah had made it in far worse conditions before. This was, of course, the same trail he, the Morrells, and Dominic had treaded in deep winter, the same trail he'd almost perished on not long ago. However, now in the spring, he found it to be a tolerable exercise with only the occasional burning in the muscles of his lower body. The physical pressure associated with climbing and hiking along the rocky trail was also a welcomed relief compared to the stress of impressing Varek. All the doubt and lack of confidence he felt in the presence of the Grand Chieftain made him worry he'd never have what it took to claim his fallen father's role as Chieftain of the Riverlands. At least he'd had good news come from his sister.

"You should speak when things trouble you," Orrin said over his shoulder without turning his head in the slightest. As he led the way back, he moved with such speed at times that it grew difficult for Hanzah to keep up.

"The news from Latera was exciting, uncle, not troubling. Nothing is troubling me, except my curiosity as to why you are in a near sprint."

Orrin's jogging came to an abrupt halt, the slide of his feet kicking up dirt in the process. "Yes, indeed. I am sure proud of that sister of yours and all she has done for the V'ahani of the Riverlands. But you *did* see Clovis moving north, did you not?"

"I did, yes."

"Well then, we have no time to waste, do we? Should we not be sprinting?" In his moment of pause, Orrin stroked his thick beard.

"So, you believe me?" Hanzah asked, catching his breath while he had the chance. He still felt so ashamed about missing the fallen bridge.

"Hmm ... what a curious thing to ask. Why would I not believe my own nephew? We both know you are bright enough, and the vision of the hawk you summoned is sharp enough. With those two things in mind, I am certain I would not have any reason to make an assumption about you being wrong in your determination. There is the possibility of you lying, I suppose, but as you are my nephew and a good young man, logic would dictate this to be improbable without significant reason, none of which I see. Though at the same time it would be *possible* and, on your part, questionable. Hmm."

As Orrin huffed and puffed to catch his own breath after speaking so fast, Hanzah felt the need to take advantage of an opportunity to be heard. "It was no lie."

"Illogical as expected, then. As such, the only explanation, it would seem, is you do not believe in yourself. Which if this is the case—and I believe it is—then it would be—"

"Logical and possible?"

"Well, I was going to say plausible, considering the harshness Varek displayed on the matter, and sensible, since you are a youngster and therefore still entirely unsure of everything in the world. Yet it also means—as I suspected—you are troubled in a way, which certainly is not remotely comical."

Though he knew Orrin lived in a world of his own, being unable to so much as make light of the situation with his own uncle made Hanzah wonder if he could do anything right.

"Well, what can I do to fix it?"

"What do you think you can do?"

"I do not know … which is why I am asking."

"Aha, and *this* is why you are so lost," Orrin said with a wag of his finger before shifting into a running position. "Follow me."

Racing after his uncle, Hanzah slipped along the path, kicking rocks and trying to not fall on his face along the way. The formations made by the branches of the short and tall trees alike billowed out on either side of them. Some looked like wooden webs. Others hung and cascaded like brown-green waterfalls. One in particular struck him as they continued on though. It was in the shape of a triangular cone and almost looked like it could have been a man-made shelter. Since it was uncovered, it didn't seem probable, but Hanzah's mind raced with theories of who might have built such a haunting looking abode—if anyone had built it at all. *They must have been desperate and made it to escape the winter.* He imagined the builder as being someone resourceful and, though he assumed they'd have been V'ahani, he thought of Dominic. It began to settle like a pit in his stomach how much he missed the crafty illusionist and his friends, the Morrells.

"Halt!" Orrin said, causing Hanzah to snap out of his thoughts and skid along the path to his uncle's side.

In Hanzah's distraction, he had not paid much mind to what they were running toward. Now, the mountain loomed in full view before them. The path they ran along forked at the mountain's base. Hanzah recalled the left way was smoother and circled around the circumference, while the one to the right was much less walkable. It weaved upward and at times required a vertical climb to continue along.

"Which way should we go, Hanzah?"

"Which way? I am not sure what you—"

"Not sure? Okay, well, I think we should go right. Follow along."

"Go right? But we will have to go straight up the mountain." The view up the rocky, eroded cliffs was unsettling. A recent rain must have caused the dirt and moss to seep down like wet paint upon them. At parts, it seemed the climb would be impossible with no room to grab onto inverted ground.

"Well, would you say you disagree with me?"

"No, I do not disagree. I am sorry. Please, lead on." Assuming his uncle had some kind of lesson to teach in this, he figured it would be best to just follow along.

Orrin sent a grin and puckered his lips together with a squint before finally nodding. "Okay. Let us begin."

As they ascended along the steep, muddy way, Hanzah tried to find what creases he could in his steps for leverage. Several times he slipped, dirtying his pants and spattering splotches up onto his white jacket. With each uneasy step, he continued to wonder what the purpose of this was. As they approached uneven stones, which required the first true climbing, he worried about his uncle's sanity. The mud from lifting himself up covered his hands and dried between the creases of his skin before he could wipe it off each time. It became uncomfortable to extend his fingers, adding to his irritation with Orrin's decision. A short bit of a level path soon led to a mossy wall of rock more than ten feet high—*a dead end.*

"I once faced a task so tall and so true, it was one that I could not hope to get through," Orrin said aloud in a choral ring as Hanzah listened, praying not to hear the order to try and climb.

"But the longer I waited, it never abated; the challenge beheld only grew.

'So, I spoke strong and faced it and never replaced it; it was the best thing I could ever do.

'For sometimes our silence is equal to violence, so fail not to try something new."

Looking over to his uncle and back at the cliff, Hanzah was confused by the poem. "So ... you are saying we should try to climb it?"

"Perhaps this is the lesson I refer to."

"Well, if you say it is what we should do, let us do it."

Orrin darted to the wall as soon as Hanzah finished speaking, which startled him despite his initial attempt to maintain his confidence. Standing off to the side, Orrin looked Hanzah's way with his arms behind his back. "I say we climb one at a time."

"One at a time? Why? How could we ever make it up?"

"Why, you ask? To this I say ... because. Because I think it is what we should do." Orrin's tone was passive, but somehow still maintained his customary playfulness.

"All right, I can do this." For a reason Hanzah didn't understand, Orrin's eyes rolled as Hanzah tried to be strong. Did his uncle not believe he could do it? Whatever it was, he was determined to prove him wrong. Not just him though—Varek, too. One day, he swore to himself, he would become Chieftain of the Riverlands. *So, I spoke strong and faced it and never replaced it; it was the best thing I ever could do.*

Standing parallel within an inch of the wall, Hanzah looked straight up and scanned for any crease he could find to grab. Noting the height was over twice his own caused shades of doubt in his mind. *What is his reasoning? Hopefully I might understand once it is done.* His still-crusty hands would not provide a good grip, so he rubbed them together to remove as much of the dried mud as he could. There was only one root sticking out of the rock to utilize for a lift, but it was in arms' reach, so he did have a place to begin. With a yank or two, he ensured it was firm enough to hold. It was hard to spot any kind of point for leverage beyond this, though. He tried digging his right foot into a few inverted spaces until he struck one—he was off the ground—if only a few inches or so. Next he'd need another grabbing point and a place for his left foot. However, this task proved much more difficult. Over and over he tried and failed to latch different spots with each proving too slippery. Trial and error dragged on for hours, with Hanzah sliding right off to the ground and figuring out nothing each time.

With the sun beginning to set, Hanzah's thoughts snapped off his challenge and to Orrin. He noticed his uncle was sitting straight up on a rock to the side, eyes wide open and un-blinking.

"I do not think I can do it," Hanzah said.

"Neither do I. In fact, I do not think any person could do it. So what will we do?"

"We have come all this way, and our time is limited. Are we to turn back so many attempts later?"

"So, if not, what will we do?" Orrin asked.

*Father would have never wasted such time with no purpose. And why is he grinning? Is this a game to him?*

"I do not know. You said this way would be best. And I tried—I tried as hard as I could." When his voice cracked, he forced a cough.

"You did. And I did say that … so what will we do?"

"Have I not—"

"No, Hanzah, you have not. So tell me."

"Tell you what?"

"What a chieftain would say."

"A chieftain would say to go back, that we *must* go back to take the other trail because this one is not possible to pass through and is too out of our way. It was a waste of time to attempt it in the first place. That is what a chieftain would say. And why did we bother? So I could fail and be humiliated? Thank you for this *valuable* waste of several hours and for allowing Clovis Keagan to move ever closer to the Riverlands, uncle! I know this: It will not be my fault if he makes it north to terrorize all in his wake. It will not be my fault."

The regret for the outburst was immediate, not because of how rude it had been, but because as he was shouting, he could infer what his now-beaming uncle had been after.

"Well, I might be a much better teacher than I ever thought."

"Oh?" Hanzah asked, already bracing himself.

"For sometimes our silence is equal to violence!" he shouted, moving swiftly to wrap Hanzah in a bear hug. "I did it, my boy.

Do you not see? I got you to tell me what *you* believed after all this time. You were so lost before that I could offer you the most ridiculous of options, and you listened because I am your elder. I mean, at times I did not even give you a reason, and you still followed. Perhaps this is due to the teaching of your father, and perhaps it is because you are in a new place. But you must make your voice known, always. Your opinions matter as much as ours, and if you serve us blindly, you will be of no true service to us at all. So I did it!"

As Orrin gasped for air again from his yapping, Hanzah considered the point. Though he remained flustered, his uncle's excitement calmed him, and he couldn't deny the effectiveness of the unconventional delivery. It had felt good to speak his mind after the uncertainty he'd been feeling in the wake of Varek's accusations. He knew what he saw, and he knew they needed to act. It was clear now, too, he was going about impressing his leaders the wrong way.

*Orrin is different, but he is not wrong.*

"Uncle, it does make sense—the importance of speaking my mind. I get what you are saying. What I do not understand is this: How do you trust your solution is the right one?"

"You do not trust it will be the right one, because much of the time it will not be. When there are multiple parties involved, there is almost never a right answer for everyone. Instead, you must believe in your instincts—as you just did, and as your father did before you."

"But his instincts got him killed."

"Ah, they did. Yet I assure you, if he had another go of it and was given the choice to decide on the safety of his people or his own, he would go about it without alternative—he'd still choose to lead them north. And the reason is because he, more than most chieftains or people I have ever known, was in great alignment with his feelings."

"I see."

Orrin's mouth dropped wide in anticipation. "So what will we do, Little Chieftain? What do your feelings tell you?"

Hanzah's cheeks warmed and he perked up. "We will go back down and around to the smooth trail. There is no time to waste. Follow me."

*

No amount of tenderness or reassuring would have gotten Maria on board with Henry's departure back East—especially as he'd opted to take the journey alone, not patient enough for a companion who would slow him down. It was a harsh reality, but such was the situation. In the end, the result was intentionally brief goodbyes between them. Though he'd initially felt regret over this, he knew there remained no other choice. The only way to ensure the safety of both her and their children was for him to take matters into his own hands. Forrest Hayes was the threat and would continue to be unless he acted. Explaining it to the children had been difficult, but enduring a pain like he'd experienced with Judith again would be far worse. As his horse plodded along the trail through Prayer's Passage, he accepted the terms on which he'd left. They'd understand in time; they'd understand when he was finally able to assure their safety.

Henry glanced around him with the sun pushing past the crest of its arc in the sky. His path out of the Murrieta was a bit different this time. Rather than staying north of the canyon like the last trip and risking a run-in with the Highlanders, he decided to guide his horse atop the canyon walls. This way would be dangerous, as well, but he hoped he might once again find the support of Bronson, Nova, and Kai, his posse's escorts on their previous journey. With Nova's and Kai's eyes in the sky, he figured his presence would be felt.

The weather had warmed in the week since Clovis had arrived and departed the mansion. This paved the way for Henry's journey, which began at the crack of dawn that morning. The land dried as the showers of early spring came to a halt, though most of the bloomed shrubbery maintained a brilliant hue. He trotted the horse along at a reasonable pace so its energy wouldn't be depleted on the trip. Occasionally, it would spot a lizard or snake and dart off in a panic. The mare's jitters made things even more difficult for Henry, who was not the most seasoned of riders.

With each bird flying overhead, the subsequent lack of appearance from Bronson, Nova, or Kai made Henry grow antsy. He began to wonder who might be out there, if not them. When he had traveled with William and Judith before, there'd been a bit of comfort in having another set of eyes beside his when his needed a moment to blink. Now he couldn't.

*Eyes.*

To Henry's right atop a hill, lying prone and peering his way was a red-bandana-covered face—*a Highlander beyond the canyon walls?* For an instant both he and his stalker remained still. Easing the reigns into the air, he took a deep breath before digging his heels into the mare's side. Once his horse was off, he saw the Highlander jump out of hiding.

"Stop!" he heard from behind him.

Stopping was the last thing on Henry's mind. Instead, he fumbled for his gun as his steed raced on. Once it was out of the holster, he cocked it and whipped his arm behind him. No one was there at first glance, but assuming they'd catch up, he tried to keep it steadied and aimed. A rough gallop forced him to turn his attention forward. While grabbing for the reigns, he dropped his pistol.

"Oh, for the love of ... damn it—hiya!" he called his horse on in desperation.

Picking up speed again, he took another nervous look back, shifting his chin to his shoulder. He held it there for a few moments, scanning and wondering if he'd lost them.

Turning his focus forward again, he saw a large wolf stalking into his path straight ahead. With yellow teeth barred, it growled and barked, prompting Henry to jolt at the reigns in an attempt to either slow his ride or turn it to another course mid-run. Instead it switched to an awkward trot in a sudden reduction of speed. The shift caused him to lose his balance, though he remained astride. His mare came to a stop and huffed and whinnied in frustration, a frustration that seemed to be directed both at him and the predator before them.

At this point, with the wolf prowling forward and the horse retreating step by step, Henry had no idea what to do. Without a gun, he had no defense other than whatever advantage being perched on the horse offered. The closer the beast got, the more visible the colors of its thick, brown-white coat and glowing light-brown eyes were. It stopped stalking forward, though stayed in the offensive posture, and it turned its head up to the sky with a howl. From beyond the trees to his right, Henry could see the same man as before marching toward him, only now he could see how short the person was. He'd also donned a cowboy hat since Henry had last saw him.

"Why did you not stop?" the boy asked, his voice too young to be a man.

*This could only be …*

"Kai, is that you?" Henry said, with a breath of tremendous relief. Perhaps he might have a chance to make it to New Berkeley yet.

The glow of the wolf's eyes lessened before it ran off. As soon as it disappeared, another figure emerged from the same location as the child had. Was it Nova or Bronson? It was hard to tell with the apparel. Also wearing a cowboy hat and red bandana, this person wore long boots and more of a loose getup to match. On reaching Kai, the figure removed the hat to reveal long hair pulled up in a ponytail before pulling the bandana down.

"Nova, thank the heavens." With his tensed shoulders easing back down, Henry noted that Nova still held the same youthful glow she always had. Then again, it hadn't been long since he'd last seen her, only a month. He watched as Kai followed suit and revealed his own face.

"My apologies for the scare, Henry Abigale," Nova said as she gave Kai a look. The young boy looked confused at first, but soon after pulled a pistol off his person, careful in passing it in the palms of his two hands to his mother. Henry recognized it as his own, and Nova motioned for him to take it from her. "It seems we are not the only ones who have been on edge of late."

"No, it seems not. You weren't helping my case any though with the Highlander getups." Dismounting his horse, he walked over to retrieve his weapon.

Apparent relief showed on Nova's face once she was rid of it.

"We take them off the bodies to blend in when we need to. We can never be too sure here."

Henry shuddered at the thought of them living in a place like this. "I can't say I blame you." He paused, glancing over at the way the wolf had gone. "You know what, though, I gotta ask … I'm still not seasoned on the Murrieta, and when I first got here I didn't have any clue about all you natives were capable of, but wolves, too? William never said nothing about wolves."

"My mother is special. I cannot control the wolves," Kai said with a frown.

"I know you are leaving the Territory, and I believe we both know you will not return," Nova said, addressing Henry and ignoring Kai's comment.

"Well, I'm sure the former wasn't too difficult an implication at least. But for the latter, that's not true. Well, I suppose if I die trying, it would be."

Nova stared at him without a word.

"What?" Henry asked.

"I would rather the truth be between us, Henry Abigale."

It was the truth, though, wasn't it? He'd come back for his family, wouldn't he? But at the very idea of returning to the Territory every muscle in his body tensed, a physical response to his degree of resistance. Though he may be doing this to ensure his family's safety, he realized he was also leaving for himself—for his own anger and for his own disgust with this land. The thought weighed on him: Why didn't he think to bring his family with him? But he knew it was far too unsafe to do so. But what then? Would he send an escort back for them? Yes, he would. That's what he would do. Of course, it was also dependent on if he survived New Berkeley at all, so he realized he just hadn't yet considered further ahead than reaching Forrest.

He refocused on Nova, who'd been silent and waiting patiently. How did she know a decision he himself barely realized he'd made? Or was it so obvious in his demeanor … had Maria known, too?

"I suppose it wouldn't be too far from the realm of possibility that I never plan to return." He admitted it both to her and to himself.

She nodded. "And yes, to answer your question. Where the natives of the Territory are limited in their control of its children, I am not."

"Gifted with beauty *and* power. I would say your momma is special indeed, Kai."

"Such power may be considered a 'gift' by some, I imagine."

"As much as I wonder what you might mean by that, it's all a bit over my head to be honest. I don't mean to be rude, and I know I made the inquiry in the first place, but I need to get on to New Berkeley. Important business, to say the least."

"Business is always important when there is loss involved," Nova said with a telling look. His mouth opened to reply, but he didn't know what to say. "It could not be written with greater clarity on you, Henry. There is no hiding it, nor is there need to. Kai and I will be going West soon to complete some tasks of our own. None of your concern, of course, but it is our own kind of business to take care of, as you might say."

He had no idea how she read him so well but was unconcerned over whatever business she had. Not unaware of how natural selfishness came to him, he readied his next question.

"I guess if you're gonna be going West, you wouldn't be able to see me the rest of the way through the Passage after all, would you? I know William made a promise last time, and I won't be here to ensure he keeps it. But if you could at least keep the animals off me—maybe spot me a Highlander getup if you have an extra—I would remain in your debt."

"Like I told William before, no one can tame the Territory. I expected nothing from him. I only hoped our help might lead him down a new path. One on which he would not further contribute to the terrors some of your kind have brought here. We will see whether he fulfills my wish. As for you, though, there is a darkness in you, and to be frank, I would prefer you to be back from whence you came while your demons still maintain their control. So with this in mind, yes, we will see you through as you ask."

Gratitude for the protection was short-lived when he considered the demon comment further. "Thank you. I do appreciate it. Before I head off though … where's Bronson?"

Kai looked away, and Nova placed a hand on her son's shoulder. "As I said, I know your pain, though I am not sure you could understand the extent of mine. The Highlanders became aware of our presence beyond the canyon not long before we met. On a run one morning after your return, Bronson went to retrieve supplies from beyond the tributary. The bodies were still there from your skirmish, so we thought it safe."

"We should have known," Kai said.

"They ambushed him, and there was nothing we could do. He would not have wanted us to risk our safety when there was so little opportunity to save him."

"Sorry to hear it. He seemed like a good man. It's hard to lose someone you love, whether a husband or a daughter. I feel I've lost not just a daughter but also my wife. Like even though I aim to be reunited with her, all we've been through and what's still to come will shape us in a way which'll cause the people we were before to disappear. And once it happens, maybe ..." The possibility of losing his wife's love pained him as it had since he left. Saying it out loud though was much more excruciating, so he decided to continue repressing it. "Anyway, I don't know. I guess I should get going now."

"Yes, I believe you should. And it is okay for us to accept the presence of our demons, Henry Abigale. But we must not give up the fight of what they would have us become."

Nova nodded one last time before she and Kai disappeared back into the tree line. Henry spurred on his horse, Nova's warning echoing in his head.

*

"It was some days ago. I cannot remember the exact length of time. It was not long though. Anyway, I was in the pews, sitting and praying as I usually do. I like to think myself a good, devout follower of the Enigma, so sometimes I'm at the church in the late hours. It's quieter, and I feel like it—"

"Skip to the part about the man you saw," William said, storming ahead of Gregory and the old parishioner, Mary-Claire Norvell, who'd apparently seen Charles. They were approaching Fayette's Church of the Humble Followers to talk to Priest Kubler. It'd been several days since Gregory shared the news of a potential Charles sighting with him, and William was livid it'd taken so long for the priest to get back from preaching to the small settlements in the countryside. In this particular mood of impatience, he had no desire to hear about the meaningless practices of those who believed in the fantasies of Cerebism, least of all from this uppity, prude woman. Cerebism was the predominant religion for those faithfully blind back East, and his late, secular father never raised him to pay it any mind. Now, without Judith, it was near impossible for him to imagine there was any meaning to this life.

"All right. Well, he was asleep a few rows ahead of me. I did not hear him at first, but when I was reciting the Fifth of the Cereb Hymnal, I heard a loud snoring. When I got up to see who it was, the floorboards creaked loud enough to wake him, I think. He jumped up, and it was like he had seen a ghost, because he ran right off."

"And what did you say he looked like?" William asked as he stopped on the steps of the church while the others caught up. He scoffed at the dark maroon, freshly painted Cereb Crest. The crest was comprised of a crescent moon with a two-axis star inside it, which identified the religion on the building's face.

*What an ugly color to choose.*

"I didn't say yet, but I can tell you for sure, because my eyes were well-adjusted to the dark." Mary-Claire nodded and looked up at the church as if this was some place to stop her train of thought.

"Well … ?"

"Oh—yes, right. He was a larger man and had long hair on the sides of his head. The top of which, on the other hand, was smooth and bald."

William looked to Gregory, who furrowed his brows with a knowing frown.

"Okay, that'll be all," William said. "Feel free to run along home and let us know if you see anything else that seems off around town."

"I was going to go in to pray though."

"Why?" William asked. The question was an honest one more than one meant to mock, as he didn't understand what good it would do for anyone.

"Well, I … well, for one, I know you are after this man I saw. Maybe warranted, maybe not. But I know in either case *someone* needs praying for. This way, your worlds may be better in your next lives."

Staring at the woman for a moment, he sighed. With a roll of his eyes, he waved her off before entering the church with Gregory. Priest Kubler knelt before another large crest at the altar in silence and did not turn when they entered.

"Hello, Kubler, we're here to discuss a vagabond spotted in your church." William's voice returned to him with a faint echo.

"Might you have a moment, father?" Gregory asked, calling the priest by the respectful title his followers might.

The moniker made William recall he had no father anymore—and maybe he never really did.

Another few seconds passed with the priest still frozen in place, his head bowed and hands on his thighs. Craning his neck up to the crest above him, he touched a fist to his forehead before turning toward them.

He was only a year or two older than William, despite his frail disposition and smooth, shaved baby-face. The haircut atop his small head was strange—the sides and back were trimmed close to the scalp while the top fell in short-mushroom bangs around his temples.

"Greetings, and welcome to our shrine, fellow children of the Enigma," the priest said in a natural, calming tone with his arms outstretched.

"Yes, hello. Now about my inquiry. We spoke to one of your followers who said she chanced on a vagabond who was sheltering here. Might you know anything about this person?"

"We are all the vagabonds of our God-given perception, William Keagan, so I'm sure you will have to be a bit more specific if I am to help you."

"Oh, look here now, Priest, I ain't got the time or patience to be dealing in strange metaphors about your idea of what it all means. I've been wronged in ways you couldn't fucking imagine, and I got nothing left to hold on to but justice."

"Such blasphemous language is not meant to be uttered within these walls."

The calm remained in his tone and bothered William. He read it as a smug poise, and it only made him want to swear more.

"Just … please, father, tell us if there's anything you do know, and if not, you won't have to worry about us anymore," Gregory said before William could reply, which he was certain in retrospect was for the best.

Priest Kubler's looks were the same as his speech—in all likelihood meant to be welcoming, but it translated as superior and judgmental to William. "I have seen the man you're after."

"Where? When? How do you know for certain? I didn't describe him."

"I know because he told me."

*Son of a—*

"Wait … you spoke to him?" Gregory asked, speaking again in William's place as he was now too speechless to do so himself.

"Yes, I did—in confessional." The priest paused. "I am sorry for your loss, William."

It took William a moment to process the statement, though his white-hot rage burned through any reason he had in him to do so.

"He told you he had a hand in killing a woman whose wedding *you* presided over, and you gave him a goddamn roof instead of telling us he was here?"

"I cannot discuss what is said in the confessional. It is between the confessor, myself, and the Enigma."

"I don't have time for your inane bullshit! Just tell me where he went hiding, dammit! You tell me where that murdering son of a bitch ran to now!" William pulled back on his hair as if to rip it out.

"To tell you would be to betray the sanctity of my title as—"

William lunged for the priest with a scream, and Gregory's overpowering restraint was the only thing keeping William from tearing the man apart. "Fuck your title and your Enigma, you dumb sheep!"

"We'll come back another time, Father Kubler," Gregory said, struggling to maintain control as William went manic. "You know as well as I do there's much more to be discussed here though."

While he hadn't yet had much to drink, William felt as if he'd blacked out. Even as it was happening, he felt unaware of all the venom he was spewing at the priest at this point. The words were dark, muffled howls to his ears. A maelstrom of grief and fury had blocked out everything else in his sensory perception—that was, until the infuriating priest spoke again.

"The righteous and wicked always have had business together. For how else would the darkest among us become enlightened? What transpires here, beneath this roof, fulfills the Great Enigma's plan to craft us a better world to perceive in each of our next lives. I do not interfere with those who confess to the Enigma. But yes, Gregory, I have a feeling I will be seeing you both very soon." The priest stared at William with the same emotionless gaze until the moment the church doors closed in his face.

*

A brilliant morning sun rose into the sky and forced its way into Latera's tent. She knew the day had come to train the Tokali. A full day of rest and settlement in their new camp had done her well, and she felt ready to take on the task. With a yawn and a stretch, she was surprised to see Winnie and Mika had already risen but still remained within the tent they all shared, actively moving about as if in preparation until they spotted her rising.

"Happy birthday, Latera!" they both said in unison.

"Is that why you are both up so early?" she asked with a laugh. "I have been so preoccupied I thought I might have missed it. Thank you though, both of you, for remembering."

"Missed your most important of days?" Mika referred to the V'ahani title for one's twenty-first birthday and the belief it represented one's official transition into adulthood. "Well, for the sake of the Mother, it is a good thing we did not let you forget. Even with all you have already done, such a milestone still deserves a commemoration. We cannot ever lose sight of our traditions, especially in these dark times."

"Most important of days ... perhaps, but I could point to so many others, as well. I find it hard to believe with all we have been through, this day—a day I slept comfortable and free—is the first I wake as a woman."

"Well you have earned your good sleep by providing us our freedom, my Chieftess," Winona said.

"Ah, Winnie, I have been meaning to speak with you about that. While I do appreciate the title, might we refrain? I do not wish to get used to a name I know I will not retain when we return home. There has never been and likely will never be a Chieftess—especially if we are to stick with our traditions through dark times, as you say." It had grown harder for her to hear the name, both out of practicality and desire to avoid later disappointment. To think she could get close to such a role, only to be denied it due to customs she disagreed with troubled her. For now she'd continue to let her actions dictate her position, but she wanted to mitigate the damage where possible.

As Mika's shoulders sagged, Winona tensed with a snarl. "Then we change those traditions, do we not?"

It was funny how well she knew them and could anticipate their responses: Mika accepting their culture for what it was and Winona being more spirited.

"I mean ..." A sharp look from Winona caused Mika to stop. This time Latera did let out a chuckle.

Mika cleared his throat. "Of course, should someone like Latera command our respect the way she has, we might have no choice but to alter tradition for her. What you have done for our people ... it has been nothing short of remarkable, and I would fight to secure such a title for you who so deserves it."

"Since the Hold, I have wondered what my parents would think if they were still here. If you had told them what I had done, and you referred to me this way in front of them, would they have been able to fathom it? All of it from the same girl who never cared to see much of the world beyond the Riverlands—not even through the eyes of the birds."

"Having known your parents the way I did—your mother in particular in our nursing duties together—there would be nothing but pride in both of them. She would not have been the least bit surprised," Winona said.

"You think so?"

"I know so. I think she had already seen it, too. She used to talk sometimes about how there was so much of your father in you and how she believed you would make a difference one day. Of course, she would heap praise on Hanzah, too. But there was something about you, she was so sure of it."

Though her parents had been supportive throughout her life until she'd lost them, it was uplifting to hear they saw potential in her all along. It further validated her path and eliminated any creeping uncertainty. To continue on this trajectory to free her people, though, she still needed a more specific plan.

She squared her shoulders and lifted herself up on her knees. "I cannot tell you how much it means to hear new things about her. But let us not dwell any longer on those we have lost. Today we need to be the ones to teach, and I will need your help to do so. The Tokali must learn to hone their skills as soon as possible."

"Hopefully it will not be too different from our own training. The largest challenge I foresee is we cannot control the beasts ourselves. It makes the process more difficult and dangerous," Mika said as they all rose to exit the tent.

In the days prior during the march from the Hold, the group had taken the time to stop twice for one specific purpose: to allow the V'ahani to attempt to control the hogs themselves. Latera, Winona, and Mika each failed on both attempts. Mika had explained to them it wasn't a surprise—his research pointed to there being specific differences in abilities between the Tokali and V'ahani. Despite apparent differences though, they needed to attempt to control the hogs anyway, just in case, as success might have provided some insight for the purposes of teaching, as well as more numbers with which to strike the Keagans.

Now as they rose to eat and assemble the others, Latera contemplated the day's training. She decided it best for Mika to stay with Charles while the others broke off to find the hogs. Although he was tied down well, and his story had been convincing enough, she knew they could take no chances with the Easterner. Until Hanzah sent word of the Morrells vouching for him, he would have to remain their captive.

As for her and the others, their search for the hogs didn't take long, as they called up to the wind for guidance along the way. It wasn't a surprise the beasts might be easy to find here, considering the camp was nearby a source of water. They ended up to the west of the camp within the tree line, which seemed to grow sparser as they went along. Coming to a place that seemed tranquil enough and had open grounds, she decided this was an ideal spot to work.

"Before we begin, I need you to tell us how you came to discover your ability, in as great detail as possible. We also need to know what you did following that discovery to try and yield the same results."

"I am the only one to have done it so far ... so I think I might be best suited to explain, if no one else disagrees?" Hammond asked.

"Please do share the wisdom only you possess, oh-mighty-one," Elan said to some under-the-breath laughter from the others.

It did not amuse Latera. What Hammond had done was an accomplishment, not something to be teased over. Jealousy did not wear well on Elan. She said nothing, though, and waited for Hammond to begin.

"Well, we were out on a hunt with Malik—Elan's father, if you were not aware, Winona—and he challenged us to hunt the wild hogs. He wanted us to be ready for anything, as Elan was herding your people to the Hold and—"

Elan scoffed. "Herding? Some choice of words."

Latera didn't step in, knowing this was heading toward another argument. In truth, she respected Hammond's opinion on the matter—his disagreement with how the Tokali had tricked the V'ahani into coming to the Hold and being captured by the Keagans—and was always open to further political in-fighting between the Tokali. They needed to play it out on their own, and she figured it could only lead them to be swayed more against the Keagans in the end—especially given the way the situation was worsening for their people in the Hold when they'd left it behind.

"Well, I meant it as it sounds. We made a mistake in sending for the V'ahani, can you still not admit as much? Look at what happened to Pharaoh! They killed him like he was nothing. Do not tell me you still believe it was a good choice to align our people with the Keagans."

The tension among the group shot up until it was palatable. They'd left one member of their group, Pharaoh, out of the escape plan, knowing he truly believed unity with the Keagans to be the best path forward. They couldn't risk his handing them over for his idealism. But he'd been shot dead by Walter Keagan himself while protecting them in their escape. There had been little time to grieve the loss, and the boys avoided the topic. It was an intense point of contention—too intense.

Latera opened her mouth to sidestep the volatile issue, but Gannon beat her to it.

"All right, enough of this. Hammond, we all miss Pharaoh. Do not make our politics about him. Elan, let Hammond explain the hogs to Latera. We have a job to do and no time to waste." He paused a moment, waiting for an objection. When none came, he spoke again, "Latera, I will begin with what I know: Malik took us on a hunt, and we each had to face off with a hog one-on-one with nothing but a rifle and a blade. It was high stakes, and there was intense pressure. We were all terrified to start, but we learned a lot, and more still when Hammond stepped up last."

"High pressure would make sense in terms of the ability forcing its way out in such a pivotal moment, would it not?" Winona asked Latera, who had already thought the same. She nodded.

"So Hammond, what happened—both physically and mentally—when you took control?" she asked.

"Well, see, my gun jammed on the first click of the trigger," he started, a twinkle in his oak brown eyes. "I kept asking myself 'why me?' at first—I am known to get a little impatient at times."

Latera could tell he was trying to lighten the atmosphere after the reprimand from Gannon.

"A *little* impatient?" Shelton asked sarcastically, picking up on the tone.

"*At times*?" Warrick added, ever clever, to the amusement of all.

Hammond let out a laugh along with them, allowing any lingering tension to break. "For the sake of the Mother ... okay, I admit it, I am as impatient as they come. But, anyway, so I drew my knife and tried to remember something Malik had explained to me earlier. He stressed the importance of being at ease. In the heat of the moment, the word stuck with me, so I started to call it out to remind myself. And I did so until the hog seemed to hear it, as well."

"A verbal cue." Latera was the one to acknowledge it this time to Winona, who nodded back.

"What about a verbal cue?" Warrick asked, scribbling notes.

"When we utilize our grizzlies, we usually maintain full control of them," Winona said. "Full control is being within the mind—seeing through the eyes of one of the creatures of the Mother and acting through it—it is also possible for a novice to give only a single command. What we are taught is that when a command is received, we are still in the mind. But it is for such a brief instant, we may not realize it."

"Yeah, I did not see through the eyes or act through it in any way that I was aware of. As far as I knew, I was still in my own body," Hammond said before Latera could have the chance to ask.

Pacing the grounds, Latera pondered. "Okay, this is all very good to know. To start we should break off since there are five of you and two of us. I—"

"I will go with Latera," Elan interrupted.

"I, as well." Hammond was quick to follow.

"If we are to be successful here, you all must be much more focused on what I have to say." Though she only now put the thought together, she had noticed Elan and Hammond were becoming more competitive as time went by—from racing to the camp to the teasing to this moment. *Were they fighting for the dominance over their Tokali group? Did they think training with the "Chieftess" was a way to further that goal? Regardless, neither of them needed the distraction.* "Winnie, you will take Elan and Hammond, and I will work with Shelton, Gannon, and Warrick." Predictable sighs from Elan and Hammond convinced her the decision was the right one.

After talking through their strategy, they broke up into the groups, the three boys assigned to Latera following her. The first day would be focused on their mental connection to the Mother, rather than on actual interaction with hogs. She knew the Tokali were much less spiritual, and it would be an important first step, both internally and externally. All day long they took the time to meditate while she explained the process to them. Ensuring they were calm and focused on her words, she described the initial feeling of taking control. She reiterated the crucial power of and the responsibility for the bond to the creature. As silly as they might have all thought this to be, she didn't care to try and tell them otherwise. If they didn't accept the mental side of the practice first, they would never be able to be consistent in their exertion of the power of the Mother. The task of control was much different than that of command, which they were used to in calling to the birds in the wind, an easier skill they had already knew from hunting.

When the sun appeared to be going down, she decided it was enough for one day, and they began to march back. The attitudes of her three students seemed pretty good. Winona also confirmed receiving concentration from Elan and Hammond. It would be a tall task to train them, but it wasn't a terrible start.

Upon returning and having a late dinner, Latera went back in her tent, her head down to put an end to her first full day of V'ahani adulthood. She wondered how different this day would be if Elan and the Keagans had never come to the Riverlands. Despite all the horror they brought with them, she was proud at how much she had grown at this point in her life, and of who she had become. After ten or twenty minutes of trying to imagine the alternate outcome, she let it go and finally started to doze off. She could feel sleep pulling her under.

A cottage was lit ablaze—the Morrell home, she knew instinctively. Clovis Keagan stood out front watching it burn with glee in his terrible eyes. She watched as Jeannie Morrell ran away out the backdoor. When the girl was just disappearing into the tree line of the forest, a shout went out.

"Sir! Ain't that one of them?"

Clovis whipped his head toward the trees, seeing just a glimpse of Jeannie's back as she was swallowed by the forest.

"How about you and your boys go fetch, Walter!" Clovis shouted manically, spittle leaping from his mouth, as his cousin assembled some men and hounds.

Within an instant, the image was gone, and there was a flash of another scene—Hanzah in an avalanche—and another—Daniel Keagan staring up at a flock of crows—and another that rushed by her too fast to process. Before she knew it, she was back in the field before the Hold.

Craning her head back and forth, she realized she was hiding for cover again among the hog carcasses with Elan by her side. The bullets whizzed into the dead flesh at her back as Elan reassured her. But she was now watching the incident unfold from outside her body. As she saw herself preparing to run, Gannon's shot went off. Time stopped, and she saw it all frozen—the flash of the muzzle, the fear in the expressions of all those in the field, and Walter Keagan with his own rifle pointed, one of his men right beside him.

Her focal point shifted to Walter, and time resumed, as she saw him grab the man in front of him, followed by a burst of blood. The two fell to the ground, only Walter was not the one bleeding out of the head. To Latera's horror, she watched as he waited there, throwing the body off and wiping his face in disgust. He looked straight at her, making her stomach turn.

"Are they gone?" he asked in an angered whisper. A muffled confirmation followed. He turned over to his back and closed his eyes. "Good. Now listen to me. You send a group to find and kill them. Each and every one … only the girl, Latera, make sure she goes last. I don't give a damn what it takes." Another muffled question. "I'm his fucking cousin, you dolt. Clovis's permission is my permission! I said kill them all, so he did too. Now go and get it done."

Latera's eyes shot open as she sat up with a gasp. It took her a moment to orient herself and control her terror. She was back in her tent, unable to understand why she was so afraid.

*What was I dreaming about?*

One part of the dream still floated in her mind, and she grasped at it before it faded away.

*Walter Keagan.*

She could feel sweat running down her face, and she was panting, desperate for air. The sun was now creeping up, and the first move she made was to the lake. Once there, she fell to her knees and splashed her face with water to cool off. The drops were coated with the salty sweat running between her lips and stinging her eyes. When her face dried a bit, she looked down at the ripples continuing to protrude from the interruption she caused.

*Could he be alive? Can we go south still if so? Were they really just dreams?*

# CHAPTER 5

## UBIQUITY

All Henry Abigale's life he had been a follower of the Enigma, like his parents had raised him. Any good Cereb believed in the power of the mind—it was a crucial aspect of the belief and the key to life. Their God Himself blessed them with this tool through which they saw their world. However, Henry was more of a casual follower and one who'd be considered on the progressive side. He believed in a more modern ideology of the faith, an ideology that promoted the mind's ability to manipulate the world around it. His late, conservative parents would most certainly have frowned upon the concept. Though Cerebism preached free will, the Hymnal said nothing about the power of the mind to inspire change through thought. Still, he believed it was reflective of the same faith. So, whenever he needed something done, he would repeat his mission to himself each morning, certain it would guarantee action and thus change—and his current mission was no exception.

*I'll bring it all down. No less than the entire operation. Everything Forrest owns—down to the last coin.*

Since leaving the mansion, his mantra had been his most important ritual upon waking. As his ship pulled into the harbor of New Berkeley late in the afternoon, he whispered the phrase to himself several times once again.

The Henry who stepped off the ship this time was different from the one who last entered the city with William and Judith, both in thought and appearance. The first thing he had done after clearing the Passage and entering Doreshire was to get his hair clipped. At the time, it had been longer than ever, as had his beard. His original intention was for it to serve as a sort of disguise, but the mangier it got, the more he realized it would only draw unwanted attention to him. So he had it lopped clean off, down to the scalp. As for the beard, it stayed, but he was determined to keep it well-trimmed. Overall, he was sure Maria wouldn't approve of the appearance, but he could always change it back once it mattered again.

Around him the port bustled, merchants with makeshift stands calling out sales on fish and produce and all sorts of wares. What a spectacle the competition between them was. One pair of seafood vendors argued with each other as they both tried to convince a woman of their respective filets' status as the freshest in New Berkeley. They sounded like politicians, each bashing the other instead of supporting their own cause in a relevant way. It seemed counterintuitive, but it was entertaining nonetheless.

As soon as the heavier of the two salesmen won the battle for the woman's business, the other darted off to find another victim. The winning merchant looked on as he did, trying to rush his sale with the woman. As soon as the transaction was finished, though, a young fellow, who was wearing black head-to-toe, approached him. The proper tailoring gave it away—this was one of Forrest's men. A second transaction now took place, one the salesman was much less excited about. It would allow him to continue doing business on these docks, though, so he conducted it without voicing a complaint.

Despite the overweight man's silence, Henry acknowledged a defeated countenance as the mobster walked away. Once the man in black was out of earshot, he approached.

"Excuse me, sir. Do you have a moment?"

"Oh—yes. Yes, of course." A downtrodden look was substituted for a heightened state, like a wounded shark returning for the hunt. "Burly, lumberjack-bearded man like yourself? Fellow like you only eats the freshest of fish."

"Yeah, that's all well and good. But I—"

"And look, I know you're a tough enough guy—I expect you prefer your salmon torn out of the water with your bare hands, thrown onto warmed coals over a fire in the middle of the woods, and seasoned just right to sustain your ilk—keep the wife fed and, by extension, satisfied. Am I right or am I right? Oh see? Look at your grin right now. I'm right, aren't I? But how about this one time only, consider what it'd be like to do no work for a real prize. To bring home the bacon—it's an expression, but I can refer you to a great bacon guy, too, if you make a purchase—but to bring it home nice and easy and kick back while the loved ones feast. You've earned it whether you believe it or not—I can see it. So what do you say? I've got just the catch. Best you'll find in New Berkeley. One pound of flounder, only five pieces. Four pieces each if you get two or more pounds."

Realizing he needed to play along to keep the man's attention, Henry took a deep breath and straightened himself out. "Wow. Did you improvise all that, or is it a speech?"

"Oh, all improvised, sir. I believe every customer should have a customized experience."

"Fantastic. Well, hey, I'll buy something from you, but might you have a moment for a quick question?"

While the man gave Henry a nod, he also kept a sharp, distracted eye on the other fish salesman.

"Great. First, I saw you struggling with a young man after your sale—"

"No struggle. No struggle or inconvenience at all." His cheeks and extra chin jiggled as he shook his head, eyes wide.

"Right, right … of course. Look, I don't mean to get you in any trouble. I was only hoping you could tell me what you know about the power dynamic here in New Berkeley."

A squint. "You sure you aren't one of them undercover or something?"

"They do that?"

"I don't know. All I can tell you is Leonard Keagan's dead. The control he had over the city is still there, only now it's in the hands of Jackson Hayes—he goes by Forrest though, so be sure not to refer to him as Jackson around him or any of his people. As for what Forrest inherited, the organization is still powerful as ever, but there's opposition rising and has been for years. The most evident is from the labor unions sprouting in the factories he runs. They're demanding better conditions and organizing, sometimes not in secret. That's all I can tell you. We don't see much of it here by the port, and I don't have any interest to."

"I see. Good to know," Henry said as he eyed the same well-dressed collector, continuing to make his rounds. "Okay, I'll take a half pound of salmon."

"Oh. You know, I don't have salmon, sir. I do have some scrumptious flounder, though."

"Does the other guy have salmon?"

"Well yeah, but—"

"See salmon's what I was looking to buy—it's my favorite meal. So ..." Henry shrugged and backed away, finding no need to apologize. Business was business, and there was no place for pity in his mission. "I do appreciate the info though. Real helpful."

The poor sap stood dumbfounded. "I took you for a man of your word. Guess I was mistaken."

This struck Henry, and first made him think about his wife, Maria. Perhaps he should go back for the children and her himself, once he finished up here. Whether it was out of guilt from this fat man's words or not, he realized he should be more considerate of her. On the defensive, he scoffed and rolled his eyes. "How rich coming from a salesman! Go sell your shitty flounder to some other poor sap, jelly roll."

The other vendor with the salmon laughed as Henry approached, and they agreed to the sale, while the fat man marched off with an insulted grunt. Once the transaction was completed, Henry stood alone in the mass of people. He felt invisible, which was more good than bad. Though he wanted to stay hidden and keep his presence unknown, the task before him would be a monumental one, considering how large an operation Forrest ran and how small he was on his own. The first thing he needed was a place to stay though, so he made his way out of the harbor and to find an apartment complex close enough to Forrest's office to scout him out, yet far enough to serve as a hideout.

Once he arrived in the ideal district, Henry couldn't help but take a route that would pass by Forrest's office. Whether it was out of ego or interest, he needed to stare into the eyes of the beast. A thick fog rested heavy over the cobblestone streets. Hidden within it were periodic lampposts, each dim, with only a glint of a visible halo despite the hours still not having turned to evening. All sorts of passersby, wearing everything from suits to loose-fitting rags, walked along the road. He counted far more of the latter than the former, until the office finally emerged from the mist.

When it came into full view, it paralyzed him. He stood, balled fists tightened and his right eye twitching, on the corner across the street from the building. All sorts of men in trench coats filed in and out of it. Young guns and old guards alike, they were. On the steps, he could see Judith climbing up, pep in her step, as she entered with William by her side. As soon as he saw her disappear through the door, she sprinted back out of it with them in the haste of their escape.

"Hey, what business you got standing around here?" The voice of one of those young guns snapped him out of his daydream.

Two others who were older said nothing as they approached behind the first.

"Sorry, son, just an impressive building y'all got here is all," Henry said, improvising an accent somewhere between his own and William's. "I guess you could say I'm 'new' to New Berkeley— in from Alvenika, I am."

"For the love of God, as if this city needs any more of you twinks." The young man looked back at the other two, as he laughed at his own joke. Having seen this before within his former organization,

Henry was all too familiar with what was going on here: new meat being broken in. "What did you have to come here for?"

"Believe me, I get why y'all dislike the place. I don't claim it as my hometown or nothing. The reason I left though, besides the people, was I heard of all the opportunity here and wanted to be a part of it. Any openings in your organization?"

"Whoa, calm down, old man. How are you gonna come up into a dragon's den asking for its scales? We don't know the first thing about you. If you want a job, we'll point you to a factory like every other shlub who invades our fair city." The young man turned to his elders. "Which one's hiring right now?"

The second handler scratched his chin. "Pretty sure the Anderson Mill at the corner of Frontera and Dobbs is. You can't miss it. Got the name painted in big red letters on the side. Kinda silly looking if you ask me."

"Textiles right? Who owns it again?" the young man asked.

The other two guards exchanged a look. "It's called the Anderson Mill," the first said.

"Yeah, I know, but who—"

"Anderson!"

Coming out of the building behind them, Henry spotted none other than Forrest Hayes within a group descending the stairs and now filing into a string of carriages. He made a slight turn to make sure his face was hidden. How he wanted to rip the hat clean off Forrest's head and substitute a bullet in its place.

"The people have spoken! For the Fraternal Forgotten!" A man with a white cloth wrapped around his nose and mouth pushed through the unsuspecting bodies across the street toward Forrest.

The three guards questioning Henry darted back toward the scene. The assailant somehow found his way to Forrest, grabbing him and rearing back an arm holding a blade into the air. Voices wailed, furious. When the attacker's arm came down, it was deflected by one of Forrest's guards, but not soon enough to keep it from landing the blade into Forrest's shoulder.

Forrest fell to his knees, howling in pain with a bloodied hand over the wound as a few of his men rushed him back into the office. "You fraternal fucks think you can kill me? I'm Forrest fucking Hayes. I'm goddamn unbreakable and—"

Once Forrest's voice disappeared, one of the sentries apprehended the assailant and slammed him into the ground.

"You fucking rat! You're finished, you hear me? You and your whole fucking family. You'll all be at the bottom of the Chorisma within the week. If you think you're forgotten now, you don't know the first thing."

The man spat up into his captor's face before those around him kicked him within an inch of his life. When they were finished, they lifted him up and dragged him up the stairs into the office.

Throughout the ordeal, Henry remained in the same spot on his street corner in shock. A smile crossed his face as he realized what he had just seen. Forrest Hayes, attacked in his own front yard. The pain Henry saw in his enemy felt good, but this was only the beginning. A weakness had revealed itself along with the sun, which now peered through the dissolving fog.

*

It was happening to Harran all over again. This was the prevailing thought Jeannie had, as she and Harrison remained in hiding in the trees almost the entire first day of Clovis's arrival. From what they could see from afar, the people were scared, the Keagans had control, and it felt like they were right back where they started when the Morrell home was burned to the ground. One glimmering ray of light was Dominic's quick save of Debra. It brought Jeannie chills to think what Clovis might have done in his random outburst if Dominic hadn't been so crafty.

The evening was starting to settle in, and still no one had returned with any assistance or update. Fidgeting in place, Jeannie felt her stomach rebelling and let out a frustrated, deep groan. "I'm *so* hungry." This was the same whining tactic she used on her late mother to give her a nudge into action. There was no one to nudge now, but she supposed it came out this way out of habit.

"Well what's complaining to me gonna do about it? We're in the same boat here, trust me. We'll just have to—"

"Morrells."

An involuntary yelp escaped her at Frankie's whisper. She noticed Harrison jumped, too, and for an instant he had raised his fists into the air. When she spotted Frankie behind them, adorned with his Keagan pin, she also saw he wasn't alone, but flanked by Debra.

Frankie shushed Jeannie. "We must be quiet."

Her brow furrowed, and her lip curled in an unamused gesture. After Harrison un-balled his fists, his expression was much the same. "What the hell, Frankie? Were you *trying* to startle us into being caught? And Debra, it's great to see you're all right, but what were you thinking planting the sign right in front of them?"

"I didn't think anything of it because I didn't think he'd know what it meant anyway."

"Was it your decision?" Jeannie asked in a gentle whisper, ensuring she was ever the voice of compassion in her family's two-person tribe.

"Well, no. Donald told me to handle it. He's taken most of the lead around here since your father's been gone. I'm sure his intent was to make it appear we were welcoming Clovis, rather than purposefully rattling him. I know Clovis is crazy, but I don't understand why he reacted the way he did. Thank heavens for Dominic and his tricks."

Fire boiled in Jeannie's lungs. "Clovis doesn't need a reason."

They all mulled over her statement in a pitiful silence alongside the singing of cicadas before she continued. "But what of Dominic? Did he remain safe and unseen?"

Frankie nodded. "Very much so. He's the one who ordered me to bring Debra to hide with you. He doesn't believe she's safe in the town right now."

"He isn't wrong about the danger, but danger's unavoidable with Clovis in the picture," Harrison said. "The people of this town need to know Jeannie and I are here now, and we're here to stay. We won't allow him to run rampant while we sit here helpless and watching from afar. So, before you tell us what someone else thinks is best for us, let me tell you, we're going to sneak back into Harran right now. And make no mistake, we're going to lead its retaking from wherever we are within it."

The nerves Jeannie felt as she brushed her hair back over her ear were superseded by her excitement to go on the offensive. The sentiment was mirrored in Debra, who shared a beaming grin with her.

Frankie displayed the only sullen face among them. "What about Daniel ... and me? Will we be included?"

"If you want to help us, Frankie, you can make sure Daniel's reminded of the choice he made and the word he gave the people of this town," Jeannie said, wanting to support her brother. "You can tell him we won't forget, and we'll be watching."

Frankie nodded in reply, though he remained frowning. Jeannie felt his desire to be a part of their community was sincere, and he had helped escort them out of town, but it didn't keep her from wondering how far his loyalty would extend now that Clovis had returned. With Clovis here, the list of who they could trust seemed to shrink. As Frankie's pin glowed in the moonlight, Jeannie couldn't shake the uncertainty.

With a semi-polite wave, Harrison sent Frankie back off into town and turned to Jeannie and Debra. "Debra, we'll hide in the Tomorrow Room again like I did when this all began. None of them will know of it, and it'll be the ideal place to meet with the others. Oh, also, Jeannie's made it clear she's hungry ... so it'll be good for us to be somewhere we can be fed without having to do our own hunting out here in these woods."

With a sarcastic scoff, Jeannie shrugged off Harrison's teasing. "Don't listen to him, Debra. He's as hungry as I am. He just thinks he's high and mighty now since he's not making a fool of himself in front of the V'ahani anymore."

"A fool of myself?"

"Only if I was being polite about it."

Jeannie exchanged a sidelong look with Debra, who let out a squeaky, albeit quiet, laugh.

"I see good things in your futures, you two. If we're all lucky, you'll never lose your sass. Now let's be off."

The town was silent and eerie at the late hour, the Keagans having all collapsed in their hotel beds after taking advantage of the spirits at Harran's saloon. Yet even without a soul walking about, the discomfort at the gang's presence was still felt.

When they arrived at the front door of the Kennedales' house, Jeannie recognized Debra used the same odd pattern of knocks as when Jeannie had first been reunited with Harrison. There was a moment or two of restless chatter inside, which she found strange since it was so late.

When the door opened, Cassie appeared and wasted no time rushing them inside. "What the hell are you all doing here?"

"Well, hello to you, too, sister," Debra said. Jeannie realized Debra had the same sass she'd praised Harrison and her for earlier. It tickled her.

Harrison stood a little taller. "We're here to—"

The emergence of Dominic and Donald from the kitchen interrupted him.

"I spose we should be gettin' ta the Tomorrah Room," Donald said. As they were rushed upstairs and into the room, Jeannie wondered how Donald was awake at this hour. Considering his age, she was impressed old man Schneider was even still alive— though she'd never say such a rude thought to anyone else.

When they arrived in the room, the rest took seats around the table. Jeannie was too antsy to sit down, so she stood behind her chair and fiddled with its backrest.

"I'll go ahead and say it," Harrison said. "We aren't gonna hide and pray you all save our home without our help. We understand you're trying to keep us safe. We appreciate it more than you know, as we do the lead you've taken in our absence, Donald. But this is non-negotiable. We *will* be included."

Dominic sighed. "Man, it's been a day."

"Yeah ya see, I don't got no qualm with ya stayin' up here in this room. But yer involvement in any moves we're intendin' ta make ends there, kiddos."

A thump sounded from Harrison's hands landing on the table. "Can I be frank, Don?"

"Well, ya see now, yer sposed ta refer to yer elders by their surname and with a 'mister.' I'm thinkin' a boy raised the way you were should know that one there. But yer lucky Don works fer me. And even though yer name's Harry, I'd prefer for ya ta be frank, boyo."

Jeannie couldn't help but giggle as Donald winked at her with the part of his droopy eye that was open. Harrison hated when Donald called him Harry.

Harrison's ensuing eye roll and shrinking in his chair didn't reduce her amusement either, as much as she did agree with the point he was trying to make.

"Well I'm sorry," Harrison said. "But you can't tell us what to do. You can't keep us from defending our home."

"Did ya know I'll be turnin' seventy-five in—"

"Yes, I know. I think we all do."

"Well if it takes not makin' it ta that milestone ta keep ya locked up here then go ahead an' dig me a six foot hole."

Cassie laid her hand on Donald's arm. "Now, Don."

"Have you forgotten your debt to our father?" Harrison asked, shaking his head and causing parts of his combed-over hair to fall onto his forehead. "Do you think because he's gone you're forgiven of what you owed him? The man who funded your hotel and supplied you your livelihood?"

"Harrison is just saying we don't want to be kept locked up when we owe our father, too, Mr. Schneider," Jeannie said, trying to balance his intensity with her kindness again. "We owe it to him to do everything we can to save this town."

"My debt is the exact reason I can't be lettin' ya outside these walls," Donald stormed back to Harrison as if Jeannie hadn't spoken. He waved his hands around without any intentional direction. Jeannie had never seen him so worked up before. His little, cylindrical hat even fell off his head without him noticing. "Yer father gave me everythin', as he did us all. The fundin' of my establishment ain't got nothin' ta do with what I owe the man. I'll be good an' damned if I let anythin' happen ta ya."

A small puddle had formed in Donald's lower eyelid. His passion touched Jeannie. As for Harrison, he went silent.

"Look, here's what we know," Dominic said with another sigh, interrupting the arguing. "Earlier in the day, before Frankie came to you with Debra, he brought news to us from Daniel saying Clovis is after reciprocation for the murders. He doesn't believe 'justice' has been dealt here, and he intends to dish it out himself in one way or another before he leaves. There are too many of his men in town for us to revolt on our own and, thinking we had things under control, we stalled the V'ahani ourselves by destroying their bridge in the days following the negotiation. Our aim was to prevent a war by stalling them. While it has already succeeded in buying us time, I'm sure Varek will be ready for a fight once they repair it unless we do something about Clovis first. When it's complete, we'll see them coming though. For those of you who don't know, the Morrells and I also set a smoke trap on the opposite side of their bridge before we came back to Harran. It'll give us some warning at least."

"Speakin' about Daniel, seems Jojo an' him are gettin' close again. Only thing bein' this time she might be takin' an actual shine ta him herself. Which ain't a problem yet I spose, long as he holds ta his word an' lets her outta his room enough ta keep feedin' us info on how Clovis an' he are approachin' things. She seems ta have been holed up mosta today so far."

"And I'm certain Daniel hasn't taken any kind of stand yet," Cassie said.

Jeannie looked away, not wanting to believe Daniel was an enemy again. It wasn't so much that she felt attached to him—it took longer for her to trust a Keagan than a week of good behavior—but she knew it would only make their circumstances more difficult if he turned against them.

"No, no he hasn't. But he did tell Jojo he thinks Clovis doesn't know a thing when it comes ta our role in takin' Harran back. No details on the murder or nothin'. He also gave her one other juicy nugget so far she was able ta slip me, too. Apparently, William Keagan's wife, Judith, well … turns out William must have some enemies er somethin' cause the poor belle had her head cut clean off." Donald scanned the room as Jeannie gulped down her disgust. "I know it's hard ta hear, but word is somehow Charles Langston had somethin' ta do with it. And even worse thing is somehow those Keagan fellas let him get away."

"You're shitting me," Dominic said.

"So what can we do? What if Charles comes after us? We framed him for that Jesse fellow Dominic killed," Debra asked, her head jolting around the room.

Harrison sat up and straightened out his shirt. "Charles can be anywhere, and at this point, for what you say he's done, it feels like he's everywhere. At least, that's what the Keagans will have to assume. And finding him will be at the top of their list of priorities."

"We would need the V'ahani here if we wanted to fight Clovis's group off and finish them. But we'd also need to ensure they'd be on our side. Considering how we left them with a dead warrior and a demolished bridge, I wouldn't be so certain Varek won't just storm into the Riverlands intent on destroying everything and every Easterner in sight," Jeannie said, with rebuilding her father's alliances at the front of her mind.

"My sister's right. And we can't wait for Daniel to grow a spine— we have to act. So it seems the better course would be to try and get Clovis out of here first and foremost."

"And how da ya expect we might be doin' that, boyo?"

"By giving him the justice he's after. We're going to give him Charles Langston."

*

118

"I can't stay in here forever, Daniel," Johanna said.

Daniel stopped rushing around the room to look at her. He'd been holding Johanna in this room for the last three days, since Clovis arrived. He did let her come and go, but as little as possible and always when the coast was clear. It'd been an interesting arrangement between them, as they still slept in adjacent but separate beds, given his remaining trauma of her trying to kill him in his sleep. His trust for her was growing, but he still needed more time to get over their "little incident" as she cheekily referred to it.

"Don't exaggerate. You've gotten to leave with me plenty of times, and it hasn't been half a week. I mean, we went downstairs to talk to Donald yesterday, didn't we?" With her arms folded, she turned her eyes up at him, their message loud and clear. He approached her and took her elbows in his hands. "Look, baby, I told you before. Only until Clovis is gone okay? I can't let you out of my sight with those animals of his running around. If they were to do anything to you …"

"If they did, it would have happened on your watch."

"Which is my point, and this is how I keep it from happening. Trust me. You know as well as I do I can't kill him myself—I just can't—and William sure as shit ain't in the right mindset for us to restrain him any better way."

"Well? What are you gonna do about it then?"

"I'm gonna get him out of town, okay? I have a plan. I just need to show him there's nothing to see here, and he should leave. Once he's in Fayette with William and me, it'll be easier."

"And if your plan doesn't work, Daniel?"

Knowing he needed an answer, he decided to give her his worst-case solution. It was one he'd been trying to shut out, but he knew somewhere inside, he needed to be prepared for the possibility. "The V'ahani will come soon. If they happened to attack, which they promised me they would ... I don't know how I'd be able to stop them and their grizzlies, you know?"

"Are you sure that's what you want to happen? If you do, how do I know you'll be safe?"

"Oh I won't be going up north again. And yes, I'm sure. It hasn't been an easy road, coming to accept the possibility. But I have, and I need you to keep the people of this town at bay, so I can ensure it doesn't come to that. I would speak to them myself, but I can't right now, so I need you to pass along a message: Clovis feels unsure of my allegiances as it is, and I'm certain he's got eyes on me at all times, so I need to stay under the radar. I told you I'd figure this out for you and for everyone in Harran, and that's what I'm doing now. It might look passive, but my lack of action is calculated, you get me?"

Her hands fell to her sides. Pulling her close, he gave her a kiss she returned with a renewed affection.

"I trust you." As she smiled, he let go and walked to the door. "But Daniel, don't prove me wrong for doing so. Next time I won't miss, baby."

"Shit. Do you ever want to sleep with me again, crazy woman?"

"I do. But you'll have to earn it."

The second he exited his room, one of Clovis's watchdogs was there to guide him down to meet his brother out front. Before they made it outside, he grabbed Frankie, who he ensured was with him whenever possible. Besides Johanna, Frankie was the person he could most confide in. The activities of Clovis and his men during their three days in Harran had thus far been of an investigative nature. During their nights in the saloon, there was a greater tameness than usual, for which Daniel was grateful and determined to maintain. He did worry about Clovis's threats of justice once the investigation into the wolf-skin murder was done, but at the same time, it seemed Clovis had yet to find anyone to mete it on— and Daniel was determined to ensure he wouldn't. The Morrells presence remained unknown, and Daniel was even recently able to secure Clovis's goodwill in regard to allowing Debra Kennedale to walk free, despite the previous misunderstanding. It wasn't without an embarrassing apology in which Clovis got an intimidation-high off Debra, but Daniel was thankful there was no violence involved.

When Daniel, Frankie, and their escort arrived outside, his brother was surrounded by a group of his men, Devin Turpin being the first of them by Clovis's side. Though Clovis locked eyes with Daniel when Daniel exited, he continued to talk in a monotonous tone to his followers, all of whom had their heads bowed, some even with a hand lifted toward him. The devotion they showed him made Daniel uneasy, and the feeling was intensified by the grin on Clovis's face. It was all so calculated. Somehow, it was difficult to tell whether this was meant as an attempt to share a dark pleasure with him, or if it was a way of bragging at his expense. The result wouldn't have been much better either way.

"Daniel! Perfect. We were waiting on you while you and your piece were busy cuddling. You've grown awful close with these people, huh?" Clovis asked after his apparent sermon had ended.

"Such is natural when forming alliances, brother."

"Yeah, well, our search has come up empty, so we should be on our way north to formalize the V'ahani surrender soon. Seems like your town here is clean, as much as it pains me to say it. Last stop today will just be to that bastard-ass Charles's house. I can only infer it's been him responsible for all this mess. Figured you'd want to review the contents, too, so we can both be better informed on Billy's most wanted."

Struggling to find the words, Daniel forced out a reply. "Uh, yes, perfect … let's go right now and see, so we can get back to Billy as soon as possible though. I can worry about the negotiations later since that's not your thing. I'm confident the V'ahani will surrender once we've regrouped with our brother. They don't have a choice with their people hostage at the Hold." He was elated by this turn of events.

"Fair enough. Let's be off."

Devin yapped the whole way as they walked through the town. "I've been known to be quite the talker. Yes, quite the talker indeed. By the way, your woman—what's her name, Johanna? Whew! That's a pure bred bitch if I've ever seen one. And I've seen a few."

Daniel winced and balled a fist, digging his nails into his palms, but gave no reply as Charles's house came into view. A whistle rang out from Clovis, signaling a few men to the door to search for anything of note as the others waited out front.

In the interim, Devin approached Daniel, rubbing his hands together and breathing heavily. "Hey, is she one of those freaky types? The type who doesn't mind being shared? I like those types. I mean, hell, I'm pretty modern myself if the two of you want to—"

"Oh, will you just—"

There was a bone-shattering clink, followed by an ear-piercing scream. Daniel whipped his head toward the sound to see the lead man who'd entered the house was sprayed in blood, his lower leg caught in a bear trap. Confusion swamped him until a hail of bullets tore through the air. Daniel jumped to the ground to avoid them. He saw Devin tackle Clovis to protect him and several other men rush to cover him up, as well. After six shots went off, the firing stopped, suggesting a revolver. He looked up and saw the bear-trap victim had been shot dead—not the worst thing considering his circumstances—along with one other man who was behind him. Two others were wounded in front of the open door.

"Well? What are y'all waiting on?" Clovis screamed at the next line of men closest to the house. His order for them to continue in wasn't surprising, but how ready they were to do it was. "If he's in there, y'all take him alive and—"

*Could Charles be here in Harran?*

Two more bright flashes and more pained cries came from within, seconds after their entry.

"They can't keep going in there."

With a grunt, Clovis affirmed Daniel's point. "Fall back!"

A rider covered in black emerged from behind the house and stormed off to the east, before veering north. He was much too fast to get any kind of look at.

Slamming the dirt beneath him with his hand, Clovis lifted himself to his feet. "After him!"

They couldn't react fast enough, however, as their horses needed to be fetched before they could make chase. Once they were retrieved, Clovis, Frankie, Devin, Daniel, and a large group of gang members rode in the direction the rider had vanished. Their path led them to the outskirts of town, and in time, they spotted the black mare, tied to a tree and standing still before the woods of the Riverlands.

"You think we should go in there?" Daniel asked, now as terrified of the capabilities of this man as he was to enter the darkness of the trees in which he might be lurking. *Could the stupidity and foolishness have just been a façade? After having played such a sinister game to this point, how could it not have been? Who the hell is Charles Langston, really?*

The first to dismount was Clovis. "You're goddamn right we're going after him. To the ends of this earth we'll go until this man is skinned."

They went creeping through brush, following Devin's lead, who declared himself good at tracking as he analyzed the trail left behind. As they went deeper, the forest seemed to grow more still. Despite the lack of any sound other than their feet crunching on the branches below them, Daniel felt the silence screaming. It was like a voice of its own, begging for them to leave this place. He wanted so bad to appease it, especially when he spotted a claw mark torn into a tree, followed by another, and soon after, another—*the grizzlies.*

"Do you see this shit, Clovis?" Daniel asked. "This is V'ahani territory. We need to get the hell out of here."

Stretched out like a spider along the ground, Devin scanned the tracks and took a sharp look to his back-left. "Our escape artist might have thought the same thing. The trail turns back here."

"We follow it until it ends," Clovis said, as Devin doubled back, squinting down with each step.

More bear claws appeared left and right. Each sound made them wonder if their own procession caused it. The snarling of the bears that surrounded Daniel during the V'ahani negotiation came to him now. A recurring flashback of their glowing eyes made him cringe at every turn. An opening in the trees came into sight—on second glance it was the same opening they had entered from. After all the searching, they had made a big circle back to where they started, only this time, the horse from before was gone.

A frustrated roar emitted from Clovis. "We aren't done here after all. Let's get back to the house."

When they arrived back at Charles's home, they made a careful and calculated search of the entry of each room. No more traps of any kind were triggered, and there was no trace of Charles or anyone else. What they did find was a ton of notebooks and papers scattered about. There were all kinds of writings on them—some making Charles seem crazy and confirming the man was who he'd been thought he was at first. However, others were concise and contained apparent details on his connections to New Berkeley. Diary entries sat next to summaries on different things about the Murrieta, but what struck Daniel the most were letters signed in his father's name.

"Clovis!" someone said from upstairs.

Daniel followed Clovis and Devin up the stairs while Frankie remained fixed on the letters. What lay before the onlookers in the room they came to was the skull of a wolf, mounted on the wall.

Clovis stroked a hand along the bone. "You said our slain friend was draped in a wolf skin, yeah?"

With a slow nod, Daniel's stomach dropped as he realized this whole chase had to have been the people of Harran's doing. Charles was in jail at the time of the murder, but Clovis didn't know this since Daniel was trying to keep it from him—Daniel wouldn't do anything to facilitate the investigation on purpose. Now Clovis would have a ghost to chase, which Daniel thought was brilliant on the part of the people of Harran, despite the possibility it now ruined his chance for Clovis to go back to Fayette with him. He needed to meet with the townspeople alone, but he wasn't sure how he could pull it off. With Devin's vile talk about Johanna, he would now also be firmer in his refusal to let her leave while he wasn't present, ruling out her help.

Behind him, Frankie entered as Clovis continued to inspect—or rather, morbidly admire—the skull before him. "Well, if Charles is our sure target, the investigation in Harran is back on."

*Damn it.*

"What's that?" Frankie asked pointing to the skull.

Daniel rushed over to usher Frankie out. "It's nothing."

"But wasn't Charles in jail when—"

"Come now, Frankie, I'll explain everything to you another time." Daniel's stomach sank as he spoke over Frankie. The young man didn't realize what he had done.

"WAIT! Just a second ..." Clovis said, Daniel's shoulders rising as a shiver went up his spine. "Please, come again, Frankie. Are you saying this wasn't Charles's doing?"

Daniel tried to defend himself. "No, he's missing the evidence of what's—"

"Devin!" Clovis said aloud to his man standing right next to him.

"Yes, my liege?"

"Did I ask for Daniel to come again? Or did I ask for Frankie to come again?"

"If I heard you right. Which, I don't believe there's anything wrong with my—"

"OUT WITH IT!"

"You asked for Frankie, my liege."

"DING, DING, FUCKING DING, I THINK WE HAVE A WINNER!" With a sour look toward Daniel, Clovis walked right up into Frankie's face. "Now Frankie, were you saying Charles was in jail at the time of the murder?"

"I did say that," Frankie said with his head hung.

"And Daniel—now this time I'd very much like for you to talk— might you be able and/or willing to corroborate this story?"

"I mean, it is true, but you've seen what he did here. The little shit is craftier than I've given him credit for, and it's possible he escaped and was somehow still responsible."

"Possible ... maybe ... but I doubt it. More likely, someone in this town framed an easily-framed man right under your weak-sniffing nose. For this, I am rejuvenated because, my friends, now I'm certain we'll have ourselves a good old-fashioned execution!" The others in the room cheered as Daniel exchanged a dreary look with Frankie. "And you, my brother ... for withholding information from me, you're now on my shit-list. As for you Frankie, you come with me. There's plenty more for us to talk about while Mr. Daniel sits in his room with his tramp and thinks about what he's done."

As the others left the room, Daniel remained still and bewildered. A red line had been crossed here: Clovis had officially asserted a position greater than his own. Though Clovis had been erratic before, the power dynamic of the brothers always had a clear balance—a balance now shifted in a dramatic way. Daniel had become an outsider in his own organization here as his plan to get Clovis south toppled in rapid, dramatic fashion. The "smooth talker" was now locked out from talking to both Clovis *and* the people of Harran. A craving for Johanna hit him, and an instinctive dash for the hotel began. Though he prayed Frankie wouldn't break and reveal the additional murders Clovis had yet to discover, he needed to clear his head so he could think straight enough to find some solution. If Clovis found the parties truly guilty here in Harran, Daniel knew he'd never have a home of any kind ever again.

When he reached the room, his hair and vest were disheveled, and he could see his feelings reflected like a mirror in Johanna's worried expression.

"Is everything okay, Daniel?"

"Do I have you?"

"What?"

"Are you going to kill me?"

"Daniel, I—"

"Tell me. Goddamn it, I need you to tell me."

"Tell you what?"

"My brothers are all I ever had, Johanna. Now Clovis … I always knew he'd be the death of me, but the days are numbered now before he pulls the trigger. He's a lost cause, and I can't be there for Billy right now, so I'm just … I'm trying to ask you if …"

"You have me." Johanna approached him as he panted, suddenly finding it hard to breathe. Her hands came up to his cheeks, and he looked down into her eyes.

"You have me," she said. "I ain't going to hurt you again. Not now, not ever."

"Let's ride off then. Let's go find us a place far away where it can just be you and me."

"This is the place. And you ain't the type of man to run." As he tried to look away, her hands latched the sides of his head and turned it right back. "Say it."

"I ain't running."

"I said say it."

"I ain't fucking running."

With a violent jerk, Daniel's face was pulled into hers, and as one they dragged each other with haste to the bed. His lips met her lips, his lips met her neck, and he pressed them over every bit of the rest of her body as they stripped off each other's clothes piece by piece. When there was nothing left but the touch of skin to warm their bodies, Johanna turned onto her back underneath him and pulled Daniel's head down so his ear was right by her mouth.

"I love you, Daniel Keagan." Her sensual whisper flowed into him.

"And I love you, Johanna Fontaine."

As their bodies moved together to further communicate the message, Daniel accepted the weight of what those words meant. With her and Harran now a part of his life, he wouldn't run from Clovis anymore—and there was no more hope to spare him either.

# CHAPTER 6

## A MATTER OF TIME

"Wha time is … is morn'ng? Hazzben four—no five," William slurred to himself as he lurched up in bed to squint at the watch on his nightstand.

*Goddamn—it is five-thirty in the morning? It's already been five hours.*

It'd been five hours since William laid his head down the evening after he'd talked to—or more accurately, failed in his attempt to maim—Priest Kubler. William's drunk mind raced only a bit slower than it had sober, but it still darted from Judith, to Charles Langston, to the Priest with his zipped lips, back to his Judith and how he wished he could bring her back, to this all being a dream, to dark depressed thoughts of why he was even trying anymore, and once again, back to Charles and the douchebag of a priest.

He blinked at the watch again. "Wheredid the laz tweny mintz go?"

He'd lost twenty minutes on another loop of his thoughts.

This was the last straw. If he couldn't talk to the priest tonight, he needed to talk to Gregory. More than anything, though, he wanted some kind of action to take his mind off things. His moral conscious had not yet faded enough to forget he shouldn't go talk to the priest in his current state. And yet, he rationalized that there was nothing wrong with telling off Gregory for holding him back earlier. Gregory would only respond by talking him down and putting him to sleep.

There was no need to dress, as he'd gone straight to bed in the same clothes he'd worn all day. At this point, when he noted his lack of hygiene, William couldn't care less. Rising out of bed was a longer chore than expected, and his limbs appeared to be flimsier than usual, struggling to maintain his balance. They looked like deer legs for a moment, which he had a laugh about as he waved them around for a minute—a form of entertainment as short lived as any form of tranquility in his mind.

Stumbling through the halls, William only became aware of the noise he was making when he saw his twin cousins, Blanton and Donna Keagan, tossing and turning in their sleep through the crack of the door to their room. From there, he tiptoed, attempting a kind of elegant dance. After tripping himself up with his own feet, he stepped carefully down the rest of the hallway. When he finally reached Gregory's room, a greater confusion swept over him as Gregory was nowhere to be found.

"Hmm, wheredi you goff to, Gregerz?" he said to himself, amused. In his mind he was now playing detective, which prompted him to whip his body around and away from the room.

In the brief moment of silence, there was the faintest disturbance coming from down the hall. "Aha!" He crept toward the Abigales' rooms, where it seemed like the noise emanated from. It became a bit more audible the closer he came. Listening into each room, he pressed his ears to the doors of Judith's younger siblings first.

"Francis, izzit you … ? Mmmnope." And onto the next. "Henriets an' Florenz, izzit yyyou … ?" Before he could answer himself, he heard the noise again coming from Henry's and Maria's room. It sounded like a woman to him. The closer he crept, the more he was able to make out until he came to register the sound.

*Sex.*

When he reached the door, he dared not open it, but peeked beneath the crack below, where he could make out Maria Abigale, stripped down and riding his best friend, Gregory Calloway. For a moment he held his breath, ready to laugh at first, but instead he rose to his feet, staring down at the ground, feeling cold and bothered.

This indiscretion didn't mean much to him. He cared not for Henry and thought it good for Gregory, who'd been through enough as it was. But why should others be happy or fulfilled while his wife and him had suffered in the worst way? Seeing Maria in particular made him connect to Judith, too, and from there, back to …

His gaze broke with the floor and he sped-walked to his room to fetch his gun. Fumbling with it in his rushed attempt to load it, bullets fell to the ground as he missed the cylinder several times. Once it was loaded, he marched straight back down the hall, this time making no effort to maintain quiet. With his eyes fixed on Henry and Maria's door, he veered to the right and trotted down the stairs. He was on a mission now.

The walk to Fayette's Church of the Humble Followers was a hazy blur. While he seemed to teleport from the doors of the mansion to the church lawn, he also had the thought in his head of having gotten lost along the way. Whatever path he took, he was here now, and he was going to take the answers he was looking for.

Though he didn't expect the doors to be locked, he kicked them open anyway with his gun by his side. They swung on their hinges and closed on him, as he wasn't quick enough to continue in past the opening. Furious at the embarrassment, he threw them open again with a loud grunt. Priest Kubler stood at the altar, and Mary-Claire Norvell was turned around in the pews. He interrupted them from a hymn they'd be voicing together. When his gun lifted in the air, Mary-Claire let out an ear-piercing shriek, which made William jump.

"Good God, wha's yer deal, lady."

"William, please, let's be calm and put the gun down," Kubler said with his hands raised William's way.

"Father! He has a gun!" Mary-Claire hid beneath the bench in her aisle.

"Look I ain' got no problm with you cept yer name. I mean, wha the heck kinda parens give their kid two names anyhoo?"

"Don't hurt her, William. We can work this out without anyone getting hurt. Tell me what you need."

William's head tilted back with his eyes closed, grinning for reasons he couldn't be sure of. "You know."

"Why you're here with a gun? No, I—"

"You know!" The sense of amusement disappeared as he pointed his gun at the priest.

"Okay, okay … this is about Charles, isn't it? Look, I understand your pain, but I told you—" As William marched toward Mary-Claire's aisle, Priest Kubler's voice trailed off, and he started pacing parallel to him. "What are you doing, William?"

"Don't take 'nother step." Stopping before Mary-Claire's row, he swung his gun toward the priest again. Mary-Claire started crying like a maniac, ringing agony in William's eardrums. "Shut yer big mouth and sit in yer pew, bitch."

"I understand your pain, I do," Kubler said.

"Whadid you jus say?"

"I said I understand."

Before Kubler could finish repeating the statement, William had a terrified Mary-Claire in his grasp and his gun pointed at her head. "SAY IT AGAIN, YOU FALSE FUCK!"

"Heretic!" Mary-Claire said in his clutches.

"Mary-Claire, please." The priest raised a hand again and crept forward.

The movement felt threatening, prompting William to fire two shots into the roof of the church. Splintered wood fell from above. "You gotta blieve in somethin' to be a heretic, Mmmmary ... or Claire ... or whatever the hell." Now amused again after the shots, he enjoyed toying with her as she yelled out her prayers to the Enigma.

The doors to the church flew open behind William, and he turned around, still holding Mary-Claire hostage.

"William," Gregory said. "What's going on, buddy?"

"He needs ta tell us, Greg. We need ta find Charles." The sight of his friend's sorrow made him feel somewhat weaker in his conviction.

"I know, but ... and I'm sorry to say this, but you know it's not gonna bring her back."

"I don't …" His mind raced, and his watery eyes darted around. "I don't know that, no. She's not … she can't be …" As he went his voice trailed off more and more.

"We should speak in the confessional sometime, William," Priest Kubler said.

"I ain't …" He started to become more aware of his immediate surroundings again. "I ain't got nothin' to confess to you."

"No, I do not expect you would want to, whether you did or didn't. I would simply like to have a conversation. Another time, though, of course. It is far too late, and you are too drunk. I will talk to you once we have all had a chance to rest this off."

Staring down at Mary-Claire's Cereb Hymnal, resting on the pew, William stood frozen. She continued a gentle whining and panting in his clutches—much to his annoyance—but now it was easier to ignore. Much less so was the moan of pain in his head as he let her go. It was so loud that after releasing her, he merely sat with his head in his hands, placing his gun on the holy book, as the echo of Gregory's words bounced around in his head.

*Won't bring her back.*

*Won't bring her back.*

*

The hike was long and grueling, the return trip in particular, as Hanzah and Orrin hauled heavy sacks filled with the axes, hammers, and rope the V'ahani would need to re-craft the bridge to the Riverlands. By the time they reunited with Varek and the others, Hanzah felt a little better for the experience. Though his own efforts were a source of pride, there was no denying this newfound confidence was bolstered in large part by Orrin's repetitive prodding for his opinions along the way. There were times it seemed obnoxious at first—no doubt the most evident being the climb up and back down the mountain trail—however, he could not deny how effective his uncle's methods were by now, and they'd bonded further on the almost week-long trip because of it.

The progress of the builders in the early morning hours was swift upon receiving their tools, despite their reliance on torchlight. This was an exercise repeated many times over by Orrin's V'ahani of the Mountainlands, and Hanzah found himself transfixed by the spectacle of his uncle's orchestration of it. Despite it being a second-nature task to many of those involved, Orrin seemed excited as he cheered and gave orders both friendly and urgent, as necessary.

As for Varek, he provided constant inspection and oversight of the project, as well, though he was less involved in the coordination. For now, Hanzah was pleased the Grand Chieftain was distracted enough not to bother him. But he did almost wish he would be given a hard time again, as he was dying to test his own courage.

"Orrin, leave them to it for now," Varek said as the finishing touches were being arranged. "Hanzah, you too, come aside so we can talk."

The time to face the Grand Chieftain came sooner than he'd expected, and Hanzah began to crack his knuckles in preparation—a habit he realized he must have picked up from seeing Dominic do the same. He exchanged a glance with Orrin, who perked up behind his beard and pounded a fist over his heart twice. *Be brave,* Hanzah thought.

"I would like to apologize, Hanzah," Varek said once they reached him, his face softening as much as it could, given his terrible scar. "I realize if you had seen the bridge was destroyed, you would have been too distracted by it to have discovered Clovis was on the move north at all—which by the way, one of ours who took your place when you left confirmed you were right about—so it likely occurred after your hawk had passed it."

"Please, Grand Chieftain, there is no need. I should have—"

"No," Varek raised a hand. "I have been far too hard on you considering all you have been through. I lost my father too at a young age and by Eastern hands. It never got any easier for me. I suppose I thought the harshness I experienced would be how best to teach you, and I also let your association with the Easterners get the better of my emotions. You must understand I will never trust them, but I can see now it is no excuse for the way I treated you. You are not one of them, and you never will be, so you do not deserve it."

"Your apology is accepted." Hanzah gave a bow and a half-grin, happy about Varek's change in attitude, but bothered by his hatred for all Easterners.

"And where has the serpent slithered since sighted last?" Orrin asked, stroking at his beard.

"He is in the Riverlands, taking residence in Harran," Varek said. His scarred eye twitching so fast he needed a moment to rub at it.

Watching the carefulness in which Varek messed with his unclosing eyelid made Hanzah want to gag. Once his focus was regained, he thought of Harran. "Is everyone there all right?"

"It has been quiet so far, but this is also the problem. Daniel

Keagan was supposed to act. First, he was supposed to keep Clovis far from the Riverlands altogether, but if he failed to do so, he was expected to take definitive action, which he has not done. Whether or not Clovis has wreaked havoc yet is irrelevant—it is only a matter of time. It is in the Easterner's nature to be cruel, but it is in *his* nature to be inhuman."

"So I take it the war will begin in Harran?" Orrin asked.

One of the men from the bridge shouted, "Grand Chieftain, it is finished!"

Rising to his feet, Varek gathered himself. "Your take is correct. We will attack the town and lay waste to any standing in our way until we are sure the grizzlies have ended the monster that is Clovis Keagan."

"Any? No! I—" It was too late, though, as Varek had already walked off, and Hanzah's voice was drowned out beneath the commotion of the V'ahani rushing to form ranks. The Grand Chieftain's plan could not be allowed to come to fruition, and though he once again felt small, he'd not allow it to paralyze him.

As a first order of bravery, he went to the front of the group this time, marching alongside Orrin's horse. The bridge was sturdy and well-fortified now, as one by one, each of the warriors crossed, as did the leaders atop their horses. Standing in the field before the mountains again, Hanzah felt the great change in him. He was not the same as he'd been when he'd last stood on this ground. Looking out at the land before him, he hoped this time he might be coming home to stay.

As he waited, he thought about what to say to Varek to guarantee no one would hurt his friends. What appeal—what statement—

would serve to make the Grand Chieftain listen? He'd have a day's time before they arrived in Harran to convince him to spare the people there.

When the last of the men crossed, they marched ahead, making it about halfway through the field when one man's horse at the head of the group stumbled to the ground. A metallic click, followed by a whooshing sound was heard as smoke started to form at different places in the ground.

*Dominic?*

"Retreat! Quickly!" Varek said as the others scurried back toward the bridge.

It appeared the only one not in a panic was Hanzah. Well, he and Orrin, though Orrin never seemed to panic. While Hanzah acknowledged the possibility of an eruption of gunfire from the forest before them, he was familiar with this trick. It was a trick the likes of which he had only ever seen from Dominic.

*But if this was Dominic, perhaps the bridge was too.*

There was no way he could tell Varek any of his suspicions. If he did, his comrades in Harran would be wiped out for sure. As he reached a point close enough to the bridge to where the smoke dissipated, he spotted Orrin again, looking down at him with a knowing stare.

"I can see you think-ety think thinking. You do realize how loudly you are doing so, do you not?" Orrin said, low enough in volume for no one to notice.

"What? I do not ..." Looking around, he needed to confirm his thoughts weren't being heard somehow. "Please, you cannot tell him. We are safe. They are my friends."

"Of course, I will not. It would not be mine to tell anyhow. I suppose though, if this was your allies, they will now see us coming and know to hide."

"You are right. They will!" Hanzah paused, overcome with gratitude. "Thank you, uncle. For everything."

"It is what I am here for, my boy. Now though ... let us be off to war!"

\*

The Tokali boys were all becoming excited. Well, all except for Hammond. He was the only one still failing to get through to the hogs in any way. As Latera continued to warm up to him, she couldn't help but feel for Hammond, but she was also confused by his failure for two reasons. The first and most obvious one being he was the first Tokali—maybe ever—to take control of a hog, and now he couldn't connect to one at all. It was strange. She had also marked him from the start as the strongest willed in the group, a trait she thought would make for a better connection with the Mother. In his case it seemed to hinder him. Regardless of how confounding it was, she knew they'd need to figure it out soon because *all* the boys still needed to get much more consistent before they could go south to the Hold.

"Are the dreams still continuing?" Mika asked her one late afternoon as they ate roasted hog at camp. Winona and Mika were the only two who knew about Latera's dreams, and she intended to keep it this way.

She glanced around to make sure there was no one in hearing distance and replied. "Every night. But I am not sure I would call them dreams. They feel so real. By the way, do you think the Tokali will one day find eating their pigs offensive?"

Winona chuckled. "I suppose referring to them as 'pigs' will become offensive at some point. Not quite as glorious sounding as razorbacks or hogs."

"Oh believe me, it does offend them. Much to my amusement, I would add. You both should try it sometime."

After she spoke, the boys could be heard coming back from a much-deserved swim in the lake after their full day of training. Though she had already noted them in passing while at the Hold, the physical differences between the clans were more apparent with their upper bodies exposed in the fluttering colors of the setting sun. One was that the Tokali were a bit taller and had more defined muscle tone on average, due to greater difficulties of nourishment for the V'ahani during the northern winters. The other was that the Tokali tended to have darker, thicker hair on their heads and bodies in general. Latera was bothered by the boys' continued teasing of Hammond, which all stemmed from the high-and-mighty Elan. She thought he might be jealous of the attention she'd been giving Hammond.

"Back to the dreams," Mika said.

Latera was glad to have had her attention pried away from the Tokali as she refocused on him.

"So you said there were memories, too?" Mika continued.

"In the course of a night, I see ... everything, though I cannot retain a fraction of it to remember. So I focus on what I know— which tends to be memories of mine, yes. But those, too, are different because I can see them not only from my own point of view, but from all sides. I told you about what I saw with Walter. A more recent dream I had included a vision of the diversion we faced in the Riverlands, which prompted us to leave. I could see the whole thing had been set up by Hanzah and a man of magic who was helping him named Dominic. It all felt so real, though I have no way to know for sure about the parts I did not experience."

"So much to handle," Winona said, placing a hand on her arm.

"It is terrifying to say the least. The first couple nights it happened, I woke up feeling sick. It is getting better now, but there is still some dizziness. Let us not talk further on it right now though, please? We will see in time what the dreams mean, but for now I would just like to maintain some normalcy."

Mika smiled and grabbed Winona's hand. "Of course. You know me. Always curious. As you wish, Chieftess."

They ate for a few minutes in contented silence before there were footsteps behind her.

"Latera, can we talk? Away from the camp, if possible?" Hammond said as he appeared in front of her. She glanced over her shoulder to see all the other Tokali sitting in their own circle. Warrick, who Latera was beginning to note as the kindest of the bunch, was feeding the tied-up Charles. She turned back to Hammond.

"Yeah, um, sure … just give me a moment," she said as she began to gather herself. Hammond nodded and walked a ways away to look out at the lake. Winona shot her a mischievous and presumptuous grin, which made her cheeks warm. With wide eyes, she shook her head in response. She'd confided her feelings for Hammond in her friend as she did everything else, and Winona loved to tease her about it at every opportunity. *Why do I tell this girl anything?*

When she was ready, she approached Hammond, and they walked off together away from the camp and along the bank of the lake. The blue-green water glistened as if with yellow diamonds as it reflected the setting sun. Hammond was a step ahead scanning their surroundings. He didn't say a word to her as they went but displayed a shy smile each time he looked back, and she couldn't help but return the same, locking her eyes with his brown ones each time. They shared the same sparkle as was reflected on the water. Now well out of sight and earshot of the camp, Hammond began to slow his pace.

"Enough privacy yet?" Latera asked.

"Yes, I am sorry. This is fine," Hammond said, taking a seat on a string of large, smooth boulders between the forest and the lake. On his cue, Latera sat next to him. "I know this is a random request, too. I hope I did not inconvenience you in any way."

"Hammond, please, it is fine. What did you want to talk to me about?"

"I just do not understand it, you know?" A subtle crack split his voice. "I was the one to stop the hog first. And now? Now I have no control, and everyone else does. And it is embarrassing."

"Well, first of all, you cannot let them bother you about it. The more frustrated you get the less focus you will have." Before he could open his mouth, she knew what was coming so continued with a smile. "And I know it is easier said than done with the way they are. But it is necessary if you want to move past this."

Hammond chuckled and looked down, scratching at the back

of his head, causing his bun to shift with the movement. "Why do I feel like we know each other better than we do?"

"Because we come from the same place. If not in geography or ethnicity, then mentality. I saw it in you when we first crossed paths. Tell me, if you would, what pushed you to take such a hard line against the Keagans? Did you lose someone to them?"

"My parents both died when I was very young. And no, it was not to the Easterners. I was told by a disease spreading through our particular camp by the others in our community—who together raised me until they decided we needed to all leave for the Hold. I always heard I was lucky to have survived. As for the Keagans, things changed in a big way once they took over. Others saw it as an agreement between our two groups. It was no mutual thing, though. As a people, we were stripped of our freedom. I saw it right away and fought against it."

"Hammond, I am so sorry about your parents." She edged closer to him and put a hand on his arm.

He flinched at first before looking up at her. For Latera, seeing his grief was like looking in a mirror.

"Am I interrupting something?" Elan asked, coming up from behind them.

A shiver of disgust and frustration whirled up Latera's spine as she pulled her hand off Hammond.

"No, it—" Hammond started.

"As a matter of fact," she couldn't help but interrupt. "Hammond came to me to train him since he is having trouble—trouble you are in no way helping with by giving him hell about it. So yes, you are interrupting."

Elan folded his arms. "Well, I just came here because I have received the news from Hanzah, but I guess you do not want to be *interrupted* so I will go."

"Elan, come on," Hammond said.

"Stop being such a child and tell me what my brother said right now."

"Oh, so now you want to listen to me." Elan paused, and Latera stared him down. With a dramatic sigh he uncrossed his arms. "Fine. Well, he said there was an incident, and your Grand Chieftain will not surrender. In fact, they're marching on the Riverlands now. He suggested you do whatever possible to rescue your people because it will be some time before they can reach us here. Last he mentioned he is no longer with the … Morrells? So he cannot ask them about their mayor, but does not remember them mentioning him either."

Her fingers came rubbing together again. "The former is good to hear. Though the latter is a concern."

"Yeah, anyway, we were getting ready to sit around the campfire and tell stories so if you two love birds are ever done, we will be waiting on you."

"Like I said, we are trying to correct issues you have contributed to. We will return when we are ready."

"Some way to speak to the guy who saved your life." Elan said under his breath as he stormed off.

"What did you say?" she called after him, but he only kept on walking.

Yes, it did seem he was jealous of the time she was giving Hammond, but Latera felt no guilt. He had saved her life twice and she, in turn, had mostly forgiven him for the utter betrayal he'd committed against her and her people. They were even. And he was acting like a spoiled child. She rose in irritation and stared after Elan's retreating back.

"So, we are going to train now?" Hammond asked.

"That is what you wanted, is it not? Some one-on-one guidance?"

"With you, yes."

She looked his way, and her irritation over Elan's childishness faded a little further into the back of her mind.

"Ready your blade. We are going to figure this out tonight," she said with a smile as she led him into the forest.

Once they reached a location Latera determined to be appropriate, she started by meditating with Hammond for about a half an hour or so. This was a common training warm-up to clear the mind and connect with the Mother. After she deemed enough time had passed to have centered themselves, she opened her eyes and observed him. His were still closed, appearing to be squeezed shut. There was something about how hard he was trying she found cute, but she needed to focus herself on the task at hand and block out her attraction … at least for now. It'd be much harder to get this accomplished—and as a result, her people saved—if she didn't.

With an exhale, it was time to begin as the evening started to set in. "Okay, Hammond." Despite the intentional smoothness of her tone, he jumped. "Are you ready to begin?"

"I think … wait, no. I know for certain I am ready, yes."

"Well your reply was about as telling as your body language has been."

At the joke Hammond sat more upright. It was a bad attempt to hide his doubts, of which Latera was ever too sharp to miss.

"Tell me what is on your mind right now," she said.

"Honestly?"

"Honestly. The first thing … and maybe the second if it is not just one thing."

"Having heard the urgency from the message your brother sent, I do not want to be the one holding us back. And I … under no circumstances do I want to let you down."

"And there is nothing more?" Latera asked. She made her tone attentive but flippant, suggesting she believed it was something they could overcome for the sake of his confidence, when really she had no idea how she was going to lead this lesson.

"I believe so. I do not think I am too worried about the others bothering me anymore. Though I have been friends with them for so long, I have always felt somewhat distanced from them by my disdain for the Keagans. There was not anyone like you in the Hold."

"Well, this is all good to hear." Determined to stay focused on teaching, she tried to mask her enthusiasm with his further acknowledgement of a connection between them. "When it comes to letting us down, know we believe in you, Hammond. However, no one but you can define expectations for what you will accomplish. So you can never let us down in truth, you can only let yourself down. By coming to me, you showed you want to put in the work for us, and you have already made us proud."

Hammond bowed his head. "Thank you, Chieftess." This was the first time she heard someone not of the V'ahani of the Riverlands say the title. In a way, this made it feel more official and helped her to feel more comfortable with it.

"Of course. Now let us face this together."

It was a humid evening, and the birds made it clear to her they would have their pick of the litter with regard to the hogs as they called to the wind for guidance. They stalked their way through the forest and had no trouble in locating a sounder of swine grazing. A group might be perfect, too, since Hammond would not be pressured to reach a certain one. She explained to him again and again he needed to try and be one with the hogs' minds in order to control them. Though she remained patient in her teaching, she did struggle with how little he seemed to connect with them. Hammond's easy frustration didn't help either.

After several failed attempts, they gave up on the group and tried the opposite: finding a lone, docile old pig with which he could speak out loud to. She thought maybe it was a matter of him believing the beast could hear him, given how he connected with one previously through this method, and perhaps it would allow him to get through to it. However, this too failed.

When the night's full moon was all there was left to light their way through the trees, she thought of one last option. "You said you were hunting before … when it worked the first time," she said as they trekked again through the trees to their next destination, at the guidance of an old owl.

"That is right."

"And the target—it was ferocious and charging straight for you, yes?"

"Not a position I was thrilled to be in, but yes."

"Well, I had hoped it would not come to this when we started, but we are going to put you in that same position again."

"Do you think it is necessary?"

"Your desperation triggered something. We have seen it in some V'ahani before with the grizzlies, though we try and avoid putting someone in a dangerous situation when possible. It is okay if you do not wish to. I would understand, and it does not mean we will need to give up altogether. But for now it is all I can think of. We could always get Gannon, too, if you would like, to provide backup."

With a sigh, Hammond stopped in place. "No. If he is there, I will not feel desperate like you said."

"Very well, just be sure to keep your blade at the ready, and I will be prepared to assist you with mine also." Despite her assurance, a crooked frown remained on his face, prompting her to grab his hand. With a smile she professed her belief in him, "You can do this, Hammond."

It worked. His expression shifted, and as his smile outshined the moon, he said, "I know I can."

When they found their mark, Hammond darted out into the field without hesitation. It was far off, but Latera could already see the rage overtaking the hog as it kicked at the dirt. It didn't like a threat making such quick movements. She would not admit it out loud, but the animals were fiercer than she imagined. Perhaps, she thought, she might not be so joking in referring to them as pigs.

As the razorback shrieked and drooled and charged toward Hammond, Latera grew worried. Hammond's stance now fixed, he betrayed no sign of outward fear. As the hog grew closer, she shut her eyes and prayed to the Mother with increasing intensity, resting her thoughts in direct line with Hammond, trying to perform the act in her own mind, as if she were in his place. She opened her eyes and was petrified to see the hog barreling straight for her. Despite the sight, she knew she was still in her cover behind the brush and could see Hammond ahead of her, too. She had no idea what was happening. The hog barreled closer.

*Oh Mother, aid me!*

"EASE!" she screamed in a panic, hearing Hammond yell it in unison with her.

Within an instant, the creature stopped dead in its tracks. Latera blinked and the double vision was gone.

*What was that? What is happening to me?*

Falling onto her backside and hyperventilating, she remained in a state of shock and terror.

"Do you see this, Latera? The hog is still! I did it!" she heard Hammond say as if from far away. She found herself incapable of formulating a response. Unable to breathe, she let out a strangled cry, scrambling to her feet.

"Latera? Latera, are you all right?"

*What is happening?*

Seemingly of their own accord, her feet began to move, and Latera was off and running as fast as she could back toward the camp. On her way she couldn't comprehend what had taken place. All she knew was that for the first time since leaving the Riverlands, she was experiencing true, unmitigated fear. Overwhelmed and lost, she felt something shatter inside her, and like a dam bursting forth, she let out an anguished cry. Maybe it was the pressure of the title she'd been given, the pressure of the task before her. Maybe it was losing her father, being separated from her brother, or being a pawn to both the councilmen and to Walter Keagan. Maybe it was reaching near starvation, being attacked and shot at. Maybe it was all those things at once. But she knew when she exited the forest and emerged upon the bank of the lake, she knew something had changed.

Running to the water, coming to her knees before it, hysterical and crying, she plunged her hands into the lake and threw the water over herself. The release wasn't enough though, and soon she submerged her entire head in the water, keeping it there until she could no longer hold her breath—needing the quiet of the water in a way she didn't understand. Bursting back out for air, she stayed kneeling on the edge, rocking back and forth weeping. If time passed, she did not notice it. She recognized nothing but her pain until Winona approached at her side, absorbing her sobs with a forceful embrace.

# CHAPTER 7

## THE PLEDGE

After a couple of days getting settled back into New Berkeley and securing an apartment, it was time for Henry to further explore the opposition to Forrest's hold on the city. The Fraternal Forgotten was the perfect place to start. Wherever they were and whomever the group consisted of, Henry would need to find them and assist in any way he could. From what the merchants told him, they seemed related to the discontented labor unions the fishmonger claimed existed. He knew little about it, but the more he could help exacerbate the chaos, the better. So, after some thought, he decided his first step would be to secure a job at the Anderson Mill to better do some digging.

The day was rainy, and the streets were slippery as he pattered along to the mill. By the time he reached the address, his hat and coat were drenched. Sure enough, though, there were the big red letters on the side of the building Forrest's men had spoken about. The red was the only spot of color on the place, as the rest of the walls were a terrible, dull shade of gray.

Before he left New Berkeley the first time, Henry was aware this mill was being constructed, but he hadn't found out much more about it after he'd retired. What he did know of it was its owner,

Torrance Andersen, who was a weird, uppity fellow from what he recalled of their single, brief interaction. In fact, Torrance might be the only owner who wasn't familiar with Henry, as he was the only one to enter as Henry was exiting the organization. As such, Torrance was least likely to recognize him with his new look, which was why he needed to make this work.

Despite his familiarity with the conditions of the mills, the volume of the place took him aback as he entered. From the machinery humming to supervisors yelling to employees grunting through fatigue and injuries, the mill was a loud place, to say the least. Looking around, he noticed an above average number of children in the workforce, too. He knew this occurred, but he didn't realize it did to this extent.

"Hey! Why are you standing around? If you're on my floor, you're working." The shouting voice came from a bone-thin man who was sweating through his dress shirt.

"Fraternal Forgotten," Henry said, as under his breath as possible, biting his tongue at his own nerve. While he knew there could be a risk, he couldn't help but hope for luck.

The floor manager got right up in Henry's face. "What the hell did you say? You should be careful where you utter those words, old man."

*No luck here.*

"I think you misheard me, son. I'm looking for the office!" Henry said, though he knew where it would be.

The man gave a snarling nod pointing up some stairs, which led to a room windowed on all sides. Within it stood a much heavier Andersen than Henry remembered. With arms folded, Andersen looked down on the bustle of the factory with an eagle's eye. While this fellow in particular had rubbed Henry the wrong way in the past, factory managers were never the most favorable people. Their need for control over their unskilled flock tended to result in intense personalities.

As Henry entered the room, Andersen remained in place without turning around. Despite his letting himself go, his office was immaculate in its organization.

"Hello, Mr. Andersen," Henry said. "I was wondering if you might be hiring."

"What?"

"Um … my name's Emory Wallace, sir. I was hoping you might have some openings."

Breaking his observation to glance Henry's way, Torrance pulled up his pants and marched toward his desk. "Of course. Sit, please. I hope you understand I'll need to ask you a few interview questions first if you want to be a floor manager. If you could go ahead and fill this out for me, we can get started … assuming you can write?" Andersen handed over a clipboard with a paper and pencil on it.

"Uh, yes, I can, but actually, I'm not looking for a job myself, Mr. Andersen."

"Great." After a brief moment or two, Andersen shook his head and put the clipboard back on his desk. "Wait, no. Then who are you here for, and why aren't they applying on their own accord?"

Henry had been thinking of claiming to have a few strapping sons or something along those lines, but after looking at the average age of the mill floor, he improvised.

"Well, I just got a job at the orphanage on the north side of the city, and—"

"Oh, you're with Settler's?"

*He would know of it.*

"Yes, that's the one. You see, we raise our youngsters right and believe they'd factor into your operation well if you gave them a shot."

Andersen's attention was now fixed on Henry, and he sat back with a grin. "Not to be rude, but your orphanage is some ways from here, and I can't be paying for transport. I'm not sure it would be best practice within my organization to be inefficient cost-wise. My bosses wouldn't be fond of it."

*Fucking pencil pusher.* "Okay, well thanks for your time." As he went to stand up, Henry shook Andersen's hand. "But hey, how about this—would you mind giving me a tour of your factory before I head back?"

"I'm afraid I'm a busy man. I can't—"

"It's work-related, I promise." Henry sat up in his seat, sure to be as animated as possible with his hands to make his proposition feel business-like to the shallow man before him. "You see, Mr. Andersen, I was impressed with what I saw when I walked in your doors. So impressed, in fact, I'd like to make you a special kind of offer for the fantastic talent I can supply you with. If you show me around now, I'll have the details I need to come back in a week's time and knock your socks off. I know I don't have an impressive offer waiting yet, but in a week, you'll make the other managers look downright wasteful with the deal I'll make you. And transport will be no concern of yours. You have my word."

With a beaming nod, Andersen looked like he'd woken from a trance. "Well, why didn't you say so? Of course, I'd be happy to show you around. I take great pride in this place, too, so thanks for noticing!"

They descended the stairs to the first level, and before Henry could get a question out, Andersen launched into a detailed history of the still-young factory's construction and business. As he outlined everything from funding to mechanical development to where the outhouse was, Henry heard several familiar details and names from within the organization. The name-dropping seemed as great a pride to Andersen as the factory itself.

"And this brings us to the main floor where the magic happens," Andersen said, his hands extended out toward his workers and machines. One of the boys on the line let out a chilling scream. His hand was bloodied, and he fell to his knees crying.

"Hey! Get him stitched up and switched out for one of the reserves! I'm sorry you had to see that, Mr. Wallace. I assure you, he'll be cared for."

Sure enough, the injured boy was ushered off and brought to a back room, while another—who looked a lot like the first—was brought out to take his place.

Having spotted the thin floor manager responding to Andersen's order with a dirty look, Henry saw an opportunity to gather some information. "Part of the job, I suppose. Teachable moment for a young man. I'm curious though, have you had any issues with your employees forming unions here with such occurrences?" He leaned in to ask in a whisper, "One particular name I heard was the Fraternal Forgotten?"

Andersen's face reddened. "I appreciate you keeping your voice down and will be grateful for you to not repeat the name. What do you know about them?"

*Probing. Interesting.*

"Of course. Not much, if I'm honest. I'm new to town though and witnessed an attack the other day where the assailant shouted it out. And if such violence is normal for them, I want to make sure my kids don't get involved in whatever they are. So, I ask because I want to know any issues I should nip in the bud, and because I also want to know what I'm getting into with this city a bit more, too."

"They are agents of chaos trying to destroy the fabric at the foundation of this society—that's what they are. They're fighting to give the corrupt 'politicians' here the power they think they should have. Which is absurd because they don't contribute anything real like we do. Their only goal is power, and they aim to secure it by scapegoating capitalists like us as some kind of villains." Andersen paused for a breath before asking, "Where are you from, Emory?"

He had a hard time remembering his new name himself and was glad for the reminder.

*Emory Wallace from …*

"Alvenika."

"Aha! I knew it the moment I saw you—no offense meant, of course. But you came here for work because you couldn't find it there, I bet. Am I right or am I right? I don't mean to trash your home, but Alvenika is a damned government-run welfare state. The difference between what makes this place grow and thrive and what makes places like yours fail is industrial geniuses like Forrest Hayes and the late Leonard Keagan. Now we got unions like the bastards you mentioned trying to ruin what we provide? They are more selfish than they care to admit."

"So, do you have a problem with them here?"

"God no. My mill is the most efficient, purest one there is."

*He would say that whether it were true or not.*

"You know what my secret is? The secret that's allowed this place to skyrocket?"

"What is it?" *This idiot really loves the sound of his own voice.*

"Other managers stress not hiring older men for a job a child can do for a quarter the wage. Me on the other hand, I say, why hire an ordinary child for a quarter when there's a motherless one I can hire for a tenth?" Andersen spread his hands apart as if revealing a sign. "Turns out you're a smarter guy than you know, friend— the secret's orphans like yours! This city is filled with parentless children who need work. And if you're worried about their quality of living, we provide them this service, along with healthcare when they need it, and a basic education, too. And in exchange for our generosity, they supply us an endless workforce. Please, don't take any offense about the reduced pay, either. It's a simple business decision for me, and my job is to run as crisp an operation here as possible, so I gotta take advantage of economies of scale. Brilliant though, right?"

Dumbfounded, Henry bit his lip to gather himself to lie through his teeth. "Um … yeah it sounds like you have something there, and I'm glad I'm on the right track. I just have to say, Mr. Andersen, I have a great admiration for how much pride you take not only in the system in New Berkeley, but also in your factory in particular."

"Why, thank you. I am rather proud." Andersen rocked back

and forward on his heels again. For a moment, Henry thought that the large man might lose his balance. "Say, I like you more than I thought I might when you walked in. What do you say you swing by here Saturday with the particulars of your deal? I'd be interested to hear what you've got to offer now that you know what kind of operation I run."

Having reached the door, Henry felt his trip here had been a tremendous success. He would return in a few days to write up some bullshit contract, set for some far-off date, affirming services he wouldn't be able to provide. It didn't matter though, because in the meantime he'd be able to utilize Andersen and his mill to remain in the know. "Why, thank you, Mr. Andersen. I can be back Saturday for sure. But one more question if you don't mind. This time I swear it's an easy one."

"Sure thing, Emory. Shoot."

"I noticed your full name on the application. Why 'Anderson Mill' with an 'o' and not an 'e' like in your name?"

"Again, a simple decision. More appealing look and more familiar spelling." Tapping the side of his temple, Torrance grinned. "I'm always putting my business first this way, and I wouldn't be where I am now if I hadn't. You'd do good not to forget it if you have hopes of reaching my level of success one day."

"Man, you're brilliant, Mr. Andersen. Thanks for the tip. Saturday?"

"Saturday."

*Saturday.*

*

The confessional was nothing more than an old, wooden confinement. The coating of dust and the appearance of molding corners didn't make the time alone in the stall any more enjoyable. If it weren't for his burning need to hunt down Charles Langston, William would have gotten up and left. Since allergies were already an issue for him at this time of year, his nose also ran during the entirety of his wait for Priest Kubler to join him. Fidgeting in place on the grainy, un-cushioned seat, he had no choice but to sniff in and wipe his nose with his hand to keep his upper-lip dry. For a moment, he was disgusted with himself, but he shrugged. He cared little for the details of living anymore.

The door to the opposite stall let out a prolonged, high-pitch creak when the priest entered. William doubted this experience could get any more uncomfortable. Without a word, William could make out Kubler ensuring his robe was taut, his pendant centered on his chest, and his Hymnal book adjacent to his person before he took his seat.

"Thank you for joining me, humble penitent."

In this midday hour it was still dark in the confessional, but through the partition William could also see the straight back and resting hands of Kubler's immaculate posture. It bothered him, though so did everything else about the man who had been withholding the information he needed.

"Hey, I told you I ain't here as no penitent. If penance is what you're aiming to get out of me, you got another thing coming."

"In order to get to where we desire to go, we must first understand two things: where we have been and how it led us to the place we now stand. I'm afraid without laying down this groundwork, the information I possess will be of no benefit to you. And I could not provide you with something useless and also keep my conscience intact. By the grace of the Enigma, no."

Pressing his hands down into his thighs while stretching and clenching his fingers, William could feel his right eye beginning to twitch. "I've waited a week for this meeting only because Gregory suggested I take some time—once again—to cool down. My meditation was anything but ... 'meditative' though. I've pretty much blacked out every single day so I could be unaware of the misery I'm feeling. Now here I am, not sober by any means, but of sound enough mind out of forced respect alone. If my best attempt at temperance was for naught, please go ahead and tell me now."

"Are you armed, William?" The words still flowed out of his mouth like a tranquil song.

"I'm here to find out where Charles Langston is one way or the other, and I ain't leaving till I do. So, of course I'm armed."

William heard a rapid fluttering of wings outside the confessional before there was a thud on the top of the stall. Through the partition, Priest Kubler didn't move a muscle.

Looking up to see only the ceiling above him, the sound of tiny steps pattered through. A bird must have landed above them. "The hell is—"

*CAW!* The shriek of a crow echoed in the church.

A chill ran up William's spine and caused a shiver to escape him.

*Is it a sign? No. Of course not. There are no signs.*

"Some architecture y'all got here."

"These walls are sacred, despite their age. Why do you mention it?"

*CAW!* As if to answer the question the bird sounded again, somehow more shrill than before. William wondered if there was any connection to the ones at his wedding.

Shaking his head and raising his palms, William turned toward the priest. "I don't think there's any need for me to name the vocal, winged elephant in the room."

"A vocal, winged elephant." Kubler remained still and forward facing. "What a sight that would be. Is that what you hear? I only hear a crow. The Enigma provides each of our minds so many interesting gifts, no?"

"What? No. It was a figure of—"

"I know—I know it was. I was only trying to assist you in reaching the understanding."

The interruption showed an odd, almost reluctant hint of frustration William wanted to explore. "Understanding of what?"

*CAW!*

"Goddamn it." William flinched.

"Of the real reason we have been brought together. You think you are only here for information on a player in your wife's murder—"

"I *know* it's why I'm here."

*CAW!*

"But the real reason is you now seek answers." The characteristic calm of the priest's tone was now substituted with a zealous fury. "Answers you need, as any would need after undergoing such trials, and which I myself have needed."

*CAW!*

"Get out of here, you." Standing on the bench in the tight stall, William reached up and banged on the ceiling of the confessional.

Feathers fluttered as the crow reacted and flew around the church.

The priest did not react. "You are here to discover why this has happened. To find a way to cope and to grieve in a constructive way."

Above them, the crow landed on the confessional again.

*CAW!*

"Please. Make it stop." William hadn't been so claustrophobic in his life. The room was spinning.

"To find purpose and meaning in this life you now question with such poisonous ire."

*CAW!*

Unable to take it anymore, he reached for the door. It wouldn't budge. "Let me out!" A powerful kick did the trick, and he sucked in a breath as it burst open.

"To bring her back."

Craning his head on its axis like an owl's full turn, he darted right back into the tight space he'd wanted nothing more than to escape from not three seconds ago. He threaded his fingers into the grates of the partition. "W—what did you say?"

The crow was silent now other than a brief pattering of its feet.

A deep, satisfied breath emanated from the stall. "Take a seat."

The bench no longer pained him as William sat right back down into it. Eager to hear what was to come, he straightened himself out and folded his hands in his lap. For a full minute, no follow-up was returned.

"Please," William said. "Just tell me what I need to do. I'll do anything you say."

After all this time, the gaze of the priest only now turned toward him. Though he couldn't be sure in the darkness, William thought he could make out turned-up cheeks. While there was always an obnoxious, relaxed smile on that face, this appeared to be more of a smirk.

"It has nothing to do with me and what I say. Only through the Enigma can we find the answers we seek."

"So help me if you're bullshitting me …" William reached for the holster on his waist with all the subtlety he could.

"Not in the slightest. You know of Cerebism do you not?"

"Sure."

"Then take your hand off your weapon and tell me what it is you know."

Snapping a glance at him, William could see Kubler was somehow facing forward again, and he tried to be more covert in moving his hand back to his leg.

"Wasn't reaching. But I don't know. Something about reincarnation."

"Is that really all you've heard?"

"I was never raised on it or anywhere near it. Only other thing I know is your god—'the Enigma'—considers our lives some kind of simulation. Always sounded kinda sick to me."

The priest sighed. "It is a sad state of affairs in the cities of East Duresia when our children are not raised with faith in the glory of God. The lack of faith is why you are so lost now, you know. But there is still time for you to see the light. We Cerebs don't usually appreciate the term 'simulation' either, by the way—though it isn't the worst of the language you use. Anyway, no world truly exists as we know it to, William. There is only our perception of a world the Enigma—our generous God—creates for each one of us. And we do reincarnate, but we are without memory of our past lives in a newly perceived world, one that is improved in ways God learns it must be for us to live as our best selves."

"So, under your logic, I should kill myself, and this will all get better. Noted. Good talk." There was no way William could resist rolling his eyes. Cerebism was always a thing he had a hard time understanding, even given how widespread it had become in New Berkeley.

"Goodness no. Anything but suicide. There is no greater sin. By killing yourself, you steal a chance for the Enigma to learn. For this there is the greatest of punishments. I said before our world improves with each life, but only if we provide our Creator with His greatest desire: knowledge."

Focusing on a tiny scuff in the door before him, William leaned forward and brought his elbows to his knees. "Well … what about murder and … other things?"

"We are given the gift of free will for a reason. The will to inflict pain exists within some. For them, the next world will be shifted to one of which they are better suited. What such a place looks like, I cannot say. But it is the way of things."

"And what does this all have to do with bringing her back?"

"Judith was already a part of your life, was she not? And if we live as good Cerebs, our worlds improve, as I've told you. Do this, and in the next life you will be with her for longer and without such a heartbreaking loss," the priest said.

There was silence as William pondered the thought, his face resting in his palms. His mind revolved around thoughts of being with her again, and he knew there remained parts of him struggling against so easily folding into a belief he hadn't granted any merit until a moment ago. He knew this and yet … to see his Judith again? So far this man was the only person who'd suggested it was possible—even if it was in another life.

"However."

William looked up through the frame. The priest had turned toward him again, staring straight at him, not saying another word. "However? However what?"

Still, no reply came. Kubler's hand came up to grasp the chain around his neck, rubbing his thumb over the crescent.

"However what!"

"However, there's another possibility. Rare, but possible."

"What is it?"

"If you fully and completely follow the will of the Enigma with *true* dedication and purpose, you may be reunited with Judith … in *this* life. And I can show you how to do so, William."

William stopped breathing.

*In this life?*

*In this life.*

*In THIS life!*

Pressing his hands to his knees, William lifted himself up and exited the confessional. He felt his heart might break out of his chest as those three words repeated over and over in his head. He came to the beginning of the closest pew and crouched with his back against the side arm rest, elbows on his knees, and hands around his head. The crow from before remained and tilted its head at him without leaving its perch. It made its call again, but the sound was muted to his ears. He felt lightheaded. Was it possible?

Out came the priest as the other door cracked open. At William's side, he squatted in the same position against the row beside him and began speaking. "When I was eighteen, I came to the Murrieta as a missionary. Just eighteen years old. I was sent here by my own church with one other—my best friend, Paul—to bring Cerebism to the natives. At the time, we both considered the duty an honor. We didn't think it too tall a task either when we learned of Fayette. We knew your gang had influence here and was expanding, so all we'd have to do was get on your good side and hide behind your veil."

"Withholding information is a *great* way to get on my good side—really."

"Hold on now, I'll get there … so, it was as difficult arriving and settling here for us as anyone, but we managed it. Around that time, we even built a bit of a following. Mary-Claire, whom you've met, was actually one of our first. We appreciated all the support, but they were Eastern folks, and we didn't want to get distracted from our purpose. That's when we went north to talk to the V'ahani."

"Because we were still fighting the Tokali at the time?"

"Exactly. We didn't want to chance the danger filling the Southern Murrieta then. Little did we know of the V'ahani and their demonic beliefs."

*CAW!* The crow came to life.

The priest's lip turned up at the interruption. "The group we came upon ridiculed us when we tried to talk to them about the Cereb way. Paul was as devout as they come and stubborn, so he didn't give up trying to convince them. In fact, he became argumentative, and it didn't end well. But we were allowed to leave when their Chieftain came along to end the bickering. The same night, though, we made camp not far away from the Riverlands. While I was asleep, Paul must have gone off to urinate or something. By the time I found him, the grizzlies had gotten to him. When we had spoken to the natives before, they told us some nonsense about those grizzlies ... and their 'Mother' god as they called it."

*CAW!*

William's patience burst again, and he stood up and shooed the bird off. It disappeared into the rafters of the ceiling. He paused, looking up, and thinking about the only important words the priest said.

*To bring her back.*

What would he do to bring Judith back? And to do so in *this* life?

*Anything.*

He looked back at the priest. "This place really needs some renovating. I could help with it if you think it'll benefit my case at all?" He thought maybe favors to the church meant favors to their god, too.

"I appreciate that, and it pleases me to no end you are beginning to see." The priest stood up and over him, placing a hand on his shoulder and reaching the other into a chest pocket. He removed a Cereb crescent pendant and handed it to him. "Take this. Know it represents the beginning of something special."

With a steady reach, William took it and placed it around his neck. The crescent fell right next to the Lion's Paw pin at his heart. He'd adopted the pin first and later made it mean something.

Maybe the crescent would grow on him the same.

"Thank you, father."

"I want to tell you something, William. When my friend was taken by those animals, I was as you are now without your love. Angry. Lost. I had a hard time believing in anything anymore. But it helped me to see in the end. Now I understand my true purpose." A gentle shake of William's shoulders caused him to look up. "We must convert the natives. It is why we have been bonded here in the sorrows we have each experienced. Yours is the wing they have been shepherded under, and mine is the voice that will show them the way."

With an expression twisted in uncertainty, William began clasping his hands together. His tragedy had nothing to do with the natives. "Are you serious?"

The priest moved in and placed his hands on William's shoulders. Their eyes locked.

"Yes. I am certain it is the only way for us both to see our loved ones again. They must be cleansed, as must this territory be cleansed of any non-believers. This is where your brother, Clovis, will be best utilized."

*CAW! CAW! CAW!*

The bird was growing more agitated. *Is it still in the church?*

"Clovis? But he doesn't believe. And how did you—"

*CAW!*

"Though you may not have known it, your friend, Gregory, is a good Cereb. Every now and then we talk in my confessional. As for Clovis's belief, it will be developed in his new mission. Think of it, William—a real meaning in life for your long-troubled brother, a territory unified in faith with you as its founder. There could be no better gift you could provide the Enigma. And for such devotion, I am certain He will return Judith to you again in this life and *every* life thereafter."

The church fell eerily silent, awaiting William's answer—not even the bird twitched.

"I … I would give anything to see her again. Can I have some time to consider?"

With a nod, he was escorted to the door. "Take your time. Oh, and Charles left Fayette some time ago, by the way. Before Gregory and you came to me about it."

"That suddenly means a lot less to me." And it did. He now had other things to mull over.

A grin that might have pissed William off when he walked into the church earlier stretched across the priest's face.

"Good. As it should. You are beginning to see there is only one way to be reunited with her, and it is through God. Accept this feeling in the coming days. We will talk again soon."

Outside the church, a glint of the sun was now peeking through a sky that had been gray the same morning. With his hands dug into his pockets, William headed home to think. A flapping from behind him caused him to turn, and he spotted the crow departing the church. His middle finger followed it along its path like the sight of a rifle until it reached the hills that looked down on Fayette. Atop one of those hills stood a small figure who made him jump. The figure was soon flanked by a rider with long hair. The crow landed on the rider's shoulder. He remained frozen, ready to run at a moment's notice when he squinted in close.

"Nova?"

Being stuck in a room, hiding from a gang that murdered your family, is never a scenario Jeannie would have described as fun. However, being holed up in the Tomorrow Room for the past few days with her brother and two friends as interesting as the Kennedale sisters were, was as close to enjoyable as such a situation could get. She also felt fortunate the windows of the room were all covered with decorations, which kept Harrison and her from needing to hide in the small, hidden closet at all times.

"Thank you both for this feast. Mother never made pressed duck before. This meat is so tender and delicious," she said as they sat around the table and ate together. The sisters had gone big on this evening's meal.

"Yeah, and this thick, red sauce, too. What's in this sauce?"

Harrison spoke with his mouth full, and Jeannie shot him a look. Unsurprisingly, he looked confused as to what her issue was. When she pointed at her mouth, he rolled his eyes and gave her a dismissive wave.

"You're both very welcome. But Debra's the one you should be thanking. She was in charge of the hardest part of the process."

With a humble wave, Debra reached for a bowl of extra sauce and passed it over to them. "The sauce is ... actually, I don't know if you want to know what the sauce is."

"Well, now I *need* to know." Harrison placed a meat-stripped bone back down onto his plate.

"We've already eaten it anyway, so how bad could it be?" Jeannie asked as she continued to chomp away.

With a grin and raised brows, Debra turned to Cassie, who waved her forward. "Okay, just remember you asked. It's made with the duck's … juices. I had to strangle the poor thing and—"

Harrison coughed. "All right. I think we get it." With a mouth full of duck juices, Jeannie froze. Looking down, with her face scrunched, she acknowledged the red had been blood. Her manners told her to hold it in and finish chewing, but her senses told her to spit. Appreciation for the sisters was the only thing to keep her eating.

"It's a new thing we heard about from this couple in town who hail from a coastal city in the far-east called Al-ven-i-ka," Cassie said, imitating the snooty way the couple spoke their home's name.

"Oh, Harrison, remember when mother and father used to talk about Alvenika and how beautiful the ocean is there?"

"I'm sure they were right, but those coastal folk think they're all sophisticated, so they talk this fancy crap up while they sniff their own farts."

Picturing the image Debra described amused Jeannie.

"The thing I can't stand is they tend to be so good at being snotty for some reason you end up wanting to do what they're doing, even though at the same time you hate them," Debra continued.

"And they use this fancy presser thing they *insisted* we borrow," Cassie said, mimicking the neighbors in question as she curled a lip and batted her lashes.

A snorting laugh from Debra became contagious, and soon Jeannie and Harrison were laughing, too.

"They kept on about it, and after a time they almost seemed mad we didn't want it. You remember, Deb?"

With a nod, Debra cackled. "She isn't kidding. And once we couldn't take it anymore and took it off them, those maniacs carried right back on being all friendly with their giddy, creepy-ass smiling."

"We had no choice but to use the damn thing. I mean, you have to see it. It's like a shiny little brass bell-slash-non-sharp-guillotine-device contraption. You know what? Let me go get it."

As Cassie left the room, Harrison turned to Debra. "Wait, I think I remember who you're talking about from my runs." The banter distracted them enough they now had almost finished their plates. It didn't taste bad after all, once you forgot about the description. "It's the Bensons, right?"

"You are Adonis's son, that's for sure," Debra said with a nod. Harrison's shoulders straightened at the comment. He loved being told he was like their father.

"They always used to try and convince me their wares were worth more than my father said they should be. Not in a hostile way or anything. They weren't polite either, but they seemed to want people to understand the value of their 'finer' things. It was like they were missionaries, but instead of coming here to spread religion, they came to spread the good word of how to live with their superior sensibilities."

Sitting up on her leg in her chair, a light bulb went off in Jeannie's head. "You didn't come up with the last part yourself, did you?"

"What? Yes, I—"

"Oh, big brother, please. It sounds an awful lot like something Daddy would say." Another snort by Debra made her giggle.

"Well, this time it wasn't." Harrison turned his head in frustration and crossed his arms.

Jeannie was still recovering from her own wit when Cassie returned.

"Where's the guillotine bell?" Debra asked.

But one look at Cassie's face made them all fall silent—Dominic entering the room only confirmed it.

Covered in sweat and panting, he blurted out, "The smoke … it has risen."

Without a word, they all walked out the door of the Tomorrow Room and toward the hall. Crouching down to remain out of sight of the hallway window, Jeannie looked toward the Mountainlands to the north and, sure enough, a gray cloud billowed over the trees. They made their way back to the Tomorrow Room again.

"What are we going to do?" Harrison asked. "The stunt you pulled to frame Charles and get Clovis out of here hasn't worked yet, has it? We need more time."

"Time is something we're running out of, I'm afraid," Dominic said.

"What options do we have?" Jeannie asked, now pacing and brushing her hair back over her ear. "If the V'ahani make it here, our town could be left in ruin."

Cassie fell back into her seat. "*When* they make it here."

"There will be no stopping them now," Debra said.

Dominic looked down at the ground, defeated. "As sorry as I am to say it, they're right. And there's little we can do until the V'ahani come." Dominic paused, a look passing between him and the Kennedales before he turned to Harrison. "If all hope is lost, our people will fight and defend this place for you." He looked toward Jeannie. "But they need you alive for morale, if nothing else."

Harrison planted his hands onto the table with a dish-clanking thud. "What are you saying?"

*What is he saying?*

"I think you know what I'm saying, Harrison."

"No, you can't."

Jeannie didn't understand what they were talking about, but she didn't like the feeling filling the room. She whipped her head toward Harrison and back to Dominic again. "Harrison, what is he talking about?"

Dominic looked at her, steady in his gaze. "We need to kill Clovis, Jeannie. And you all know as well as I do there's no one better suited to do it than me."

"But they won't give you the chance, and even if they do, they'll—"

"It's a risk I have to take."

*No.*

Harrison sighed with his face in his hands. "How will you do it?"

"No," she said.

"Jeannie—" Harrison and Dominic began in unison.

"No, Dominic."

"Listen to me, Jeannie. Frankie says he's gotten close to Clovis, and we've talked about it. When Clovis is going to be away for a bit, Frankie will give Donald the signal, which Donald will relay to me. Frankie will buy me time. When they're gone, I'll rig his room to explode. If we're lucky, it'll take some of the others out with him."

The thoughts of what could go wrong raced through her mind. "You can't leave us again."

"I made sure Donald and Frankie knew this was *your* plan. I knew it'd be best to help you two get back to where your family deserves to be, and I figured you'd—"

Harrison lifted his head. "Dominic, stop. Our restoration means nothing if we don't have you here with us. If you give us no say in this, like I assume Donald has assured you won't, you make sure you go undetected all right?"

"No, we can't let him do this," Jeannie said to her brother in a panic. It infuriated her when he didn't look her way.

"I can do this, okay?" Dominic said. "This is my payback for your father saving my life. After all these years, I now get this chance. All I need is for you both to trust me."

"We trust you," Harrison replied. Jeannie ran over to hug Dominic, tears falling from her eyes. Squeezing him as tightly as she could, she heard Harrison sigh. "But you owe the Morrells no debt, Dominic Turner. You never have."

# CHAPTER 8

## DIVE, DON'T JUMP

"Keep breathing. It will be okay."

Latera clung to Winona's embrace, needing a moment to gather herself.

"Is everything all right?" Mika asked as he appeared with Hammond by his side, the two dashing onto the bank from the trees. Latera kept her head down, but she could feel Winona motioning at Mika. "Perhaps it would be best if you head back to camp, Hammond."

"Did I do something wrong?" Hammond asked, with a pause. "Latera, I am sorry if I did."

She wanted to tell Hammond that it was okay, that it wasn't his fault, but she couldn't find the courage to do so.

"Just go; we will stay with her," Winona said.

"I … okay. Whenever you are ready to speak, Chieftess, I … you know where to find me." Hammond bowed his head and ran back off to camp.

Mika approached and rested his hand on Latera's shoulder. "You do not need to talk until you are ready, my sister. But please, if he hurt you, just nod … I will rip his heart clean out of his chest with all the malice of the—"

"No. He did nothing wrong. He did nothing at all." Wiping at her sniffling nose, she shook her head, knowing the truth and yet unable to understand it. "It was me. I am a monster."

The admittance made her break down again, and Winona shushed her gently, pulling her in close. "No, no, no. I will hear none of it. You are the furthest thing from it, Latera. The furthest thing."

"But I saw the hog, Winnie! It has been nightmare after nightmare, only they all feel real, and now this occurs while I am wide-awake. I have broken down in front of him, and I am certain he will be terrified of me."

"What do you mean when—" Mika began, but Winona cut him off.

"Well, it would not be the worst thing if he was terrified. We can have this effect sometimes, you know? A little fear of a woman is a good thing. Just ask Mika."

Mika let out a sarcastic scoff. "For the love of the Mother, Winona. I mean, you are not wrong, but—"

"No, you do not understand," Latera said, interrupting them.

A soft hand from Winona came to her shoulder. "Please help us to. Whatever it is, we would do anything to support you."

"I told you … I saw the hog."

"All right …"

"I *saw* the hog," Latera repeated, the vision playing over in her own head as she recounted it. "I mean, as it ran for him, I saw as if it were running straight for me. Only, I saw him too—and I saw me—and I do not know. I do not know anything anymore, except that our people are trapped and in danger every day while we sit here. Whenever the sun rises or sets, it is all I can think about. How can I get them out of there?"

Mika and Winona shared a wide-eyed glance before Mika spoke up. "So you had another dream … but you were awake, and this time it was a kind of … double vision of the present moment you were in?"

Latera nodded. It was the closest she could come to explaining it.

Mika ran his hand through his hair. "You know, I had an idea when you first told me about the dreams about what they could mean. At the time I was not sure and did not want to speculate. Now, though … now I am certain. You are a seer, Latera."

*A seer? What is a seer?*

Winona shot Mika a look. "Oh, love, look … I know you are well-versed as any on these things, but you do not know for certain."

"Well, if you admit I am well-versed, how can you think I would not know? This is what I am good at, Winnie."

Winona grinned and rolled her eyes.

"What?" Mika asked.

"Nothing."

"Opposite."

"Not opposite."

"Liar."

*A seer?*

While she normally loved watching their antics, at the moment it was delaying Mika's answer and prompted Latera to speak up. "Hey, do not mind me. Just kind of falling apart over here while you two are bickering."

Winona and Mika turned toward her.

"Now, what is a seer?" Latera asked. "I have not heard this term."

"There have been rare cases of some natives—V'ahani and Tokali alike—who have … visions. One belief is that these seers can call to the wind subconsciously and maintain control of the birds while being aware of their own surroundings. This is how they—you, I mean—might be able to see certain things without any apparent memory of seeing them yourself."

Latera raised her hands to her forehead and puffed out a breath. "Do you think this is really the case for me?"

"Well, we do not know for sure, but—"

"What else would explain why her dreams are focused on things she herself was involved in?" Mika asked to interrupt Winona's doubt. "What about those not of her experience or vantage point? This is what my research suggests, and I have plenty of sources with sources of their own."

Winona moved her hands to her hips. "Friends of friends? How reliable."

Mika ran his hand along the stubble forming on his cheeks. "Yes, rumors for certain, but I find it hard to believe these things could ever be complete fabrication. I do find it … fascinating."

"Fascinating? Do you realize …" Latera gulped down another rising tide of emotion. "I will never be the same."

Winona's head snapped toward her husband. "Seriously, Mika? Look what it has done to her. We cannot know the burden."

"I am sorry, Chieftess. I only meant to say how special you are. It is very rare, this gift."

"Well, I suppose I cannot blame you for your interest as much as I can your timing," Latera said, blushing as she deflected the compliment.

"And for that I apologize."

"So, I am calling the wind and do not even know it? It would explain the different vantage points." As much as having an explanation was aiding her to pull herself back together, Latera still worried. She didn't know when the visions would come and go, and she didn't know why this was happening to her now.

"Yes, and this much is clear," Mika said, interrupting her thoughts, "It is not something we can afford to look past. We must continue observing it to understand it."

Winona gave her a curious look. "If this is something you can continue to hone, and the visions turn out to be real, we should use them. There's plenty we can learn."

"Your plans sound … brilliant. But let me take it slow. I am going to need plenty of time to process all this. Also, the Tokali cannot find out, okay? It is strange enough for me to deal with on my own, and I do not need them to know yet—if ever. Mother knows it would be the only thing on their minds."

"As if you are not already in their heads," Winona said with a wink. "Are you feeling up to heading back to camp now so you can get some rest, my dark, little witch?"

"Winnie! That is not funny." Giving her friend a light shove, Latera couldn't help but laugh as she wiped her eyes dry.

"If it was not funny, why did you laugh?" Mika asked, playing along.

"You know, I am the Chieftess now, and as the Chieftess I do not appreciate you two ganging up on me." With her hands on her hips, she pointed her nose up into the air and released an exaggerated huff of affront.

Winona grinned at Mika. "Well, how long did it take for our praise to get to her head?"

Latera burst out laughing. "Hey! Ahem," she forced herself to stop giggling and frown, "I am sad again. Be nice to me."

"You may be special in some ways, sister, but you are no actress. Come, let us head back."

With Latera's spirits lifted, they returned to the campsite as Winona suggested. On arrival, the Tokali shot her a fair share of looks, each of which she noted: *Elan, upset; Hammond, apologetic; Gannon and Shelton, worried; Warrick, buried in his notes.*

Charles, on the other hand, had a look she couldn't read— though she had to admit this had been the case from the start. He did seem to be somewhat content with the fact he had nowhere else to be, but she wondered why this was. Since Hanzah wasn't able to provide her any info on him, it remained an unresolved concern.

Despite how much Winona had made Latera feel better, she knew her friend was wrong about one thing for now: an early night's sleep would be the last thing to help clear her head. With this in mind, she left her tent once the others had fallen into their slumber and headed straight for Hammond. Feeling the need for privacy, she entered his tent as quietly as possible and was gentle in waking him. When his eyes opened, she placed a finger to her lips indicating the need for silence. Grabbing his hand, she pulled him out of the shelter.

Still holding his hand, she began to run away from the camp

with him at her back. Once they were out of earshot of the tents, Hammond spoke.

"Latera? Is everything okay? Where are we going?"

Stopping in her tracks, his body bumped into hers. She tugged on his hand to bring him forward and looked up into his eyes. "Do you trust me, Hammond?"

"Of course, but—"

"Do you think … I am odd?"

"No, Latera. No. You are perfect."

She smiled. "Then follow me and do not speak except to repeat after me, okay?"

Off she raced again. Yet, they didn't go much further. All she needed was to be alone with the Mother—and Hammond—for a bit.

In a whisper, she recited an invocation she'd been taught when she was younger. "Oh great spirit of these great lands, when my head rests it shall be in your hands." Walking along the lake, her pace slowed now as she soaked in the moonlight on the water where the setting sun had been earlier in the evening. Hammond repeated the phrase, slow to spit out the words.

Stopping for a moment, she struggled with the next part now like never before, unsure of how grateful she was for her own gifts. They felt to her like a balance of benefit and burden, and she knew little about her new sight. Yet still, she pressed forward.

"But until my day comes I can only thank you, for these gifts you have granted provide us the truth."

Hammond echoed her again, more confident this time. She continued as she once again began to walk.

"So we honor your kingdom and all it nurtures, with the faintest of touch and with intentions pure." She approached an inverted hill slope, knowing it was an ideal place to lie down. It would allow her to see both the lake before her and the fire of the campsite in the distance to her right. She lay down, and to her left, Hammond did the same. The urge to rub her fingers together hit her again, the dormant anxieties waking, but before she started doing so Hammond gently wrapped his arm around her, easing her to his side. With his warmth beside her and his heartbeat beneath her cheek, she calmed and turned her attention to the stars. They littered the sky here as far as she could see, which was much further without the depth of forest she was accustomed to in the Riverlands. Some stood alone, forced to shine and earn their place on their own strength, while others rested in clusters, splatters of reds and yellows and oranges upon the ubiquitous black.

Finally, she spoke the final line. "Holding hope it is with us each day you might ride. Hope with each day we might earn your pride."

This time, Hammond didn't repeat after her. As she lifted her head from his chest to look up at him and see why, his hand came to her cheek. Still for a moment, she shivered when he slid his fingers up into her hair and pulled her lips up to touch his. Their kiss electrified her—as the V'ahani were a conservative people, and she was a Chieftain's daughter, it was her first. The feeling intensified once she eased into it. She wrapped a hand around his shoulder, pulling him closer. But after a moment, she eased up to lay her hand on his cheek, looking into his eyes.

He smiled at her. "Latera."

He raised a hand to match hers, and she smiled back. She felt the spark charging along their skin even from so innocent a contact, and she felt the gentle tug as Hammond pulled her in for another kiss. Only, this time when she was a breath away, she pulled back and sat up.

"Are you all right?" he asked, sitting up beside her.

"Yes, I am. It is just," she peeked up from beneath her lashes at him, "there is a lot happening all at once, and I … can we take this slow?"

"Well, you are the Chieftess after all, so I suppose you set the pace." He winked at her, lightening the moment, and she grinned. His face turned serious as he placed a hand on her own in the grass. "But, of course, Latera. I am not going anywhere."

"Good. I do not want you to." Then she playfully shoved him back down and, once he was lying flat, curled herself into his side. He wrapped his arm around her back and drew circles on her arms with the tips of his fingers until she felt his breath slow in sleep.

For a time, she lay awake in his arms, admiring the view before her again. Soon she let out a yawn, and her eyes grew heavier and heavier, until she could no longer fight off her own exhaustion.

The dreams passed by like a stampede across the plains. And like the herd of such a stampede, Latera could not catch them all. She needed to pick one, and she needed to pick it wisely. Charles appeared, alongside another man she did not recognize, who was holding a silver covered dish. Like a knife hurled at a moving target, she dived for the dream and latched onto it.

They stood together in a kitchen, where a man dressed as a chef lay dead on the floor.

"Did I need to kill a man who makes food for people?" Charles asked aloud as they waited by the kitchen door.

"Yes, Charles," his companion said in a hissed whisper. "For the millionth fucking time, yes, you did need to kill him to prove your loyalties remain where they're supposed to."

"But I killed Daniel's messenger on the ride here, too. Did he not count for nothing? How many more times am I going to need to prove myself?"

"So help me if you open your goddamn mouth again and William hears you—"

Latera's vantage point shifted to a passing conversation at the front of the mansion and a man identified as William Keagan. He entered the dining room, Lion's Paw pin shining on his breast. Once he sat, Charles and his associate stormed in. What unfolded thereafter disturbed her to no end. Once the head of William Keagan's wife was revealed on the table, her vantage point shifted to Charles, who managed to make an escape out of the mansion and into town.

In this moment, Latera was aware enough to realize she was in a dream, so a voice in her head commanded her to wake.

When Latera's eyes opened, she was still with Hammond on the slope, only now the sky was beginning to shift from black into the darkest of blues. As soon as she'd realized where she was and what she had just seen, she jumped to her feet.

"Latera?" Hammond said behind her as he rose.

"Come with me now—questions later." She was too focused to expand further, so she began to run toward the camp. This would be her chance to find out if her dreams were real or not, and she was determined to get answers from Charles. As much as she hated the Keagans, and as much as she knew that in being the Keagans' enemy, Charles could still be an ally, Latera needed to hear what story he would tell. Though in her opinion, the heartbreak William Keagan had endured was just, considering all her people had been put through, the cruelty of Charles and his associate's acts toward William's wife needed to be answered for.

When they arrived back at the camp, Latera found a bucket, and directed Hammond to stand guard. She filled the bucket with lake water and marched over to the sleeping Charles. He remained in the same place they had first tied him up, both hands tied together and then to a nearby pole he leaned his back against. The snoring he emitted thundered through the air as well, giving her yet another reason to wake him. Once in dumping distance, she motioned Hammond to get back into his tent. Understanding she wanted it to appear like he was only just emerging, he winked at her, and disappeared inside. When she proceeded to hurl the water on Charles's face, the response from the brutish man was immediate.

"Ah—what the hell is going on?"

The others were drowsy and beginning to stumble out of their tents as Hammond also emerged from his. She was prepared to address them all. "What is going on is you are going to tell us the truth right now."

"The truth about what, Latera?" Winona asked from behind her. "What happened?"

"Yeah, the truth about what? I've just been sleeping here," Charles echoed.

"You know what I speak of, liar. Tell them. Tell them now." The hope was her open-endedness might get more out of him than she'd already seen, assuming there was more.

"I mean … okay—you know, I admit it. I was framed for murder in Harran." Despite the intentional bait she'd cast, she was surprised his immediate response contained additional information.

"You what?"

"Yeah, that's right, framed! And I didn't even do it neither."

"But of course," Mika said, jesting under his breath.

"I swear to you I didn't. But they convinced Daniel I did. Those devils. They took everything from me. And it's all thanks to those miserable witches. Every bit of this shit is thanks to them."

"What did they say you did?" She squinted at him in confusion, as he seemed to be losing his wits. "Did they say you were one of the men who murdered William Keagan's wife?"

"He did *what*?" Mika asked.

Coming toward Charles, Elan stood tall as if to intimidate. "*Him*? How?"

"Oh, well … yeah I guess I had a hand in the William thing too. But I wasn't the one to kill her and I would have never gotten involved in that mess either if I hadn't been yanked from my position!"

There were now more questions than answers in Latera's head. "Let me get this straight. I follow up with my brother, who is as close with the Morrells as any still alive, and he says they made no mention of you whatsoever. Yet at the same time, you claim to be the mayor of a town their family built, who was framed for a murder—a murder I still have not heard you clarify at the moment. Now you admit to me you are powerful enough to have had a role in the murder of the wife of William Keagan, in his mansion home. And after all this, I am left to wonder who you are, sir. Because if I do not know who the real Charles is, how can I possibly trust you?"

As he looked them all up and down with inverted brows, he still remained a blank page to her.

"But I've now told you who I am," Charles said. "So, I'm afraid I'm lost. I mean, isn't the rest obvious?"

"Is he serious?" Winona asked.

Turning back to her, Latera shrugged her shoulders. "To be honest, I have not the slightest."

"Out with it," Gannon said, pulling back the hammer on his rifle.

"All right, all right. If you somehow still don't get it, I'll spell it out for you. I'm a spy from the East. An important one, too, as you now know." Charles's nose hung in the air with anticipation while Latera and the others remained silent. She could not believe him, yet, somehow she also could not find a way to doubt him either. His cheeks turned red, as if he had something still to prove. "They wouldn't have assigned me my title of 'mayor' otherwise, you know. William Keagan made enemies with my handlers, but it became personal for me when his brother, Daniel, made a mockery of me in my own town. He allowed me to be framed for the murder of one of his men without a fair trial. So I brought William great pain like his kin gave me. But we didn't get the chance to take him out, too, since his people came in and killed my assistant first."

A grin on her face turned into a laugh as the dream she had replayed in her mind. "*Your* assistant, Charles?"

Looking away, Charles frowned. "Of course, we were partners.

Look, what do you know anyway?"

"So you are an enemy of the Keagans, too?" Hammond asked.

"Have I not been clear here? I was a part of the murder of William Keagan's wife. In fact, my sick-ass assistant went and beheaded her after he killed her. Not in front of me—I turned around and closed my eyes real tight. But between her and the murder they *thought* I did? Hell, I shot down a messenger and chef of theirs, too. We're talking about a guy making all the feasts for them in the world, and someone goes and kills him? Who would go so far if not an enemy?"

The others all traded glances. "As sick as the things he has been a part of sound ... Perhaps, to us, he's an ally?" Mika asked aloud.

No one replied, so Latera decided she'd heard enough. "Thank you for your honesty. The more of it you give us, the better things will go for you."

"Well you hadn't asked so ..." Charles said. Latera rolled her eyes.

After Charles's interrogation, Latera, Mika, and Winona returned to their tent.

Upon entering, she plopped down onto her back and stared up with the back of her hand on her forehead. "I suppose now we know."

"Yeah, at least as much as it seems we need to know about him for now," Winona said.

Turning over to her friends, Latera debated whether she felt confidence or sorrow about what would come next. "No, Winnie. The murder of the wife of William Keagan—I saw it. Now we know that my dreams, they are real. It seems the stories you heard are true, Mika. I am your proof. I am ... different."

Mika's posture straightened. "Not different, Latera. You are *magnificent.*"

∗

In the five days leading up to his second talk with factory owner Torrance Andersen, Henry spent the bulk of his time becoming Emory Wallace. The more he had heard Andersen talk about the state of affairs in New Berkeley, the more he embraced the idea of a political movement. Beyond being a means of vengeance, it also seemed to him like a good cause and one he started to repeat to himself along with his morning affirmations. Falling into his new character's progressive past life in Alvenika only helped his passion grow.

The meeting didn't have a set time, but he decided he'd head over at about noon. So the morning of, with time to kill, he decided to take a carriage ride through the city's suburbs. He never did get to do so last time he was here with William. As his old chauffeur took them through the streets, the chauffeur went into great detail about the history of every corner. Though Henry knew most of it already, there were a few tidbits he wasn't aware of, and the animated man's storytelling was entertaining, so he was happy to hear it.

As time passed, he started to wonder why they hadn't arrived yet. The city seemed to expand out much further than he remembered.

"Okay, it's been a pleasure, sir. Here we are," the old rider said.

"What? Oh no, I think you must be mistaken. This can't be where—"

"I'm sorry to tell you it is. The expansion here has been ...

without end. We used to have pretty places still close enough to visit. Unfortunately, no more."

"Can you give me a second before we head back?"

"Sure thing."

Stepping down from the carriage, Henry was horrified by what he saw. Gone were the homes surrounded by gardens their owners took pride in. No longer were there smiling, neighborly faces on either side of white fences. The separation of city and countryside had been replaced by an endless string of apartments and storefronts. Simple, dirt roads were substituted for cobblestones. Now the balance he loved about New Berkeley was broken, and a desire in him to act on it was cemented.

The ride back felt longer than the trip there. It might have been the historical tour being over or the disappointment in what became of his old, quiet town, but the mood had taken a turn. Within a few blocks of the Anderson Mill, another factory came into view with a crowd built around it. The closer the wagon came, the more Henry could hear the protesting.

"Double the fare if you give me fifteen minutes to see what's going on here."

"I'll give you twenty, but I ain't parking it nearby. I'll be a block up."

"Great, thank you." Henry jumped out and rushed up to the crowd. There were both men and women, varying in age from their twenties to forties, yelling and raising fists outside. Leaning over one angry woman's shoulder he asked, "What's all this about, ma'am?"

"The pigs stick us in terrible, dangerous conditions for shit wages, so we band together and ask for more. But when we do, they fire us and bring in children who they pay less," she said as a chant began. She turned away from Henry and joined in. "Fair work for all or the towers will fall! Cause when they drag us down, the Forgotten heed the call!"

The doors to the factory were guarded by some large, shady characters, who would let the occasional worker out every now and again. Whenever one would leave, the crowd would howl "scab" at the top of their lungs. The children were apparently fair game for such ridicule, though they didn't seem to understand what was going on, as an adult of some kind would hurry to usher them away.

The riots continued, but from what Henry could see, it didn't seem they were disrupting any operations of the factory itself. It was good to see the unity anyway, though. Somehow he would need to figure out who the leadership of this Fraternal Forgotten was. As he went to approach the woman again to ask more questions about the organization, he spotted four men in black trench coats coming around the corner. One look, and he knew they were Forrest's. He watched as they whipped guns out of their coats.

Without conscious thought, he started pushing through the crowd. "Everybody down!" Surprised onlookers looked at him perplexed until they spotted the guns. "Down, I said!" Shrieking, they quickly followed his order and ducked to the ground. As the weapons were raised, Henry stood tall in the crowd and raised his hands. "Stop! Don't shoot! I'll make sure they disperse and cause y'all no more headache."

"And who are you to make such a guarantee?"

*Who am I?*

*I'm Emory Wallace.*

The people around him stared up at him as they cowered. Somehow, he felt responsible for them now by claim alone.

"My name is Emory Wallace." The name came out with a boom as he looked around at the strikers and back to the young guns. He'd need to convince all of them of the story he was about to tell. "I'm no better than any of these people. My background is as humble as theirs. And like them, I only want what's best for this city. It's what we all want. Y'all too, I'm sure."

"If all you got is your name and the shit coming out of your mouth, make your peace with God now." The weapons clicked.

"Wait! Look, *I* organized this rally in the name of the Fraternal Forgotten to protest the unfair conditions at this mill and so many others. These workers deserve better. New Berkeley deserves better. But I can see now perhaps disturbing the peace wasn't the best way. Let these people go."

There was a pause as the lead gunman stared him down. "They got sixty seconds to disband like you said, or you'll be nothing more than the first to meet our fire, Emory Wallace."

Some in the group retreated right away while others were slower to leave. With his hands still raised in the air, he urged the stragglers on.

"Value your lives, my comrades. They are worth far more than this single moment. Live for a greater day." When the last of them turned the corner and were out of sight, Henry bowed his head toward Forrest's men and started off back-peddling, too. "My apologies, gentlemen. You will not have any more trouble."

"Where do you think you're going?"

"I said we'd be off."

"We allowed for them to be off. Ain't never promised for the damn ringleader to go strolling into the night. Get on your knees. Do it now."

All four guns were raised his way once again. The order was not one Henry was eager to follow. Only now did he realize how foolish and brazen he had been. Being taken before Forrest would be the worst thing possible with so much left to do. It would be suicide to resist, but suicide might be preferable to the humiliation he could face.

"He said get on your knees now, asshole," another in the group said as they made their gradual approach, circling him.

His shoulders sank in defeat with a sigh as he locked his hands behind his hand. One knee at a time he came to the ground, stalling the impact as long as he could. Once he was in the position, the men rushed him. They slammed him onto the ground, bound his hands behind his back, and blindfolded him. Unwilling to give them the courtesy of walking, he made them drag him for a distance before they threw him in the back of a carriage.

From his place in it he could hear them talking for a bit. One agreed to stay at the factory, while two would sit on the front to guide the carriage and the fourth would be inside it with him. His travel companion gave him a nice kick when he climbed in. "You pathetic quacks are real brilliant, huh? You'll never know what it's like to taste success—not with your communist fantasies."

"Don't judge a book by its cover."

He received another kick to the ribs for his quip, one hard

enough it forced him to grunt and cry out.

"You good back there?" one of the riders asked.

"Oh, don't you worry, he'll be just fine."

With a snap of the reins, the horses jolted forward, and the wheels started turning in the last direction Henry wanted to be going. In the agony of his failure and without saying a word out loud, he mouthed his mantra to himself for comfort. "Jackson 'Forrest' Hayes … no less than all of it—the entire operation … Find a way—any way. Find a way—any way."

*

Though the temperature was mild that morning, Daniel was sweltering. His nerves made the day feel like it carried the heat of an oven ten times over. This was the day he would take action. He could no longer rely on a V'ahani attack to bail him out of a problem he should have solved long ago—especially now with Clovis having ripped Daniel's control over Harran right out of his grip. Daniel finally found a place to build something, and his brother wanted to tear it apart piece by piece to "cleanse" it. He couldn't stand by and allow it. He was also aware making a move only now, when Clovis's presence was against his own direct interest, was selfish. But it didn't matter what anyone else thought. The intentions he had to protect those he cared about were clear to him, and after so many years of pushing this issue aside, Daniel knew it needed to be him to put a stop to his brother. Clovis's followers were still Keagan men, and when separated from their leader, he'd be able to control them.

Like a sign from the heavens, about two days since the incident at Charles' house, Clovis had summoned Daniel to show him the findings of his investigation. Whatever they were, it wouldn't matter soon. Waiting at the door of his hotel room was Frankie. Giving Johanna the longest, most affectionate kiss Daniel had ever given, he was fortified when she returned it with equal vigor. Daniel took one last long look at her. He hadn't told her of his decision to act today, but he didn't need to. She knew. They were getting better at reading each other, and some things didn't need to be said. With a nod, he slicked back his hair and was off with Frankie.

"You got any idea what Clovis's investigation found?" he asked as they headed for the lobby.

"I don't have a clue. He hasn't told me."

"Welcome to my world, man." He was so sick of Clovis's demented, manipulative mind games, though at this point he welcomed any fuel to add to the fire.

After an exchange with Donald they exited the hotel, but Clovis was nowhere to be found. However, across the dirt road from the hotel sat the "Welcome to Harran" sign, or rather not the original sign, which he'd watched burn to a pile of ash, but another sign with words painted in black. Then, in red, over the text, was Daniel's name and an arrow pointing to his left.

*Why go through the effort?*

This meant one thing: Clovis was about to perform some theatrics. Tilting his head back with a sigh, he knew he should have seen this coming. "You've gotta be fucking kidding me." Storming off down the road in the requested direction, Frankie walked at an uneven pace behind him to keep up.

"Something happen to your leg?" Daniel asked.

"I took a tumble and rolled my ankle. All good though."

They walked on until they came around a bend and saw Clovis and Devin standing before the rubble of the jail. Straightening out his vest, Daniel stormed over to them, hoping to cut off whatever spectacle his brother had planned.

"What are we doing here, Clovis? We know Charles is the source of all our ills. You know the true crime he's committed against our family. Yet you obsess over things I told you I've handled. You're wasting time here in Harran "investigating" instead of finding Charles Langston, *and* you're doing it while Billy's alone in Fayette. What if Charles was on his way down there right now? How could we live with ourselves knowing we let him get hurt?"

Clovis looked up with an eerie calmness as he cleaned his pistol with a handkerchief he carried. "Are you done?"

"Am I what?"

"Done. As in, 'arrived at or brought to an end,'" Devin said with a grin. "Used in a sentence—"

"Oh, save me the fucking definition, lackey. Who do you think you are, trying to play with me?" Daniel sent a look of disgust at Clovis's second in command and back to Clovis. "Look, I'll ask it again: What the hell is all this about?"

There was a tense silence for a few minutes, making Daniel more uneasy than he'd ever been around Clovis. It was a different beast being on the receiving end of his brother's malice. Clovis turned toward the jail as if to admire the ashes, before shaking his head from one side to the other. He clicked his tongue in disapproval. "I gotta say this because it's the first time in my life I've ever had the opportunity. And it might be the last, too, but I honestly don't know anymore, Daniel. I really don't."

"Don't know what? Enough of this shit, brother. Say what you want to say."

"What I want to say is I now know the feeling of being the good egg. For once it's you who's been the bad boy and me who's gonna have to bail you out."

*What did he know? How could he ... Frankie.*

Daniel tried his best not to let his terror show in his expression as his mind ran ahead with possibilities. Details came to him: Frankie's pale skin and limp far more pronounced than it should be for a "tumble." So Clovis had tortured the boy. Daniel had a hard time getting mad at Frankie, even as things were falling apart around him.

"This rubble!" Clovis said, lifting up a bit of it. "Tell me what once stood here."

"May I?" Devin asked Clovis, who nodded in response.

Devin was the last person Daniel wanted to hear speak now. "Please, don't bother."

"I was gonna say he already knows the answer, boss. It's one of those things that's kind of like a rhetorical question, but I mean ... is it? He did wait for you to answer, and a rhetorical question is not meant to have an answer, so—"

"A jail, Clovis," Daniel said, cutting off Devin. "My jail. A jail that once imprisoned the man who helped kill Billy's wife. He's the only person in the world we need to be hunting down right now. The only person our brother cares about us hunting down. I don't know how many more times I need to say it or how much more incentive you could need. After all Billy's given you, you should have one focus right now."

"It was a jail," Clovis began, ignoring him. "Much like the one you trap me in when you question my work."

"How could you—"

"You aren't supposed to do that, Daniel." Clovis was screaming now as tears streamed down his face.

"Look at how much he cares for you," Devin cried, feeding off his idol's hysteria. "How could you do this to him?"

"You aren't supposed to restrict me," Clovis said. "Of all fucking people, you're supposed to be the one who's there for me. If you aren't setting me free, who will? You're supposed to set me free!"

It wasn't odd whatsoever for Clovis's emotions to overtake him, but he looked more insane now than Daniel had ever seen him. His eyes bulged as he screeched each word, snot and tears running down his red face. Daniel dared not move, but he was careful to mind his holster. Perhaps now was the time to end it.

"And now I come to find you're hiding things from me, too, Daniel! Big things, with no explanation whatsoever."

"Please, take a deep breath. I—"

Clovis lifted his own gun and pointed it at Daniel in one fluid motion.

"Whoa, whoa, whoa, Clovis," Daniel said, his arms coming up automatically. Pulling his own gun now would get him shot for certain. And yet, despite Daniel's defensive posture, Devin pulled his gun on him, as well. "What the hell are you doing, bitch?" Daniel asked, trying to hold on to any shred of power. He couldn't take them both.

"TELL ME! TELL ME WHY YOU'RE LYING TO ME!" Clovis's

voice cracked as he yelled the words. His arm straightened out taking aim as he did so.

Though Clovis was manic, Daniel had some confidence his brother wouldn't go through with killing him. Clovis had one limit, and William and he were it.

"I can't …"

"YOU WILL TELL ME."

*So be it.*

"Okay. Okay." Daniel took a deep breath and forged on. "Look, we can't go on like this anymore. It won't work. You're my brother, and I love you to my core. You know I do. But this chaotic world existing within you ain't the one we can force everyone around us to inhabit anymore. We just can't. And this town has grown on me, you know? There's something about the people and everything. It's helped me to see what we've been doing to this point isn't the way. There's still time to fix it, and together our vision can still come to life. But it needs to be a peaceful one, Clovis. And if it can't be peaceful, it can't be at all."

"But … but I can't go back, Daniel."

There was honesty in Clovis's plea, and Daniel recognized it better than any other could. Despite the gun still pointed at him, this moment was one of the most raw he'd ever had with his baby brother. There was no one else in the world except for William who would understand. If he didn't approach it right, though, this might be the last time this connection would find its way through the black ocean of Clovis's internal self.

"I'm sorry, buddy, but it can't be this way. We can get through this though, okay? I promise you. We will figure this out together like we always have. Please. Give me a chance."

Clovis looked like a malfunctioning machine, un-moving but ready to fall to pieces. With an anguished cry, he lowered his arm and returned his pistol to its holster. Following suit, Devin did the same. The man mimicked his brother's every move. It was dangerous, but Daniel couldn't pay it too much mind right now.

"Thank you. Thank you so—"

"There's something I need you to see," Clovis said, his face losing all emotion. His voice turned monotone, and his shoulders slumped. Appearing blank and defeated, he transformed into a different person before Daniel's eyes.

"Of course, show me."

"I have to make a stop first in my hotel room, okay?"

"Whatever you need, I'm here for you."

Clovis marched past Daniel and Frankie back toward the hotel. The faces of Harran's citizens watched them from windows and porches. There were so many places this road could lead, but it was about time he'd walked it.

Inside the hotel, Clovis's pace slowed until he stopped at his door. With a heart-breaking tear in his eye, he whispered, "I didn't want this, but you've left me no choice. You've changed, brother."

*Oh no.*

Daniel reached for the gun on his waist, but the barrel of Devin's gun was already on his temple. Clovis kicked open the door to his room. Crouching within it, fiddling with something underneath Clovis's bed, was Dominic Turner. Dominic reacted in kind, darting for a dresser where a revolver sat. Clovis was too quick though, and they grappled with each other. As Clovis grabbed the pistol on the dresser and clubbed Dominic between the shoulder blades, Dominic somehow managed to get a hand on the gun on Clovis's waist. Again, Clovis reacted, preventing Dominic from getting any real grip on its handle, but not from opening the cylinder, emptying the bullets onto the ground, and slapping it away to the floor. In an instant, Clovis went berserk. Dominic had stood a chance when his brother was fighting like a man, but not when he transformed into the monster inside him. Backing Dominic up against the dresser, Clovis swung wildly at him, pounding him without pause.

"Clovis, please!" Daniel shouted, held still by Devin's gun.

Clovis froze, and Dominic fell bloody to the floor. Lifting Dominic's gun, Clovis let out a guttural howl.

*He's going to kill him right here.*

"Don't do this!"

Clovis turned to Daniel, letting out an enraged scream right in his face. He turned to Devin next. "Assemble the townsfolk for an execution."

"No!"

Devin lifted the gun from Daniel's temple for an instant, but before he could blink two more of Clovis's men appeared behind him and restrained him.

"They need to know the Keagans will not tolerate murder and disorder against our own in any way." Clovis took a deep breath and approached a petrified Frankie, who was shaking with his back against the hallway wall. "You've done well, kid. For giving up this killer we've been searching for, Billy and I will see to your promotion as promised."

"Clovis, stop. You can't do this. I won't let you."

Clovis turned to him slowly. The look Daniel received made it clear their bond had been severed forever.

"I didn't do this, Daniel. You did."

# CHAPTER 9

## ꝒAINTED

As he stepped into the forest, the presence of grizzlies radiated in Hanzah's bones. All V'ahani shared an inherent connection to their home, yet at times it felt to him like there was more to it. The moment his feet touched the earth of the Riverlands, it felt like a direct link to the Mother came alive. It wasn't the same in the Mountainlands or anywhere else he'd ever been. The Riverlands were simply a part of him. He was born into this place. The blood of his fallen father ran through its river. His mother had lost a battle with the same waters when Hanzah was young, and his father had always told him the river still held her. Somehow, he could feel the presence of both of them now—in the air, in the water, in the earth. They tied him to this place, and if he was to see war in the coming days, there would be no place more familiar and advantageous than here.

A few hours away from Harran, he marched alongside his Uncle Orrin's horse, looking up at him with a smile on his face.

"Have you ever been in such a battle as we are marching toward, uncle?"

"Not a one, no. None of us have. Do not get me wrong, we have had our fair bit of skirmishes. But no larger conflict we ever lacked the upper hand over. The Easterners we have dealt with were either lost, ill-equipped, or over-confident. Not even Varek has seen this kind of fight, as far as I know. As much as relations with the Tokali have remained chilly for some time, the space between us—the literal, geographical space between us, I mean, as opposed to the ideological one—has kept our war with them a cold one." Orrin took a deep gasp of a breath, having winded himself again. "Whew. Am I talking fast or what? I suppose I might be a little nervous to be honest."

"*You* are nervous? There would be no telling it if it is so."

For the first time—perhaps ever—Hanzah watched Orrin look to the ground in sorrow. "I just never thought I would be marching into any big skirmish without your father. Let alone one in the Riverlands. And if he could not stop the threat then …"

"Then we must," Hanzah said, reaching up to place a hand on his uncle's knee. "We must stop them and get our people back for him. I will not let his loss be in vain."

Orrin's calming smile returned, affirming Hanzah's words. He took the winter hat he always wore off his head and placed it onto Hanzah's. The fur inside was a bit damp, but the sentiment was more important than his discomfort. It was also more important than the hat's being too big to fit his head.

When Hanzah pulled it down, and it fell over his eyes, he turned his head up playfully toward Orrin, who laughed out loud on seeing the upper half of Hanzah's face covered.

"You are not supposed to be the one pepping me up about getting through this, but I am far too proud of you to feel any shame about it," Orrin said. "He would be, too, you know."

Fixing the hat in a position where it would stay in place, Hanzah's spirits lifted. "I am not supposed to be the one making you laugh either. But I have learned so many things from you, Uncle Orrin. Humor principal among them."

"Perhaps that has been a little heavy in the curriculum," Orrin said with a wink.

"An important lesson nonetheless. I suppose we should get serious now though, with Harran approaching?"

"No. This is action. When we take action we do not prepare mentally other than to shut off all thoughts. Seriousness is the enemy. Levity is the enemy though, too, if we take our obstacles too lightly. And do not get me wrong. You must understand this before we engage in combat. We *will* prepare as much as possible. In our time of preparation we will be thoughtful of our advantages and develop a strategy for victory. But we *will not* think beyond that point. There can only be action in line with instinct, based on our outline beforehand."

This was too much to absorb for Hanzah to offer an immediate reply. There was something direct about what he'd said, but it also required some consideration. As they continued on, Hanzah pondered it for a long while—all the way until they came upon the area where the forest met the outskirts of the town. The time would soon be upon them.

*I need to talk to Varek.*

He'd taken all the time he could to craft something to say, but he still didn't know how to convince the Grand Chieftain not all Easterners were enemies. The lives of his friends would be at stake if he failed.

The large cluster of V'ahani warriors waited while Varek, Orrin, and their respective Masters and Councilmen crept up to scout out the town. As the leaders broke off and the larger group retreated a ways back, blending into the trees and awaiting orders, Hanzah found himself in an awkward place in between. Uncertain of whom to follow, he stood alone for a moment, equidistant between the two segments.

*Forward or back?*

With a deep breath, he plunged forward and ran to catch up to Orrin.

Looking out on Harran from the trees, Orrin whipped his hat off Hanzah's head, plopped it back on his own, and rubbed a hand over Hanzah's messy hair. With a roll of his eyes, Hanzah fixed his hair as he beheld the bustling town before him. There was an antsy, agitated vibe to it now, which he didn't remember from the last time he was there. While he was certain some of it had to do with the presence of Clovis and his men, something else seemed amiss.

With a nod at the stirring crowd, Varek rested his weight on his elbow over his knee. "It would seem they are all out in the open today. There will be nowhere to run once we attack."

"How will we do it, Grand Chieftain?" one of the Masters asked, leaning over Varek's shoulder.

There was a contemplative pause before Varek pointed along the tree line. "We will attack from all sides of the north. Maintaining the element of surprise is imperative, so we will launch an overwhelming strike all at once on my orders. I need to see a storm of grizzlies, followed by an army of every man not controlling a beast … Oh and not a single shot is to be fired from our side. There will be no need for it, and I will not chance one of our own getting caught in the line of fire."

*Now or never.*

Hanzah clenched his fists for courage and dived in. "How are we to identify the townsfolk?"

Varek did not so much as glance Hanzah's way, but continued on. "We aim for Clovis first, if he is identifiable, and if not, we tear this town inside out until we find him among them."

"But this crowd is not just members of the Keagan gang," Hanzah insisted. He broke off a nearby branch as he spoke. The frustration with its blowing in his face might have been amplified by his worry about the Grand Chieftain's sensibilities when it came to the Easterners.

"There is no way we could properly identify them all," Varek said, now addressing Hanzah directly. "We will treat the situation like any other fight. Women and children will be helped to safety where possible, and if there is a clear ally we will do our best to fight alongside them rather than with them. But there can be no hesitation for even a moment. This is about *our* people being returned to us. That is the priority more than the safety of any Easterner, no matter how nice they might be."

How could he argue with such a statement? How could he choose anything over his own people? With eyes fixed on his feet, Hanzah nodded. "Understood, Grand Chieftain."

"Good. Well, Masters, you have heard my orders. Get the men in position and prepare for my signal."

It was time to assemble the grizzlies. Taking to a knee by Varek and Orrin, Hanzah looked down to the ground and began his call.

"Oh Mother. Oh Maiden of the Land. Hear my thanks as true as you hear my prayers. For your humbling gifts. For your glorious Territory. Let us utilize the beasts of your forest. And take this as my vow today the same as all days that I shall do so only in the defense of your children."

"Good, Hanzah," Varek said with wide, war-hungry eyes.

The excitement he showed didn't impress Hanzah, who had done this ritual many times before and didn't need his approval.

In his mind's eye, he saw his grizzly. "I have you." Sure enough, trampling through the brush tranquilly behind him was a massive bear. It stood on all fours with a tamed, panting growl and eyes with a glow about them. All that kept Hanzah's beast from unleashing its fury was his word. This was as empowering to him now as it had been the first time he experienced it.

Walking over to it with grace, Orrin grazed a hand through its rich, brown fur. "A fantastic sow indeed."

"I am ready to put on my face now, if you allow me to borrow your paint."

"Of course. As mentioned, I would be happy to apply it for you if you would like."

"Thank you, uncle," Hanzah said. "But if I have learned anything from you in days past, it is that I must do this myself. I hope you will understand."

Orrin agreed with grace as Hanzah spread a white, vertical line down his nose and chin, with two horizontal lines on his cheeks under his eyes. He was ready.

A commotion started in the center of Harran, grabbing Hanzah and the two leaders' attention. Being careful to maintain his connection with the grizzly, Hanzah could make out a mass of Keagan men, corralling the people of Harran into one group. The people protested with vigor at first, but were brought to silence by an array of weapons pointed in their direction. Though Hanzah squinted with all his might, he could not spot Dominic or the Morrells in the crowd.

Once there was organization and calm, Clovis Keagan appeared at the front of the crowd. Daniel Keagan followed him but not of his own volition. He was restrained by two men, one on each side of him, and was shouting at Clovis though it was difficult to make out anything he said.

A menacing grin crept over Varek's face. "There he is. There they all are. We have them right where we want them."

"What is our move?" Orrin asked, inhaling with heavy, audible breaths as he rubbed his hands up and down his legs before unsheathing his blade.

Varek raised his hand in the air, looking across to different points of the tree line where his Masters were awaiting his order. The V'ahani warriors assembled with either bears or weapons according to the drills from their training.

Clovis raised a gun into the air. "I will waste no time!" Hanzah could only just make out his shouting. "Bring out the murderous fiend!" A moment later, one of Clovis's men escorted someone to his side. As the crowd roared—the Keagans in excitement and the people of Harran in fury—the prisoner was thrown down to his knees. His head was hung, but when he glanced up Hanzah could make out Dominic's bloodied face.

"Are you both ready?" Varek asked with a whisper.

*Only in the defense of your children.*

The words of the ritual, of his prayer to the Mother, came back to Hanzah, making his hair stand on end. Who were the Mother's children?

In a moment of desperation, Hanzah grabbed the Grand Chieftain's lifted arm. The shock on Varek's face was less than Hanzah's own surprise at the nerve he showed.

"No," Hanzah said, realizing an attack now would result in an immediate massacre. "We must wait."

"Take your hand off me, boy," Varek said as he pushed Hanzah away. Hanzah's grizzly rumbled with a low growl, and Hanzah dedicated part of his mind to calming the bear, though he heard Varek's next words as clear as day. "Have you lost your senses? Every minute we allow him to live puts us at risk."

"We must hear the boy out," Orrin said, with a large smile on his face and placing a hand on Varek's shoulder.

*What will make him hear me? How can I give my friends a chance?*

"I have only just now found my senses, Grand Chieftain." Out of the corner of his eye, Hanzah could see Orrin with his brows raised, mouthing the word "good" as he spoke. "I can promise you I would not have had the courage to do what I just did otherwise. I failed to speak my own mind earlier, and I must do so now. If we attack this very moment, we put in danger lives we must once again coexist with when we take back our home. They will resent us for it and if that were to happen … then one day we will have another gang on our hands and the cycle will continue. So for the sake of the Riverlands, please wait."

"In all honesty, Varek, I had not even thought of any of what he mentioned," Orrin said. "Whether he is my nephew or not, he has spoken wisely. We cannot afford to inspire our next enemies in the process of vanquishing these."

With his forehead pressed against his spear, and his hands now ringing the handle, Varek appeared frustrated and stressed. A deep breath and shifting on the tips of his feet seemed to alter his mood. "Fine then." Another sigh, and he continued, "Well done, Hanzah. We wait for now, as suggested. But the instant we have our opening, we are going to take it. No matter what it means for future enemies. Do you understand?"

Hanzah nodded. It was fair enough.

He released a breath as he, Orrin, and Varek all turned back to observe Clovis's spectacle.

*

The crow resting on Nova's shoulder flew off once William spotted her. There was too much he'd just had to absorb, and the promises he'd made about clearing Prayer's Passage of Highlanders were the last thing he wanted to hear about right now. He ignored them and continued back toward the mansion. He needed to consider what the priest said, and he couldn't deny he now felt different about the natives. Dancing around in the recesses of his mind, spoken in Kubler's voice, were words once foreign such as "heathens" and "non-believers" as he increased his pace through the town. Nova couldn't help him get to Judith, but maybe the priest could. And that's all that mattered.

Nova and Kai followed his path, walking parallel to the left of him, along the outskirts. With Kai now up on the horse, they increased speed at the same rate he did his own pace. Agitated for some reason beyond his understanding, he broke into a sprint. Coming up on either side of him were a saloon to his left and a funeral parlor to his right. Once between the two he'd have a moment of being hidden, so he decided to cut left into the saloon, needing a drink anyway.

The saloon was empty other than the bartender, who was cleaning some glassware, and a ragged older man, who was hunched in a defensive position over his beer.

"Hey there, Mr. Keagan," the bartender said. "Scotch?"

William had become a regular here—especially over the past week—so he was aware of the back room, where customers could go for some privacy. He made a break for it now. Before this moment, he'd always wondered if it had ever been used.

"What else?" he said. "I'm not here though, you got me?"

"Of course." The bartender slid a bottle and glass his way, and he caught them before heading to the back.

Along with being separate from the main bar area, the back room was entered through a door disguised as being part of the wall. Picture frames were hung from it, and the paint job was consistent over the cracks and hinges. There could have been no better place to escape, drink, and avoid the promises he'd made when he was a different man. He kicked back with a sigh, before removing his gun from its holster and placing it on the table. He couldn't imagine he would need it, but he couldn't seem to fight the urge.

A consistent rumbling or two of conversation could be heard outside the room. It helped him relax. Staring at his half-finished drink, the sudden silence on the other side of the door made him alert. He drummed his fingers against the table, waiting for it to resume. When it didn't, a sense of concern he felt made him rise up and lean forward, bringing his ear to the door. Footsteps sounded, and he began to relax.

*CAW!*

William jumped back. "I'm gonna kill that fucking bird."

Careful to hush his voice and tiptoe his feet on the floorboards, he nearly tripped on a chair as he rushed for his gun.

"They are gone, William." It was Nova's voice. "I know you are in here, and I sent them off. Please, I would only like to talk."

*If that barman sold me out, I swear.* He remained silent, figuring she couldn't know about the private room if they hadn't told her.

There were faint steps on the other side of the door. At first they were far off, but they moved around the place inch by inch.

"If you will just hear what I have to say, it should be the last time you will ever have to do so," Nova said. "After this conversation, you will owe us no debt for our protection in the Passage—none at all."

He guessed she was searching in the back office. Perhaps he should just hear her and be done with it so he could go back to his life. He leaned forward.

"I know what you have been through, William. I know about Judith and Cassius and Charles."

"You couldn't possibly," he said on reflex. He was furious by the suggestion. Eyeing his bottle, he poured a glass and downed a shot. Then a second.

"I can, and I do. But you are and have been a catalyst to the

Territory. Whether a positive or negative one, I did not know. It had seemed after our encounter you were moving in the direction of the former. There has been a change though."

Wiping the remnants of the second shot off his lip, he leaned against the table where he was previously sitting for support. "A change? Ha. Well, isn't that the understatement of the year."

"Perhaps. I did not mean any offense by it. But you must listen to me, please."

He could hear Nova was now right outside the door. It did not sound like she had made any attempt to open it, but she'd found him.

"The priest you spoke to is leading you down a path you cannot return from. His teachings are ridiculous, and you must ignore his vision for the natives."

"Oh please. You don't know what he—"

*CAW!*

"Did you think it was just any crow in his church, William?"

His heart sunk as he lumbered toward the door. Taking a seat with his back to it, he cradled his bottle and glass.

"Do you think any of the wonders of this place are really coincidence?" Nova asked. "Mere projections some god places into your mind? Why would a deity give you such pain?"

"I suppose you'd have me believe it makes more sense for this place to be watched over by some maternal she-god?"

"Yes, I would."

In his sulk, he mustered a brief, sarcastic grin and raised his brows before throwing back another shot.

Understanding and ease were present in Nova's tone. "But not because I would expect it to make any more or less sense to you. It is because I have experienced Her firsthand, William. She has lived through me. That is how I know as much as I do. I am not meant to tell you this. Kai is outside right now because even he cannot know the full extent of it. However, I am afraid there is no other way. If you do not hear it, I am afraid you will be lost. And I worry too much about what that will mean for this place."

"What are you really saying, Nova?"

"I am saying to you the Mother is real. I am saying she has lived here through me. I am saying I am what my people pass around as only a legend by the name of the Walking Widow. And I say it all in hopes you believe me, in hope to avoid the pain you may cause if you follow down this darker road. You must trust me, William. Forget the lies of the priest and return to the path you were on prior to reaching New Berkeley. You are destined to play a crucial role in this place. If you handle the Highlanders and stop your brother like you know you must, the people of the Murrieta would be happy to stand beside you. You could give them the order, peace, and freedom they deserve. You could change this land for the better."

"And my Judith?"

A second of silence. Another.

"I am sorry, William. I will make no false promises."

Silence reigned for a time as he closed his eyes to absorb it. In a single day, two very different people had talked to him about their very different gods and expected him to believe in them. But he'd never believed in any god. He'd only ever believed in one thing. And only the priest promised he could get her back.

Looking down at the empty glass in his hand, he decided this time to place it down on the ground beside him as it was. "I can't let her go. I'm sorry. I won't."

"I understand."

"My Judith was … a still winter in the mountains. On a morning when the air is flavored with pine so crisp you can relish the taste as much as the smell. Its breeze goes far beyond filling your lungs though. It enriches your entire soul."

A smile crept across his face as his heart increased its pace and intensity. "But somehow—somehow she's more than that, too. Right at the moment you were starting to think there couldn't possibly be more, there is. Because she's also a storm. A hurricane others might try to steer clear of, but not you. No. You truly know her—her path and every bit of her form. So you run straight for the eye, straight through the bolts of lightning and crackling thunder, to her center and watch as she tears through the plains without a care in the world of what's left behind. And you love every minute of it because as much as that winter air is a part of her, so too is the storm. And you wouldn't have her any other way. Because all of it exists within you, and it feels like it always has until you become one. But then … then you lose it all."

Staring ahead with the back of his head against the door, his breathing slowed before he started to break down, as he had so many times before. "I … I need her back, Nova. I can't go on without her. This is the only way."

Not a reply or sound came.

"Nova? Are you still there?"

The silence only stretched.

William stood and tore open the door to find an empty bar. Gently closing it again, he returned to his seat and wept.

*

What gifts the Mother supplied! Latera was feeling positive about her newfound abilities. *A seer—me.* Once she'd understood it, it'd become less frightening, and she'd decided to make the Mother proud as repayment for Her generosity. She'd start with bringing others closer to Her gifts.

Each of the Tokali boys were on their way to basic control of the hogs, and though it would be another couple of months before they would be ready to make a move on the Hold, Latera could not have been more pleased with their progress. Having the help of Mika and Winona played a big part in her fortune as well, and she was grateful for that, too.

And then there was Hammond. Though she remembered Elan's initial betrayal and remained guarded, the moment she'd shared with Hammond had been magical. And she thought, perhaps, he'd be different. Time would tell.

Charles was also proving to be a valuable source of information on Keagan exploits. Talks around the campfire included descriptions of their operations and clarifications of their intentions, all of which were in greater depth than the Tokali were able to provide.

Things were finally bending in their favor.

At midday, Latera stoked the flames underneath a cooking rabbit as Charles sat nearby with a blank stare. He still remained so difficult to read.

"Charles, tell me more about the cities you come from ... please."

The request made him snap back to life with a shake of his head. "Oh, yeah, sure, well, like I've said, I came from pretty humble beginnings. It's what makes my ascension to mayor such a point of pride. My mother would have been proud of me too, if she'd known."

"Well it seems we have both things in common."

"What things?"

The meal was almost finished cooking, but her attention was drawn away from it as she raised a brow at Charles. Perhaps it was a language issue she was unsure of, but she and the other natives seemed to frequently have these kinds of conversational misunderstandings when talking with Charles. "Um … you mentioned an ascension and your proud mother."

"You have been given a title?" There might have been an emphasis on the word you. It was hard to tell if it was unintentional.

"Unofficially, I suppose. But yes."

"Oh. Well. It was a proud and *deceased* mother, sadly, in my case."

"As … is mine."

"Oh. Okay. Then yes."

There was no more talking as Latera lost her initial interest to hear more about Duresia's east … or at least to do so from Charles. The rabbit finished cooking as she spotted the Tokali boys returning from a hunt with more rabbits to prepare.

Warrick collected all of them from the others and stacked them neatly by her side. "This should be enough for everyone. Even Charles will have extra tonight."

"It sounds like you all did well." While preparing the next

carcass, Latera sneaked a look at Hammond. They caught each other's glance and both turned away with a smile.

"We believe in ourselves now in ways we did not before," Warrick said. "I can see it and have documented the changes I have observed in great detail. Whether the others admit it or not, it is in no small part thanks to you, Latera."

"I am glad to hear it, Warrick. Let us talk more about it after these are finished, okay?"

From beyond the hills to the south of them, Latera spotted Mika and Winona. The pair had gone off for a stroll and to have some general alone time. With all they had done for her, she was happy to support them doing so. But she thought it a bit odd they appeared to be running back to the camp rather than walking.

Latera dropped the rabbit and stood. Winona went straight for their tent and began disassembling it, while Mika raced to Latera's side. "We need to go—now."

"What is happening?" Elan asked.

Latera felt like sinking into the earth at her feet. She knew what Mika was going to say. "You saw them?"

"Yes. They are coming."

There was time for one contemplative sigh before her voice filled the camp. "Gather what essentials we will need. No less than one weapon each. More, if you can carry them and still run. Elan, please free Charles. Charles, you may go wherever you please. Everyone else, make all the haste you can muster because the Keagans are coming for us."

Charles stood up so fast he slipped. "Which Keagans?"

"We have reason to believe Walter Keagan is alive," Mika said, stepping forward to speak as Latera and the others started rushing around the camp in a frenzy to prepare their things. "Winona and I called to the wind and saw a group of about twenty armed members of the Keagan gang coming straight for us. They come from the south, which means they come from the Hold, and are only hours behind. While they will be slowed by the need to track us, they are traveling on horseback and will move faster than we can to shrink the distance between us. So we cannot let them find us."

By the time Mika finished, Elan had untied Charles, who began shaking his head. "You obviously know what I've done to their leader, yes? Please, let me come with you. If we die fighting them, so be it, but I will have no chance alone." As Latera attached one of the makeshift daggers the group had crafted to her person, Charles approached her. "You wouldn't really leave me to certain death would you? I could be wrong, but you seem better than that."

Frozen in place now, she looked up at him slowly. "If you think for one second you can guilt me into pitying you for your role in this you are mistaken. I am a V'ahani Chieftess, *Mr. Mayor*, and a ruthless one at that. Do not forget it again, or I will ensure they find you." A sour, scrunched face nodded back at her. She grabbed another weapon and tossed it to him. He glanced at her in surprise. "You will need this if you are to come with us. Understand the weight of my mercy."

With all their things on their backs and each person accounted for, they set out from the camp. They jogged north at a pace deemed reasonable enough to create distance without over-exerting themselves. They'd need the stamina. When the sun was about a quarter of the way through its march to the horizon, they stopped to catch their breath, drink water from their crafted sacks, and check on the progress of their pursuers. Mika took to the duty of calling to the wind again. Once he spotted them, he said they reached their previous campsite by the lake. Time was running out.

The revelation turned their jog into a dash. Along the way, Elan argued for finding a place to hide. It was clear to Latera there were no places to hide—at least none that would do them any good. They were being hunted, and they wouldn't be able to stay out of sight long enough or well enough. As they ran up and down the crests of hilly fields, she could tell they were beginning to tire. Her mind raced along with her legs, considering and discarding plans, but she kept coming to the same conclusion. In each simulation, they ended up fighting. And in each fight, they ended up dying. They needed horses to make it back to the north. It was the only destination now, with no time left to build themselves up for a surprise attack on the Hold. While she worried for her captive people in the Hold, she recalled that Walter should not have permission to kill the others without Clovis around. And she could not help her people if she was dead. A troubling thought crept into her mind.

*What if escaping was a mistake? What if we die here?*

She closed her eyes, asking the Mother for strength.

*If we must go down, we will go down fighting.*

The group huffed and puffed at the base of an extensive hill with the sun now almost ready to set.

"If we continue to run, will we not expend all energy to fight?" Elan asked as they charged up.

Like each of the others, Latera could see he was covered in sweat,

223

and she felt for their struggle. "When we reach the top of this hill, we will call to the wind to inspect the area for hogs. Ready or not, you Tokali will need to utilize them as our first line of defense. Once we have the high ground, we will no longer run, my friends. It is time to stand and fight as Elan has suggested. And I promise you, we will fight to our last breath."

With one final push through the pain and exhaustion, they soon made it to just below the peak of the hill. Hands met knees and panting ensued. There was no time to be tired though, and Latera knew it was on her to rally them. She opened her mouth to provide her instruction on finding the hogs when a faint cheering came from behind her. Far off in the distance, the Keagan gang came thundering into view.

"RUN!" Winona yelled, leading the charge.

Their sprint lasted only a few seconds though, as once they reached the crest of the hill, a tremendous house came into view.

"No, no, no, no, no, no," Charles said, flustered.

"What do we do, Latera?" Elan asked at the same time.

She held up a hand to Elan and, still heaving for breath, turned to Charles. "What is it?"

His terrified eyes met hers. "That's William Keagan's mansion. We've reached Fayette. We're surrounded."

*

Henry's hips and shoulders ached from being slumped over on the hard, wooden floor jarring his bones at each and every bump in the road. Once he had been thrown into the carriage, his feet had been tied together too, so there wasn't any way for him to get comfortable.

Thoughts of Maria and his children popped up into his mind. Perhaps this had all been a big mistake. *What was it for anyway? Were they any safer now? Would they be whether I succeeded or not?* It felt like at minimum he had let them down, at worst, he'd failed them. He was certain he'd failed Judith.

The more he thought of her, the more he rejected the predicament he was in. With a gun to his head or not, once Forrest Hayes was in front of him, Henry would try to kill him. He knew whether he was tied or chained or restrained in some other way, he'd go after Forrest until he either killed him or was killed.

The carriage stopped for a moment, and the man in the back with him stepped out. Some chatter ensued as the two at the front stepped down, as well. It went quiet. A bead of salty sweat fell down Henry's lip and into his mouth. Though he tried his best to listen, he could hear nothing and anticipated being dragged out at any moment. Steps sounded again as the man returned to the back of the wagon and took a seat. The two at the front jumped back up as well, and they were off again.

For another fifteen minutes or so they rode on before stopping again. *This is it. May the Enigma have granted me better.* The man in the back lifted him to his feet and untied the binds around them, pushing him forward once he did. No longer would he resist—not until he saw Forrest. If he was going to face him, he'd face him like a man. Still bound at the hands, blindfolded, and gagged, he was led on, trying to follow the steps of the two men before him by sound. From a small opening in the blindfold, he could see they had entered a dark alleyway. At the sound of the two men in front of him stopping, he followed suit. After a few seconds of silence, they knocked on a door. The sound of a peephole sliding open and some whispering could be heard but not made out. The door opened, and he was ushered in.

Once inside, he was brought to another room. A chair was pulled back, and he was pushed to sit into it as his gag was undone.

"When will I see him? Tell him I hope it's sooner rather than later. I want to look him straight in the eye."

"Soon enough." The blindfold remained over his eyes as he heard a seat pulled up in front of him.

"Who are you?" a new voice said.

"I … I'm Emory Wallace."

"Never heard such an uncertain answer to that question."

"I don't—"

"Why did you say you organized the riot at the factory?"

"Because I did you piece of shit."

"No. No, you didn't. Why did you say you organized the riot at the factory?"

"It's like I said at the riot. Working conditions are unfair, and it's about time a change came to this city."

"You don't really believe that."

"I do."

"Who are you? Why did you come to New Berkeley?"

"I'm Emory Wallace. I'm proud I stood up and protected those people, too. Keeping them safe from y'all is why I did what I did."

"So the story changes, huh? What other lies are you telling me? What lies are you telling yourself?"

"I don't have time for this shit. Bring me Forrest already. I never had time for low-man scrubs like you, and I never will."

"Now we're getting somewhere. What do you mean by that?"

"All right, all right. I'm Henry Abigale. The same Henry Abigale who would be your goddamn boss if I hadn't retired. You happy? I came to New Berkeley to get revenge on Forrest Hayes for what he did to my daughter. I came here to unleash all hell on him, and because I'm an idiot, now I'm stuck here. Protecting those people was a mistake, but it was one I'd make again if it gives you and the rest of your dogs even an ounce of trouble. Fuck you, and fuck Forrest more for giving me the displeasure of meeting you."

"No. You're Emory Wallace."

Henry shook his head and leaned back. This wasn't at all what he had expected to hear. "What? No, I mean it this time, I'm—"

"Why did you say 'Fraternal Forgotten' to me at the mill? Why are those words relevant to you?"

"In the mill? I … the floor manager. Am I right? Please tell me I'm talking to Andersen's boney-ass floor manager right now." Confused, but elated, he hoped it was true.

"I'm flattered. Now answer the question."

"I've been seeking out the Forgotten because I know they're my best chance to hurt Forrest. In the past few years, he and Leonard have thrown everything into those factories. Any opposition to their success would have been the best place for me to start. And believe me, I'd do anything to break him."

The man stood up from his seat now, and his footsteps paced the room. "When the carriage stopped, we took down Forrest's men and took their place. We're his enemies, the Fraternal Forgotten. You're safe here. But you're Emory Wallace now. Your place in our movement has been solidified if you wish to help the cause. What you did will be talked about within the Fraternal. Your name will be talked about. So you must become it. Henry Abigale is dead, do you understand? If you want to hurt Forrest, this is how you do it."

"I do—you can't know how terrible the want is." Henry paused, swelling with relief for his safety. His thoughts turned for a moment to what giving up his identity in total for another might mean, but his mantra floated through his mind again. *Nothing less than the whole operation.* "I will be your Emory Wallace."

"Good. Now give me a moment. The Father of the Fraternal will want to speak with the newest member of his family."

"Wait, can you also take off my—" The click of a closing door told him the man was already gone. "—blindfold?" Despite his apparent safety, Henry's heartbeat maintained a furious pace. How close he thought he had been to the end, yet how validated it turns out his actions had been. Not only did he find the group he'd meant to ally with, but he'd become an inadvertent symbol for them. It was an exciting step forward, and one he was more than ready to act on.

The door opened again, and the sounds of two pairs of feet could be heard entering. One man—who he assumed was this "father" the floor manager spoke of—came in and took a seat in the chair before him, while the other walked behind Henry and started to work off the binds on his hands.

"Thank you," Henry said. "And Father of the Fraternal, it's an honor to meet you. I admire your cause, I do."

"My cause. It's funny. I became a part of this cause the same way you find yourself becoming a part of it now, *Emory.*"

A shiver went up Henry's spine as he recognized the voice. "It can't be. Can it?"

"Oh, it can be, and it is. Old allies, allied again."

As the blindfold fell off Henry's face, his suspicions were confirmed. Sitting before him was none other than William Keagan's uncle, Jimmy Keagan.

# CHAPTER 10

## ]HE ]URN

The Tomorrow Room was silent and had been for some time. Jeannie sat next to Harrison at the table, tense as she awaited any news. Glancing at her brother, she offered a brief smile. They'd united together to gain back what their family had lost, and despite their different approaches, she had confidence in their ability to accomplish it—especially with the rock-solid support of the townspeople on their side. However, a heavy responsibility came with their position.

Downstairs, the front door slammed shut. Jeannie and Harrison shared an urgent look as footsteps pounded their way up to the Tomorrow Room.

Cassie entered, fresh tears rolling down her face, as Debra too began to wail downstairs. Jeannie felt herself begin to shatter inside and out.

"Dominic … he … he failed," Cassie said.

"No!" Jeannie shouted in denial of a truth she could see on Cassie's face.

Beside her, Harrison's head sunk and he fell into his seat. "How, Cassie? Is he … is he alive?"

"For now, yes. And I'm sorry, but Debra and I need to go. Clovis is demanding everyone gather at the center of town. They're saying he's going to … going to execute Dominic in front of us."

Although she knew she needed to be quiet, Jeannie couldn't keep from shrieking. Her control snapped. "They can't do this! Not again! Harrison, not again!"

Harrison got up to wrap her in his arms. "It's going to be okay, Jeannie. We're going to figure all this out, all right?"

"How is it going to be okay?" She hiccupped as sobs began to shake her small frame.

"What about Daniel? Will he not stop this?" Harrison asked Cassie.

Looking up from Harrison's arm, Jeannie saw Cassie shake her head. "It seems he tried and is still trying, but Clovis apprehended him before he could."

"Clovis turned on Daniel? My God. Okay, well … Go now. Don't give him any reason to punish you. We will watch from the windows."

With a teary nod, Cassie embraced them both.

After a rush up the stairs, Debra entered and hugged them too. "I couldn't be the one to tell you. I'm so sorry. We won't let him do this. If he does … Cassie and I will kill them all ourselves, I swear it."

"Don't do anything foolish," Harrison said, backing away from their huddle. "Whatever comes of this, we will respond. But please, we can't afford to lose anyone else. Go now and do as they order you to."

Once Cassie and Debra left, she and Harrison headed to the windows in the upstairs hall. Jeannie's hand squeezed Harrison's as she continued to weep. From a not-so-ideal angle inside, they could make out the crowd of townspeople filing into a mass, as they were surrounded by gun-wielding Keagan gang members. It was clear from their viewpoint there was no way out of this. Clovis entered the scene and stood on top of a makeshift raised platform—the wreckage of the jail. Off to the side next to him was Daniel, who was restrained by two of Clovis's men. It was comforting to see him screaming in protest along with the rest of the crowd.

As if snapped out of a trance, Clovis whipped his gun in the air. The crowd gasped and then murmured into quiet.

"I will waste no more time!" Clovis yelled. "Bring out the murderous fiend!"

The sight of a bloodied Dominic crushed Jeannie all over again, and she began to huff and puff. Harrison's grip on her hand grew tighter. What had they already done to him? Two escorts threw Dominic to his knees, and the crowd became re-animated.

Raising his pistol again, Clovis settled everyone back down. "People of Harran, do not be alarmed by my commanding presence. Do not be frightened by false notions of who y'all were told I am. Clovis Keagan is not an enemy to those who do not beg for him to be their enemy. No, sirs, and no, ma'ams. Clovis Keagan is a man who provides the world with justice. Which, I might add, seems to be something y'all ain't had in a good while. I mean, what could be more symbolic of that fact than the remains of this here jail beneath my feet? So, as a bringer of justice, let me spell this out for y'all, nice and simple: Y'all have a murderer on y'all's hands. Actually, shit … I guess I could be clearer. Y'all got a goddamned serial killer."

Protests mixed with cheers filled the air.

"There's only one murderer here—you!" one brave and/or stupid voice called out. Clovis let out a giddy laugh in response. Jeannie couldn't be more disgusted.

"Stop this, Clovis," Daniel shouted as he continued to resist. "This isn't what Billy would want."

"EVERYBODY SHUT THE FUCK UP!" The laugh was gone, a grim mask in its place. Everyone fell silent once again. "My brother has reminded me of this pitiful scum's *other* crime. You see, as surprising as it may sound to all of you, I had my share of difficulties growing up. As, of course, we all do." His head craned back and forth as if for someone to agree, but not a peep came. "Well, my two brothers were the only people in the world to try and help me with the struggles I faced. And now I come here, to find this man has tried to turn one of my own brothers against me." Leaning in close, Clovis sucked in and spat in Dominic's face. "Well, fuck you!"

The crowd roared again, and Dominic didn't seem to have the energy to wipe the spit away. Jeannie released Harrison's hand to wring her own together.

"Now, let's take a tally. We were brought here to investigate the murder of one of our own, bled and draped in a wolf skin. Little did we know, Dominic Turner also killed Jesse Billings by hurling a knife into the poor man's face. Jesse too was a Keagan man, so that's two big-ass strikes."

"Jesse Billings?" Harrison asked as Jeannie's head sank.

"Next on this sociopath's rampage, Turner went and framed Billings' murder on an, at-the-time, innocent man."

*No. He couldn't have taken the blame for this, too.*

"A man y'all know as being too stupid to do anything about it, Charles Langston. I mean, of all the people to take advantage of, the guy was likely dropped on his head every morning with his damn breakfast as a child. Now, in the interest of full disclosure, so y'all know y'all can trust me, Charles turned out to be a murderous, lying son-of-a-bitch himself. So, I guess I should be grateful for any harm to come his way. Nonetheless, a strike is a strike, and by my count that'd be three so far."

Daniel had stopped physically resisting his captors, but he didn't appear ready to give up. "Clovis, please."

"Which brings us to this very spot I stand for the final count. Seems y'all's illusionist friend made rivals with one of ours by the name of Collin McCormack. Dominic embarrassed Collin with his silly tricks, and Collin understandably didn't take too much of a shine to that. So these two became obsessed with besting each other until Dominic got the upper hand. This jail I now stand upon contains the ashes of that man. Collin McCormack was burned to the ground right here, with nowhere to run or hide."

Jeannie's head snapped up and her fists clenched. How dare he, the person who burned her innocent parents and brother, Donovan, to the ground now damned the very same act carried out on someone as deserving as Collin. It made her sick. She'd heard a direct taunt in his words, a dare for her to face him, a gloat over the crime he'd yet to pay for.

*No more.*

She turned and darted out of the hall and down the stairs.

"No, Jeannie. Don't!"

She ignored the concerned call from her brother. What strength she had made her rip the front door open and exit the house. Making a run for the crowd, she stopped close enough to be seen and heard. "Stop! You stop this right now!"

Every gathered soul turned to acknowledge Jeannie's presence. The people of Harran looked like they could burst, but whether it was in excitement or fear she couldn't tell. She had no idea what to do or say next, but she couldn't see Dominic killed without trying to prevent it. She couldn't hear Clovis spit his hypocritical words as he killed another good man.

And just maybe, she could inspire a riot.

"Well, if I ain't just the luckiest … ladies and gentlemen, Jeannie Morrell." Clovis raised his hands in the air and jumped, waving them in a peppy motion. His hoarse, raspy voice cracked as he called it out. "Ain't this something? Consider me elated you could make it, Jeannie. But why do you look so frail, child?"

*This is for momma, for papa, for Donovan.*

Jeannie raised her chin, balled her fists, and looked her monster straight in the eye. "When all was said and done and my home had been reduced to ashes, I'll admit, I was wounded. And how could I not be with the wrong you'd done me then? That's what you want to hear, isn't it? So, good for you, I guess. As horrible as you might be though, I measure what's happened in the same way my mother taught me to: by standing in front of a mirror. And what I see, despite any bruises, is a spirit unbroken. In fact, to be frank, it's one you haven't so much as dented, Clovis Keagan." Jeannie heard a rush of footsteps behind her, and she felt Harrison place a firm hand on her shoulder. "So you can't have our town, and you can't have our Dominic, because the only one who needs to be served justice here is you."

*

*Because the only one who needs to be served justice here is you.*

The hair on Hanzah's neck stood up at Jeannie's bravery, even as he feared for her. He'd watched, riveted, as she burst out of the house and onto the scene, followed soon after by Harrison. Now the Morrells stood exposed in front of the beast that was Clovis Keagan.

"Dominic lied about framing Charles. Cassie and I framed him," Debra Kennedale said from in the crowd.

"An' it was me who ordered the hit on yer man at the Morrell's house. Wolf skin an' all." This came from an older voice.

More proud cries of guilt followed. "I'm the one who did the killing."

"It was me who skinned the wolf!"

"I attempted to murder your brother in his sleep," a woman Hanzah thought was particularly bold said.

"And I knew about all of it, Clovis." Clovis whipped around toward Daniel, whose confession silenced the crowd. "So, now you know. We're all guilty. Every single one of us."

A glint of hope presented itself. Surely Clovis couldn't execute them all. The unity was brilliant.

Clovis's gaze remained fixed on Daniel before turning to the crowd and then back to Daniel again. His gun jostled in his loose grip. One steady step at a time, he began moving toward his brother, each step causing a squeak in the burned wood beneath him. He continued until he stopped between Daniel and Dominic, with about five feet of space between each of them. "All guilty, you say?"

"Yes, brother. And you're the guiltiest of all."

A dark grin etched across Clovis's face. "Seems you've lost sight of one thing, Daniel: I just don't give a fuck. Goodbye, brother."

Kicking and jolting, Daniel started to resist again as Clovis raised his gun at Dominic. "No! Don't! Clovis, no!"

A teary smile graced Dominic's face as he closed his eyes and croaked out three words through his bloody lips. "Welcome to Harran."

*POP!*

Dominic's right shoulder jerked back, and he collapsed in the dirt, grabbing at his chest. The crowd screamed. With labored breaths, Hanzah watched as his illusionist friend lay as a limp heap, blood spreading from beneath him.

Hanzah's blood boiled, and his eyes watered. He knew it was time to end this. "AHHHHHHHHHH—!"

The scream Hanzah emitted carried over as a thunderous roar from the grizzly he now controlled. All eyes in Harran turned to the trees as it led the charge. Behind it, a storm of war cries filled the air as a mass of grizzlies and men charged for the town. The townspeople started to scatter.

The grizzly could see a hysterical Jeannie being pulled away by Harrison, back to the house they'd emerged from.

"Dominic! Dominic! Dominic!" she cried over and over again.

Drool streamed out of the sides of the grizzly's mouth as its panting growl accentuated each syllable of her cries, each barreling step of the charge.

A volley of shots blistered through the air. Around the grizzly, men and bears collapsed to the ground. An instinctual, irate roar filled the scene. It inspired the same from others, until more flashes from rifles came, and a sting in the arm caused the grizzly to yelp. Another frustrated roar allowed it to overcome the pain. Blood dripped from the wound, but a flesh-tear was the extent of the damage.

Some of the braver townsfolk began to fight the Keagans, but the majority who tried fell, powerless against their guns. They would be avenged. A few of the V'ahani warriors with spears who had clean shots took them. Elation flowed through the air as targets were hit. The grizzly spotted Clovis Keagan next, who had unloaded his gun in the first round of the firing before throwing his pistol away. Several men shielded him now as others ran for the horses. He could not be allowed to escape. The grizzly let out another furious roar.

A Keagan man fumbled to reload his weapon in terror and stood right in the path of the grizzly. This was it. Time to strike. Time to hunt. Time for vengeance. The grizzly closed the distance by jumping through the air and pinning the man into the ground. The man screamed as two other men slammed the butt of their rifles into the grizzly, one hitting its wound. A teeth-baring growl and a reactionary swipe of both paws knocked them to the floor. The man below tried crawling away during the distraction. A swipe of its claws through his back led to another ear-rattling scream.

The other V'ahani and grizzlies had now reached the crowd too. Weapons were utilized, bones were broken, and lives were taken. Though many had fallen during their charge, it was clear the

V'ahani and their beasts had the numbers to overpower the town. Some attacked without discrimination. Aware of the importance of the V'ahani alliance with the people of Harran, Hanzah charged his beast forward when he spotted a potential conflict. A Harran man attempting to flee had run into a warrior. As the warrior shoved the cowering man to the ground and raised his spear, the grizzly raised on all fours over the target and let out a grunt. While the warrior snarled at the save, he stood down, and the terrified man ran off to a nearby structure.

After the standoff, the grizzly resumed its rampage on the Keagans, protecting townspeople when it could, until it saw Clovis again, now atop a horse with another rider beside him. As the grizzly stormed toward Clovis, it saw him reach a hand down to Daniel.

In an unexpected turn, Clovis seemed desperate. "Take my hand! Brother, we need to get out of here!"

Almost upon them.

"I can't go with you, Clovis. I won't. You did this. And I will be a part of it no more."

Clovis raised his weapon at his brother with an infuriated scream before dropping it back to his side. Then his eyes locked with those of the grizzly. There was panic in them.

"Protect Clovis!" the other rider screamed.

Kicking the horses, they darted off, but they were too late. The grizzly bunched its hindquarters, preparing to jump. It could reach him. As the grizzly leapt, there was a sharp pain in its backside, causing it to flinch and miss its target by a hair's length. With its gaze fixed on Clovis, who stared right back, the grizzly cried out in agony—more at the escape than the pain.

When Clovis disappeared in the distance, the grizzly turned. The man who shot him had finished reloading and lifted his gun to finish the bear.

Three gunshots had the man tumbling dead to the floor, killed by Daniel Keagan. Raising his weapon in the air and coming to a knee, he nodded at the grizzly, as if to ask for acceptance. With what energy it had left, the grizzly let him be and marched back to finish the fight.

At the end of it all, only three of Clovis's men remained alive, and they begged to remain as such. A number of bodies lay in the path of the weakened grizzly. It seemed fortunate the majority were Keagan men. In fact, as they emerged, the townspeople who weren't mourning immediate losses appeared grateful for their freedom.

Hanzah snapped back to himself, releasing the grizzly to wander off, thanking it and the Mother with gratitude for its strength. Despite their victory, the most important enemy had escaped. For this reason, it didn't feel like they were successful at all, and Varek didn't treat it as such when he reached the town. The Grand Chieftain executed the three uninjured Keagans attempting to surrender and ordered Daniel Keagan to be next.

There was no way Hanzah could stand for that. "No, Grand Chieftain. He fought beside us and saved my beast from certain death."

"This carnage is on him and his brother. It is past time he paid for it."

"Y'all can go ahead and kill me if y'all think it fair. I'll go down without any complaints and won't pretend like I ain't earned it. But know this …" Daniel slicked back his hair as he let out a series of coughs. "Clovis ain't my brother. Not anymore."

Jeannie and Harrison ran out from the house they had hid in. "Please don't, Grand Chieftain," Harrison said. "If we are to find Clovis, there is no one better to help us in doing it. You would be killing one of our greatest assets."

With a sigh, Varek looked to Hanzah. "Would you agree? Do you think he could help us?"

Hanzah felt Orrin come to his side. Standing tall, the two exchanged a smile.

"I do," Hanzah said.

While Hanzah knew there was still more danger and fighting to come, he was so happy to be back home. The Riverlands had been won.

*

Latera thought her head would burst from the stress of devising a plan. Glancing from the riders galloping closer to the backside of the Keagan mansion, she struggled to calm down. But much like her dreams of late, she couldn't seem to focus on any one idea.

Those around Latera started to panic. "Oh no—not like this," Elan said, pacing back and forth.

In stark contrast to Elan, Winona stood still in a fighting position. "You are a Tokali warrior, are you not? Calm yourself. You are trained for this."

"But we are surrounded on either side." For one of the few times since she'd met Warrick, Latera noted he had nothing to write with as his voice cracked. "What are we going to do?"

"We'll die if that's what it takes," Charles said, though he shook in his boots as he did. "They sure as shit won't be taking me alive."

"Latera, what do you think?" Gannon asked.

The question rang in her head over and over and over—until suddenly, she had the answer. Overcome with an immense yet uncertain hope, Latera turned and ran for the mansion without warning. She knew if she simply gave the order, she'd lose precious time arguing with them all on the top of the hill. But if she moved, they'd move. "Follow me. Hurry!"

Right behind her were Winona and Mika. Hammond, Warrick, Gannon, and Shelton followed next. Elan hesitated before sprinting after them, and Charles gave in last, albeit with some protest.

"Are you fucking insane?" Charles asked. "You're going to get us all killed."

Perhaps her plan would end up being insane, but she knew from her dream the mansion was not densely populated with Keagan men—at least it wasn't during the time of her vision. No matter what awaited them, though, they had nowhere left to run, and no other options she could think of.

Swinging around to the side of the house once she crossed the field, she raised a hand as the others filed in behind her with their backs to the wall. A quick scan around the corner to inspect the front of the property showed no one out and about. The mansion also appeared far enough from the main road of Fayette for wandering townsfolk to not be an immediate problem. Looking back, the riders hadn't yet reached the peak of the hill, but the cloud they kicked up continued to rise.

"All right, seriously, now what?" Shelton asked in a whisper.

Panting from the run to their current position, Winona rested a hand on Latera's forearm. "What did you have in mind, Chieftess? We will follow wherever you lead."

The lives of all her friends—and by extension, the captive V'ahani of the Riverlands at the Hold—would rest on the success of her decision-making. For a moment, the weight of her responsibility was crushing. She began to rub her fingers together.

"It is okay if you do not have anything specific—" Mika began, but she interrupted him.

"You know the mansion well enough, Charles?" she asked.

"Yes."

*Now or never.*

"Good. We are going to storm it and take William Keagan hostage." Eyes widened, but no resistance was given. There was only nerves and excitement on their faces. The first of the riders came over the hill. "We must go now—go-go-go!" Waving them on around the corner and toward the front porch, Latera followed once they were all safely ahead of her.

*PEW! PING!* The gunshots rang out from behind.

"They will have heard that in the mansion," Mika said. "Lead the way and go straight inside, Gannon."

Wielding a crafted blade, which was tiny in his hand, Charles emerged before Latera. "Through the door to the right will be a library. Front right is the door to the dining room and kitchen. A hall straight ahead will lead upstairs. To the left is a study."

As soon as Gannon mounted the porch, he took a breath and

kicked in the door, his rifle raised in the air. "Get down on the ground now!"

"Fuck you," A male voice in the house said.

*BANG!* Gannon's rifle echoed through the halls.

The other Tokali streamed in behind him, and screams ensued as blades met flesh of the guards who resisted. Once Latera rushed in, she saw a few men had been downed, and Hammond had an older woman by the neck. Despite her panting, she remained calm, while several children screamed from the kitchen.

"Mother!" one of the children shouted.

"Let her go!" another screamed.

"It's okay children," the mother said. "Everything's going to be all right."

"Where is he?" Latera jerked the woman out of Hammond's grasp and threw her into the nearest wall.

"Who? Where is wh—"

Steps atop the stairs. "Maria!"

*BANG!* Gannon's shot toward the call sounded instantaneously but missed as the source of the voice dodged out of the way.

"Please, don't hurt her," the man cried out.

The sound of hooves thundered outside the front door of the mansion. Shelton slammed the door shut. "They are here, Latera. They caught up with us."

Having noted the desperation in the man's voice at the top of the stairs, Latera turned her attention back to the woman. Taking her in her grasp, she placed the blade close enough to slice the thinnest of hairs lingering on the woman's throat. "I will feed her to the grizzlies, limb by limb, if you do not do what I say. Do you understand me?"

"Yes—yes, of course," the man said. "What do you want?"

Shelton peeked an eye through the window before ducking away from it. "They are approaching."

"What is your name?" Latera asked the woman.

"Maria … Abigale."

Latera's tone needed to be loud enough to address those inside as well as out. "I have Maria Abigale at knifepoint. Whoever you are up there, tell your men outside not to take another step, or her blood will be spilled through the halls of this mansion. We have the children here, too. They will be next."

It hurt her to hear the children whimper at her threat, but she forced herself to ignore it.

"Stand down y'all. Do it now." This command came from a different voice, one that sounded like …

A silhouette that could only belong to William Keagan appeared at the top of the stairs, his hands in the air.

The rifle in Gannon's hands snapped upward again. "Do not move!" It was strange to see such peace on William's face, given the situation.

Once William nodded, the other man popped out of cover. His face sagged when he spotted Latera's captive.

"Maria, are you all right? Tell me you aren't hurt."

"I'll be fine as long as my babies are okay."

Spotting a gun on the man's hip, Latera ensured her body was covered by Maria's. "They will not be harmed as long as you empty your weapons and toss them toward us. Do it now."

Both men followed her order, as the guns and bullets clanked to the floor.

"Good now—"

"Die, you son of a—!" Charles burst out of the kitchen and ran toward William, his small blade ready to attack.

"You," William said before Charles heaved the blade through the air.

"No!" Latera said, raising her non-weapon-wielding hand.

The dagger Charles threw missed by a long shot, clumsily bouncing off a wall beneath the stairs and falling to the ground. A pathetic sulk covered his face before Elan came up behind him and slammed him in the head with the blunt end of his spear. With Charles unconscious on the floor, William Keagan sprinted down the stairs, grabbing framed pictures off the wall and hurling them at his body. "Wake the fuck up, you ape."

Trying to stand his ground, Gannon pointed his rifle again. "Do not move!"

Likely knowing Gannon would not shoot or not caring, William barreled past him and began kicking Charles in the ribs. "You'll never kill me you fucking hear me?" It took the efforts of Hammond, Elan, and Mika to pull him off Charles and restrain him. "Let go of me. I'll give you whatever the hell you want if you just give me five minutes with this waste of breath. You don't understand. He took everything from me."

"We know he did, but you have done the same to us, and you must first right your wrongs if you wish to be given what you desire," Latera said. Winona peeked out from her place in the kitchen where she had been restraining the children. The drop of her jaw and wideness of her eyes communicated to Latera that she now saw the greater purpose of the abduction. "We will leave him here with your men, on the sole condition you order our people free from the Hold and guarantee our safe passage back to the Riverlands without issue."

William was practically foaming at the mouth to get near Charles, but said nothing for a moment. His hands fisted at his side, he shook his head as if to clear it.

"We'll send you with an escort south, and they'll have my orders as—"

"No," Latera said, jerking Maria close. "They will hear the order from you, the freeing of the V'ahani and Tokali will be overseen by you, and you will remain our captive until the minute we are safe back in the Riverlands where we belong. Only then may you return to your prize."

"I just need a few minutes once he wakes. I give you my word I'll follow through after that."

"Shelton, Warrick, carry Charles's body to the door. We will set him free after he wakes."

"No! Wait!" William exploded, but froze. There was a battle within him—it was clear from the way his eyes shifted back and forth between her and Charles, as if he was weighing cost and reward.

*Yes*, Latera thought, *surrender is difficult, isn't it?*

"I agree to y'all's terms, okay? I agree. Let Maria go, and leave him here, and I'll do whatever you need of me. Please."

As Latera's grip on Maria loosened, the boys' grip on William tightened. Once freed, Maria ran into the embrace of the man on the stairs. With one last look back at the couple, William told the man to ensure Charles' captivity and survival at all costs until his return. Next, the boys guided him out of the mansion and onto the front porch, where he ordered the riders to return to the Hold. Once they saw he was captive, they did as he ordered. Just outside the opened door, Winona and Mika embraced Latera.

While Latera laughed with relief in their arms, Winona cried with joy. "You did it, Latera. You told us you would, and you did. You saved us all."

Mika pulled back, smiled, and bowed his head. "The Mother bestowed a great gift upon us in such a Chieftess."

"*We*, Winnie. *We* saved ourselves. And thank you, Mika. The Mother is generous in her blessings today and we look to Her for the task ahead."

As soon as she finished the statement, William shot her an undecipherable look, his eyes narrowing on her. She felt a chill run down her back and the color leech from her cheeks. A calculation had entered his gaze and a myriad of emotions flashed across his face: hate, glee, desperation, determination, and then … no emotion at all. A deep sense of foreboding flashed through her. When he finally shifted his eyes away from her, the feeling was gone, as if it was never there.

She shook herself mentally. Why did this one hard look cause this reaction? She was a Chieftess who needed to save her people. She did not have the luxury of intimidation or self-doubt. Yes, her captive was furious. Of course he was, she realized, because his rage was centered on the single most important fact in all of this: William Keagan was no longer in control.

~

# CURIOUS ABOUT WHAT HAPPENS NEXT?

Continue to Amazon to buy the next book in the series now:

**https://www.amazon.com/author/nbaustin**

Need more than that?
Check out Nicholas Austin's website!

**linktr.ee/nbaustinbooks**

# About the Author

N.B. Austin is the author, screenwriter, and blogger behind the Civilands Series. His first novel, *Crimson River*, was a finalist for the *2016-2017 BooksGoSocialDaily Book of the Year Award*.

Based in Austin, Texas, but hailing originally from Long Island, New York. University of Texas at Austin educated. His experience as writer and editor for several scholastic newsletter publications combined with a passion for song writing, soon inspired him to divert his attention to storytelling.

Find more about N.B. Austin, including his blog and details on free book giveaways, at:

**linktr.ee/nbaustinbooks**